BLOOD KIN

BLOOD KIN

Matt Hilton

SEVERN
HOUSE

First world edition published in Great Britain and the USA in 2021
by Severn House, an imprint of Canongate Books Ltd,
14 High Street, Edinburgh EH1 1TE.

Trade paperback edition first published in Great Britain and the USA in 2022
by Severn House, an imprint of Canongate Books Ltd.

severnhouse.com

British Library Cataloguing-in-Publication Data
A CIP catalogue record for this title is available from the British Library.

ISBN-13: 978-0-7278-9096-2 (cased)
ISBN-13: 978-1-78029-795-8 (trade paper)
ISBN-13: 978-1-4483-0534-6 (e-book)

All Severn House titles are printed on acid-free paper.

Typeset by Palimpsest Book Production Ltd.,
Falkirk, Stirlingshire, Scotland.
Printed and bound in Great Britain by
TJ Books, Padstow, Cornwall.

ONE

O rson Keeler Burdon boasted that he could put an arrow through a dime at twenty paces. It was one thing shooting at a static target, another when it came to taking down a nervous buck at twice that distance and currently mostly obscured by foliage. Twice already he'd missed shots that should have been a walk in the park for him, and now he wasn't as confident of filling his freezer with venison. He must get closer.

It was hunting season, but this was private land and he'd no right to be there. He was there illegally, a poacher. He didn't wear the hunter's orange, he was clad in military surplus jungle camouflage, and to further disrupt his outline he'd smeared grease paint on his face and wore a shapeless net through which he'd entwined some of the local moss and leaves. As long as he made no sudden moves he would be indistinguishable from the landscape, but the instincts of prey animals bordered on supernatural. The slightest sound and that buck would spring away, and he'd miss.

He kept low, moving on cat's feet, his attention darting from the deer to the ground underfoot: he mustn't step on a fallen twig. For now he was downwind, so his scent wasn't an issue. He moved at a tangent to the deer, aiming to both close distance and if it came to it, funnel the beast towards a gap in the deadfall of trees to his right. If it ran, he felt he could still shoot before it cleared the bottleneck of fallen branches and bring it down. The deer flicked its ears and tasted the air. He stopped, as still as the trees around him, and held his breath. The deer looked all around, then lowered its head, returning to grazing.

Orson set his teeth in a grimace of effort as he slowly drew back the arrow, lining the broad tip up a few inches behind the deer's foreleg. The draw weight on his compound bow was sixty-five pounds, and his arrows were heavier grain, ideal for bringing down larger game such as elk and moose, perhaps excessive for a white-tailed deer. When he was drunk and boasting to the ladies about his sexual prowess, he'd remind them that it was all about girth and depth of penetration. He rarely impressed any woman with that kind of dirty talk, but that was Orson Keeler Burdon for you. He struck out romantically more often than he did taking a killing shot at a game animal. Third time would be the charm, he hoped.

At full draw, he held the deer under his aim. He slowly exhaled, a bare second from releasing his arrow.

Something crackled, and it was as if the deer was on a tripwire release of its own. As he shot, the deer sprang forward, and his arrow glanced from its rump rather than embed deep in its heart. The deer kept going, a flash of dun color and flicking white tail, and then it was at the deadfall. His quiver was attached to his bow for easy access. Except there was no possible way that Orson could fit and draw another arrow before it fled from sight. It wasn't even in his mind to reload; he was too busy cursing his bad luck, while looking for whatever had spooked the darn animal. He turned and the curse caught in his throat.

Standing behind him was a man cradling a rifle.

The guy was dressed similarly to Orson, in top to toe camo, but he hadn't bothered with the face paint or ghillie net. He wasn't a poacher and had no need to hide. He was a big man, thickly muscled across the chest and shoulders, with a bushy blond mustache riding his top lip. The rifle he deliberately leveled at Orson was not designed for bringing down game, it was a M4 carbine, a man killer.

'Did you get yerself lost or somethin', boy?'

Orson dragged off his ghillie net and held his bow out to the side. Without an arrow nocked his weapon didn't pose much of a threat but he didn't want to give the gunman a reason to shoot. 'Look, buddy, I was going to take one buck and that's all. Got me a brood of kids in need of feedin' and—'

'You're trespassing.'

'Yeah, I maybe wandered in and—'

'You ignored the signs.'

'I saw them, but—'

'Take that bow off him.'

Orson flinched as another figure materialized from the foliage. The second man wore camo and carried a more conventional rifle.

He was a younger man, muscular but with an expansive belly, and looked enough like the first man to be kin. He flicked the end of his rifle at Orson. 'Give it here.'

Orson shook his head and addressed the older man. 'Look, I've done wrong. I trespassed on your property . . . I was poaching. But gimme a break, man. I'm just tryin' to feed my kids and I can't do it without my bow.'

'Take that bow off him,' the man repeated, as if oblivious to Orson's words.

The younger man came forward, and shifting his rifle to one hand, he reached out and grabbed the bow with the other. Orson didn't relinquish it. The man stuck his rifle in Orson's gut.

'Gimme it.'

Orson let go of the bow and stepped back, holding up his hands in surrender.

The older man gestured with the carbine. 'Search him for other weapons.'

A third man had moved in on Orson. He wasn't sure if the trio had already been here when he'd stalked the deer or if they'd encircled him after: it was as if they'd materialized from the very earth. Discounting the crackle of branches that had startled his prey, they had given him no hint of their presence or approach. He guessed that they'd deliberately made the noise, purposefully ruining his shot.

'You've no right searching me,' Orson said.

'I've every right,' said the first man. 'You're a goddamn thief and you snuck onto my land. Gonna make sure you can't do any of mine any harm.'

Showing his palms, Orson said, 'I did wrong, and I apologize, man. But just let me go, yeah? Gimme back my bow and I'll leave. I promise I'll never bother you again.'

He was ignored.

He was brusquely searched, and his belt knife taken away.

The eldest man was the leader. Orson had heard of him. 'C'mon, Eldon, you don't have to—'

'So you know who I am?'

'Yes, you're Eldon Moorcock, you're an important man here abouts,' said Orson, hoping he could appeal to the man's ego.

'You know who I am, and that I'm important, but still you come onto *my* land to steal *my* game? How many different ways can one man disrespect another?'

'This isn't about disrespect, man, it's just about—'

'Feedin' your kids?'

'Yeah. Sure. That's it. You're a family man, a father. You wouldn't hold it against me for tryin' to put some food in their mouths, would ya?'

'I wouldn't.'

Orson shrugged disarmingly.

'Except I know you too, Orson Burdon,' Moorcock went on. 'I've been watchin' you sneakin' on and off my land these last few weeks. I had you checked out, boy, makin' sure you weren't no fed, pretending he's a poacher. I'm satisfied you ain't no fed, but you ain't no father neither. You're a bum, a drunk, and you live alone. You don't have any kin hereabouts to speak about, let alone a brood of kids. So not only are you a thief, you're a goddamn liar too, and they're both aspects of a man I don't care for. Stick him, Darrell.'

Orson was too surprised by Moorcock's pronouncement to understand the seriousness of his final words. It was only when the man who had searched him suddenly lunged forward that Orson flinched. The man was Darrell Moorcock, another son of Eldon, and his fist thudded into Orson's gut. As Darrell's hand withdrew, Orson was horrified to see it was still holding his belt knife, and that his blood smeared it.

He cupped his hands over his belly, but could do little to stop the blood gushing out of him; the cut was longer than both hands could cover. Darrell had opened him up the way Orson had his kills when dressing game: he always began by removing the gut pile. Orson opened his mouth in dismay as he sought pity from Eldon Moorcock. There was no pity in the man. Darrell wouldn't help, so Orson tried to beseech the other of Moorcock's sons.

'You go ahead and stick him too, Randolph,' said Moorcock. 'Stick him good.'

Randolph had slung his rifle, but it was so he could nock an arrow and draw back the string on Orson's bow. The heavy grain arrow with its broad tip point went through Orson's heart and stood out a foot between his shoulders.

'Nobody disrespects me and gets away with it, boy,' said Eldon Moorcock as Orson collapsed in the undergrowth.

The father and two of his sons stood around Orson. The arrow had stopped his heart, killing him instantly, though it hadn't been a mercy shot.

'D'you think he saw anything he shouldn't't've, Pa?' asked Darrell.

'Far as I know he didn't get close enough. Wasn't about to take any chances, though.'

'What d'you want us to do with him?' asked Randolph.

'Strip him of anything useful,' said Moorcock, 'then put him down Booger Hole with the others. He doesn't have any kin, but he might be missed in one of those bars he frequents in Muller Falls. We don't know if he's boasted about poachin' here before. Best be on the lookout for any of his drinkin' buddies comin' out here lookin' for him.'

'If they do,' said Randolph as he admired the bow, 'they can join him in the booger's den.'

TWO

The vintage Ford Mustang prowled Commercial Street, bypassing the wharves of Portland Harbor. Its driver hung an elbow out of the window, trailing a cigarette pinched between his fingers. The sleek lines and glistening black paintwork gave the muscle car a predatory look, as if it were a shark stalking the shallows on the hunt. The car was a common sight to the locals, but it drew the approval of tourists, some of who took snapshots of it on their cell phones. On those occasions the driver averted his face. He wasn't doing anything untoward. Nicolas 'Po' Villere was simply killing time as if it was a lazy Sunday morning. It wasn't. It was a Thursday afternoon, but he was at a loose end with nothing better to occupy his mind.

He checked the time and wondered what was keeping his partner, Tess Grey. It was more than two hours since he'd dropped her off at the Maine District Courthouse on Newbury Street, with a promise from her that she wouldn't be long. He wasn't impatient, and Tess couldn't be held responsible for the turgidity of court proceedings. He was only happy he had followed instinct and kept well out of the way. As an ex-con he had experience of courtrooms and they were not happy memories. He far preferred the freedom of the open road than kicking his heels in a waiting room, even if it was just here on the bustling harborside where he found few opportunities to drive faster than at a snail's pace. It didn't matter; the slower he drove the more he got to people watch. Occasionally he spotted a familiar face and he flicked his hand in greeting; mostly he just flicked ash. These days he rarely smoked in his car, more for Tess's sake than for preserving its leather interior. Without her beside him, he made the most of it. He still drove with all the windows down so he didn't stink it out: being a person that'd quit the evils of nicotine she was particularly sensitive to its 'godawful smell' these days.

He took a right turn, then another, following the loop back up towards the main thoroughfare of Franklin Street, where he'd be in pouncing distance of the courthouse should Tess summon him. Tess didn't call though, so he headed down Fore Street, one of the areas that attracted nighttime drinkers, and also hearty numbers of diners during the day. Po owned a retro-style bar-diner called Bar-Lesque, but it was out on the edge of town, and he had often considered shifting his business here where he might attract more custom. Beyond keeping an eye out for any appropriate venues coming vacant, he hadn't given too much thought to the idea. On his behalf, Jasmine Reed and Chris Mitchell, the front of house and bar managers respectively, had helped turn the one-time strip joint into a destination eatery, and he was unsure they'd be as successful surrounded by so much competition. Nevertheless, it did no harm checking out potential venues, should he decide to expand his empire. For now there was nothing that caught his fancy.

Back on Commercial Street he swung into a parking lot and took a stroll. He was tall, rangy of build, with dark hair tending to grey at the temples, a weathered face and denoting his Cajun heritage he had eyes the color of turquoise. Wearing a black leather jacket with contrasting cream stripes down the sleeves, black jeans and high-topped boots he dressed like an aging rock star. He caught glances, some admiring but others tentative, because he had an aura of potential danger surrounding him. Po was as striking a figure as the muscle car he drove. Some of the locals knew he'd spent time incarcerated for killing a man, and avoided him, but others admired him: they knew the man he'd killed had murdered his dad, and what man given the opportunity and skills wouldn't try to avenge his loved ones?

He set up in the sunshine outside a coffee shop with the largest unsweetened Americano they sold and lit up another in a long string of Marlboros. The outside seating area was on a boardwalk overlooking the mooring spot for the Cushing's Island Ferry. From where he sat he could see a triptych monument wharfside, formed of three segments of the historic Berlin Wall, transported there after its demolition in 1989. From past experience he knew the slabs of concrete carried original graffiti – including the hammer and sickle of the USSR – but also a message to never forget the tyranny of the wall or the love of freedom that made it fall. The memorial attracted tourists seeking a photo opportunity more often than his muscle car did. As he killed time, he watched people come and go, pose by the slabs for their selfies, then wander on as they sought new delights. After a while the faces all blended together and he began to lose focus. He listened to the shrill squawking of gulls competing over some morsel of food dropped by a careless tourist and watched a pleasure craft returning after a trip around Casco Bay.

He looked away from the monument for half a minute and almost missed spotting a familiar face. His gaze slipped back from the pleasure craft as the skipper maneuvered it snugly to the wharf, and settled a moment on the tall, red-haired woman lining up her cell phone's camera to get the best shot possible of her kid posing as if he was presenting the star prize on a TV game show. Po barely registered the boy, squinting instead to bring the woman's features into focus through a blue pall of cigarette smoke. She looked older, naturally, because he hadn't seen her in more than a decade, but little else about Elspeth Fuchs had changed. She was still willowy but in an athletic way and dressed in those bohemian skirts and blouses she'd favored in her twenties, and she still held back her thick mane of hair with a knotted scarf. She wore huge silver circlet earrings and at least a dozen rings and bangles. She'd always reminded him of a free-spirited artist, or even a New Age pagan priestess, and nothing about her dispelled the image now.

Before he met Tess, Po had enjoyed the company of other women, but few of them seriously. Elspeth Fuchs was one of the small number he had dated for longer than a week or two, and the only woman before Tess he'd ever considered settling down with. Until she'd upped and left him with barely a goodbye said. He had missed her and regretted that their relationship had ended so abruptly. She would be approaching forty years old now and, if anything, her maturity made her more beautiful than ever.

A trickle of guilt wormed its way through him. He loved Tess and was betrothed to her; he shouldn't be admiring an old flame like this. But it was difficult to look away. He watched her smile and coax the boy to strike a different pose, and then she snapped away. She lowered the cell phone, checking the screen for how well the pictures had come out, and then she raised her gaze to the boy again. The smile froze on her lips, and she straightened up. She was looking across at where Po sat looking back.

He was torn, as to whether or not to wave in greeting or just turn away and pretend not to have noticed her. But then the kid must have picked up on his mother's unease, because he turned and sought what had caused her sudden change of mood. The boy was tall and slim, but with a wiry strength undisguised by a black T-shirt and jeans. He had a shock of wavy black hair and deep-set eyes. The boy stared at Po, with his mouth hanging slightly open, before he looked up at his mom for clarity on an unspoken question.

Po felt that worm of guilt turn into a river of icy water that washed the length of his spine and caused the back of his neck to tingle.

Without warning, Elspeth grabbed the boy's wrist, turned and walked briskly away. Po stood, watching them go, trying to decide whether to chase after them. He had an unspoken question requiring clarification too.

If he didn't know otherwise, when he stared at that boy, Po would swear he was seeing a ten-year-old version of himself.

THREE

Annoyed and overheated, Tess Grey pushed out of the court-house and stood on Newbury Street. She breathed hard, exasperated at how most of an afternoon had been wasted. She had sat for hours in a stuffy room where the air-conditioning unit groaned out the barest trickle of air, waiting to give evidence in a case against a man accused of theft. In her role as a private investigator, Tess had tracked down the stolen property to a pawn-shop, and identified the suspect on the corresponding CCTV footage, before sending for the cops. She had been summoned to court to testify to the chain of evidence. Playing the system, the accused had eked out his freedom until the last moment and offered a guilty plea just as the proceedings commenced. The case had been adjourned for sentencing at a later date. With no trial going ahead Tess's evidence hadn't been required, so she'd been released. It was as frustrating as all hell. It reminded her of the eternal hours she'd wasted waiting in court when she was with the Cumberland County Sheriff's department.

She had dressed professionally in a suit and blouse and sensible loafers. Her clothing wasn't fit for a hot day in Maine, and she couldn't wait to get into something lighter and more comfort-able. She looked up at the sun, as if divining the precise time from its position in the vault of blue sky and thought that Po must be royally pissed off by now: she'd promised she wouldn't be too long in court, but that had been hours ago. She walked stiffly out onto the sidewalk, and checked for Po's Mustang parked at curb-side, but it wasn't there. She took out her cell phone, then after pushing back her fair locks, and blowing out a hot breath, she brought up his number. She should apologize to him for wasting his time, but was too aggravated to concoct the few sincere words necessary. Instead, when he answered, she said, 'You can come get me now.'

'You're done there?'

'Yes. Otherwise I wouldn't be asking you to pick me up.' She caught herself; it was unfair speaking to him so brusquely, and after all it wasn't his fault another damn criminal had decided to play the system for all it was worth. 'Sorry, Po, yeah, I've been let go. What a waste of time it's been here.'

'Can you maybe gimme ten minutes an' I'll come get you?' he said.

'Something wrong?'

'No. Nothing's wrong.' He sounded a little breathless. 'It's just I'm outta my car, so I'll have to go fetch it.'

'Where are you? Is it easier if I walk on over and meet you at the car?'

'No, Tess. Just stay put and I'll come get you. I only need ten minutes.'

There was something off in his tone.

'Po. Is everything OK? You sound—'

'Everything's fine. Stay put and I'll be along in ten minutes.'

He ended the call.

Frowning, she shoved away her phone. When she first met Po, she'd found him difficult to comprehend. Sometimes getting him to speak more than a few words had proven as difficult as drawing a rusty nail out of a weathered plank with her teeth. On other occasions he had a way of saying nothing, but exuding meaning through his actions. He wasn't very verbose, and what he did say was usually after some consideration. In the passing years she'd learned to understand him, and these days didn't need him to verbalize when she could read a quirk of his lip, or a crinkle of his eyes as plain as the words in a book. His clipped, hurried manner here was plain *wrong*.

There was a one-way system around the court buildings. Tess decided to cut Po off at the pass, by walking around the block to Lincoln Park. It would be cooler there under the shade of the trees, and besides they were nicer surroundings than reflective stone and overheated asphalt. She took off her suit jacket, opened a couple of buttons on her blouse, and set off. She slung her jacket over her shoulder for the short walk, while her purse bumped softly against her hip. It was hot in the afternoon sun, but there was a cold sensation at the core of her. She considered ringing Po back and demanding to know what was going on, because something was troubling her man.

She didn't call. He'd explain what was going on when he saw her, and that would have to do.

Many times in the past she'd sat in Lincoln Park, listening to the tinkle of the fountain and chirping of birds in the trees. There was no play area for children, but young mothers used the park when pushing their little ones in their strollers. Sometimes they'd sit and chat a while and Tess had found herself cooing at a baby or tickling a toddler under the chin. Today Tess had the park to herself. She sat on the grass in full view of the turning where Po would have to join the one-way system.

She waited. Ten minutes came and went, and soon it was approaching twice that long. She had no right to be annoyed with Po for keeping her waiting, not after he'd had to hang around for her all afternoon. Besides, annoyed wasn't the correct word for how she felt; she was more concerned, and that was what was making her antsy.

She took out her cell phone, about to ring him after all, but thought if he were driving he wouldn't answer. Instead, feeling a little underhanded about it, she opened an app on the screen. A few months ago they had become embroiled in a case involving blackmail and coercion, and Po had gotten himself abducted in an ill-advised attempt at finding his way to the ringleaders. Tess had suffered a worrying time before discovering his whereabouts, almost too late to save him from torture at the hands of a sadistic thug. After that they'd both installed a GPS tracking device on their phones so that they wouldn't be placed in the same untenable position again. Apart from trying out the app, this was the first time she'd had cause to use it, and it felt a bit like snooping. But, still. She brought up a map on screen and saw Po's tag was static outside an ice cream shop on Portland Pier. Maybe he'd decided to treat her to something cold and delicious to counteract the heat and had gotten held up in a long queue. No, that explanation was far too hopeful. There was something else going on.

She watched the cursor, hoping to see it move. It did, but only to roadside on Commercial Street. What on earth was the fool man up to? Had he forgotten she was waiting? She closed the app and hit his number. It rang but went unanswered. Now she was particularly worried. She stood, and hit his number again. Slinging her jacket over her shoulder once more she set off marching, her phone pressed tight to her ear. Po didn't answer. She again pulled up the app and saw he had still not moved. It was only a five- or six-minute stroll from the park to the pier, with her head down and a steady pace she could cut a couple minutes off the time. It was a straight path down Pearl Street, and in all likelihood it would be the route Po came by if he ever recalled that he'd left her hanging. Periodically she checked the app, ensuring he hadn't set off and was taking a more roundabout route to the courthouse. Nope, he was still there, on Commercial Street.

Sweating, but still with that icy sensation clutching at her gut, Tess reached the intersection with the main strip. Portland Pier was a block down to her right, and from where she emerged she could see the ice cream shop, and true enough there was quite a long queue outside, as well as dozens of tourists and locals milling about. She couldn't see Po. One last time she checked her app and saw that he'd moved, but only across the road to stand outside a Starbucks from where she'd regularly grabbed a latte. He was two blocks away, but trees decorated the sidewalks here and their branches hung in full bloom, making it difficult to see beyond a few dozen feet. Tess began walking, and so he didn't realize she had been snooping, she shoved her cell phone away in her bag. She walked a block and was held up by a delivery truck turning out of the side street. As the truck cleared the junction, Tess checked for Po and this time caught sight of him. It was useful that he was taller than most of the other people on the sidewalk. Where he was standing he had his head tilted down, and looked to be in conversation with somebody shorter. Actually, his inter-action looked more intimate than that: he was holding the hand of a woman, beside who stood a little boy. The boy studiously kicked at the sidewalk, wanting no part of the adult stuff he was party to.

For a reason she couldn't fully explain, but which felt very much like suspicion, Tess halted in her tracks and watched. Some of the other pedestrians on the sidewalk had entered shops or returned to cars parked at roadside, so she had a clear view to where Po suddenly leaned in, and embraced the woman. After a moment she returned the hug, before Po set her loose and she stepped back. She raised a hand to her mouth, then turned away, but if she hadn't blown a kiss in parting then Tess was blind, stupid, or both. The boy followed the woman, but walked backwards a

few paces, staring up at Po, before Po offered a wave. The boy
didn't return it; he spun about and trotted after the woman. Po
stood, thumbs in his belt as he watched them go around the corner
onto Market Street. Po stood a moment longer, then took a glance
in both directions along the sidewalk. Tess backed into the doorway
of a café advertising a Mediterranean-influenced menu, but she
needn't have been so clandestine, as Po's gaze hadn't traveled the
entire length of the block. He turned away and trotted through a
gap in the traffic to the wharfside, and as he reached the sidewalk
he dipped his hand in his pocket and pulled out his cell phone.
Her phone began ringing.

She took out her phone, watching him still as he strode –
unusually hurried for Po – towards where she assumed he'd parked
his Mustang.

'Hey, Tess!' he said breezily when she answered.

'Hey!' she replied, but the word felt like chalk in her mouth.

'You still at the courthouse?'

'I waited,' she said, 'but thought something must be wrong.'

'Uh, yeah. Sorry I took a bit longer than I promised.'

'What was so urgent it needed doing?'

'Uh, nothing much. I had to see a guy about a dawg.'

'Really?'

Po was involved in some legitimate business enterprises, no less
his ownership of Bar-Lesque and also Charley's Autoshop, but he
also dabbled in areas skirting the law and they had an agreement
that he would never involve her in any of them. In her role, often
sub-contracting to a specialist inquiry firm working on behalf of
the Portland district attorney's office, she must remain above
reproach.

'Don't ask . . .' he said, making light of their agreement.

'And you won't have to lie to me,' she finished off their dictum.

Except he was lying to her and he couldn't know how badly it
hurt.

'Where are you now?' he asked.

'Pearl Street.' She realized that she too was lying and it made
her feel even worse. 'I walked. I'm almost at the front, so you
can pick me up outside the old Custom's House building, if you'd
like to?'

'Sure I will. Gimme a minute.'

'Where are you?' she asked, trying to sound like the model of innocence.

'Just down the road apiece.'

He wasn't exactly lying this time, but there was no committing to divulging his exact location either. She assumed his Mustang was in the public parking lot at Fisherman's Wharf. She trusted she could make the walk back to Pearl Street well before he arrived, be waiting there for when he pulled in to collect her, and giving him no idea that she had witnessed his intimacy with the woman outside Starbucks. It wasn't that he'd hugged a woman that troubled her or that she'd blown him a kiss. Hell, she too was a hugger and often squeezed the life out of their mutual friend Pinky Leclerc, garnering no hint of jealousy from Po. It was the fact he had stood her up for going onto half an hour now, and had concocted a lie to cover his sneaky ass. To Tess, they smacked of actions to be suspicious of, and it tore her up to even have the slightest reason to distrust her man.

She was still stewing in her own juices when the Mustang growled to a halt at curbside, and Po waved her across three lanes. She crossed, watched all the while by Po, and she climbed in alongside him. She dumped her suit jacket and bag between her feet in the footwell, and without asking permission reached to turn the A/C to its highest setting.

'It's hot,' he said needlessly.

'I'm boiling.' Tess didn't explain, but there was a deep crease between his eyes as he stared a moment at her. He understood he was in hot water with her, but was man enough not to try worming his way back into her good book.

'Where d'you wanna be?' he asked.

'Home.'

Yeah, the privacy of home, she thought, would be the best place to broach a subject that could have them raising their voices before long.

She didn't speak to him at all during the drive back to his ranch-style property north of the city limits near to Presumpscot Falls.

FOUR

P o swigged at an open bottle of beer, hardly tasting the brew. His thoughts were elsewhere.

Bangs, thumps and soft curses emanating from inside the house spoke volumes of Tess's mood. He hoped she would join him outside, though he was a tad anxious how things would go if she did. But they must speak.

If not an apology, he owed Tess an explanation at least. He'd left her waiting in the hot sun, and prompted her to march to find him. When he had finally picked her up she had been drenched in sweat, and her feet had been chafed raw because of her unsuitable leather footwear. He suspected her mood was as much about her discomfort as it was his inattentiveness, but whatever the cause, he was responsible. Since arriving back home she'd barely uttered a word to him. She had gone to shower and change into something less restrictive, and he'd taken himself out onto the porch and sat on the swing chair to think. He wanted to tell Tess everything, clear the air, and ask for her help. He simply didn't know how to broach the subject of Elspeth Fuchs though, not without possibly complicating matters and further darkening Tess's mood.

There were aspects of his life that he kept from her. He had secrets he held, but only to protect her from any fallout should they ever come to light. His secrets weren't criminal per se; they were more about flouting and bending laws and regulations rather than breaking them. Tess was a licensed private investigator, and she was bound by rules. He was not. Yet he assisted Tess when she was working certain cases where she needed somebody to step beyond the lawful boundary that constrained her. It was best that his involvement never compromise Tess's employment, or in fact her trustworthiness as a witness in court. He kept some of his dealings close to his chest, so that a desperate defense attorney couldn't challenge Tess with them. They had held to the dictum of 'don't ask and I won't lie', and the agreement had worked for them.

He'd been open with her from the get-go. He had told her about his past, how he had killed the man responsible for murdering his dad, and how that had affected the entirety of his adult life. He had made no bones about having to defend his life several times while in the Louisiana State Penitentiary, and how – to survive The Farm – he'd had to become a more frightening creature than the monsters that wished him harm. He told her how he had become a guardian to Jerome 'Pinky' Leclerc when the Aryan Brotherhood had targeted the young, gay, black kid, and how doing so had formed a lifelong friendship between two men vastly different and yet so alike. Hearing his story, Tess had judged him, but not negatively. She came from a law enforcement background, while he was a convicted killer, but in their hearts they were both protectors, the difference being she'd carried a badge while he hadn't. Occasionally he did things some people might deem wrong, but never to anyone's detriment that didn't deserve it. There were some things he'd done that he wasn't proud of, but until now, nothing he should be ashamed to admit.

And yet, there he was, reluctant to raise the subject of Elspeth Fuchs because in doing so he might break Tess's heart.

Tess came out of the house. Po looked up at her expectantly but she wouldn't meet his eyes. She was carrying a six-pack of beers from the fridge. She had foregone make-up and her blonde hair was still damp from the shower, curlier than what it was when she dried and styled it. She wore one of Po's old T-shirts with a Harley-Davidson logo and the sleeves fully cut off, and pared-down denim shorts, frayed at the edges. Her legs and feet were bare, pale as milk except for where her shoes had rubbed her skin raw. She smelled of shampoo and something citrusy. She was stripped back and to Po she was a vision of beauty.

'Budge along,' she said, inserting her backside on the chair, and wiggling for room, 'I'm not a string bean, you know.'

Po made way. Tess tucked her feet under her backside, turning so she was partially facing him. Often they sat on the swing chair together, listening to the roar of white water, or trickle through the rocks, dependent on the season. For now the Presumpscot River was running low, and there was more of a rustle caused by the hot breeze through the canopy of trees than sound from the falls. On cooler nights Tess wrapped up under a blanket, sometimes

with a woolen hat pulled down over her ears, but today was the
antithesis to winter. Po was warm enough to have taken off his
leather jacket. He could feel more welcome warmth radiating off
Tess's bare arm, and through his jeans where their thighs touched.
He put his hand on her knee and was relieved when she let it rest
there. She passed him a bottle of Budweiser. It hadn't occurred
that he'd finished his other beer, and was holding the empty bottle,
swinging from his fingers by its neck. He put the empty down by
the chair, and worked the cap off the second bottle. Tess opened
a bottle too, and they tapped the bases together.

Po angled his beer towards her. 'Does this mean I'm forgiven?'

'Forgiven for what?'

'For leaving you standing.'

'You didn't leave me standing, I walked.'

She adjusted so she could touch her chafed toes on her right
foot.

'They look painful,' said Po.

'I've blistered,' she said.

He gently touched one of the risen sores, and Tess hissed, over-
egging the pudding a little.

'I'm sorry,' he said.

Tess didn't comment, she left her feet alone and instead pressed
the pad of a thumb into her thigh. She took away her thumb and
watched the dimple in her skin take a few seconds to smoothen
out. 'Am I getting fat?'

'You have lovely legs.'

'Wouldn't you prefer it if I was taller, a bit skinnier?'

'Tess, what's this all about? I love you just the way you are.'

She shrugged. 'So you say. I just wonder what your *actual*
type is.'

He turned and stared at her. Tess was always conscious of her
weight. Her mom – a mother to three children no less – was
decidedly pear-shaped, and Tess occasionally fretted she'd end up
the same build. But this wasn't about the propensity of genes she'd
inherited from her mom. It explained her comment about not being
a string bean, and asking if she was growing fat.

'You saw me with her, didn't ya?' Po sighed.

'If you mean that tall, ravishing redhead, yeah, I saw.'

'Tess, it wasn't what you think.'

'What am I supposed to be thinking?' she challenged, her face serious again. 'That I was stood up because you wanted to spend time with a beautiful woman taller, skinnier and younger than me?'

'Elspeth isn't younger than you,' he said, and instantly regretted it.

'Oh, well that makes it OK then!'

'No. That's not what I meant. It's just, well, whatever you saw, I guess you misread it.'

'If you mean seeing you embracing, and blowing kisses like a couple of teenage sweethearts, there wasn't much to misread.'

'That's not how it was, Tess, and you know it.'

'Explain to me then, tell me what it was I really witnessed.'

'Elspeth's an old flame—'

She stalled him with a sour grimace.

'Hang on; you knew I'd been with other women before I met you, Tess. I got released from prison, not a darn monastery.'

She nodded several times, admitting she was being unfair. They had never gone into specifics before about his relationships, but she knew he wasn't a forty-year-old virgin when they met, and that was fine because she'd slept with a few guys in the past and had just come out of a long-term relationship with a previous fiancé too, and they'd never allowed any of those partners to come between them.

'You've never mentioned her to me before,' she said.

'Why would I have? I haven't seen her in more than a decade; as far as I was concerned she was ancient history.'

'You haven't seen or spoken with her in all that time?'

'Nope. Bumped into her outta the blue today. The thing was, when I went to say hi, she acted like I was the boogieman and tried to gimme the slip.'

'But you chased after her? Why not just let her go?'

'I had to know why she was so frightened of me.'

'Apparently you cleared that up, you parted on friendly enough terms from what I saw.'

Po took a long swig of beer. It was as tasteless as the first one he'd consumed. He took another gulp, while considering his next words. 'It turned out it wasn't me in particular she was afraid of. She just panicked when she realized somebody had recognized her who might carry tales back to her husband. She didn't go into details, but it sounds as if she escaped an abusive relationship and doesn't want to go back.'

'And she thought you'd be likely to tell him where to find her? She doesn't know you the way I do.'

'We were both young back then, and we were only together a month or so before she upped and left me. She was fearful I might be bitter and enjoy taking my revenge on her.

'Anyway, you know that ain't me. But Elspeth wasn't to know that, I guess.' He pursed his lips. 'I said if there was anythin' we could do to help, she need only ask.'

'You told her about me?'

'Why wouldn't I? You're my fiancée, and my partner. I told her if her husband was causing her trouble then there was perhaps something we could do. You saw when she hugged me, right? That was her thanking me for the offer, after she turned me down flat. She said she'd be better off goin' elsewhere where there was less chance of him findin' her. That kiss she blew? That was her way of sayin' goodbye, said she owed me it from when she walked out without an explanation last time.'

'So she's leaving town?'

'I guess she is.'

'Why come here in the first place if she didn't want to be recognized?'

'I don't know. I didn't get chapter and verse of her life, Tess. I only spoke with her a few minutes. Remember I said she ran away from me at first, I had to track her down to an ice cream parlor and wait until she came outside to speak with her.'

Tess started picking at her feet again. Absorbing his explanation, and he supposed he'd put her mind at rest for now. Pity he'd have to broach the other subject regarding Elspeth's presence in town. He cleared his throat with another long swallow of beer. 'Did you see the kid?'

'Yeah. I take it he's Elspeth's son?'

'Yeah. Well, that's the thing, Tess.'

She cocked her head to regard him and he could tell she suspected what was coming next.

'He's called Jacob and he's ten years old.' He exhaled. 'I think he could also be mine.'

FIVE

Eldon Moorcock supervised the unloading of the truck from the comfort of his own pickup's cab while he took a phone call. His sons, Darrell and Randolph acted as overseers on the actual ground, ensuring there was no loafing around by the workforce. Larger boxes and crates were transported on stacking barrows and handcarts, whereas the smaller stuff was manhandled from the flatbed truck into the hangar. Men, women and even some of the older kids had been drafted in to make the human chain, and they mostly worked without complaint. There was always a dissenter in most groups, somebody unwilling to carry an equal load, but it usually only took a stiff warning from one of Moorcock's boys to get the slacker moving. Occasionally, things had to be handled differently, take what happened with Mikey Stewart for instance, whom most people here assumed had moved to California: he hadn't.

All but the oldest or weakest members were expected to work; it was an ethos that had been agreed upon during the establishment of their community almost a quarter century ago and had carried through to the present. Back then the agreement had been mutual, now Moorcock and his closest allies enforced it.

After his telephone call ended, he put away the phone and Moorcock hit the pickup's horn to beckon over Darrell. With his first son Caleb gone, Darrell was the elder of his two boys present and by default in charge of the unloading of the truck.

Darrell gestured a few curt orders for where to stack some drums, then strolled over to his father.

'Everything in order?' Moorcock asked.

'Yup. I checked everything off the manifest. It all seems to be there.'

Moorcock nodded. 'Hand-pick me four of our most trusted men, I've another job for them.'

'Sure thing, Pa. You want them now or when we're done with this load?'

'Randolph can finish off here. Get your men and have them come over to the bay. I'll meet you there.'

Darrell walked away, hailing a couple of the nearest guys. Moorcock started the pickup and reversed away. He pulled a turn and drove down a trail formed of poured concrete. Over the decades the road had weathered, and it had crumbled in places, with some of the concrete sections sinking at their joins. It was a bumpy ride.

He pulled the truck to a halt outside the bay. This was not a coastal enclave, but the large opening into the side of a wooded hill. The entrance was surrounded by reinforced concrete and protected by sturdy pneumatic steel doors. With the doors open there was space to drive a couple of freightliners inside, with room to spare. At its far end, raised concrete platforms made unloading direct from the backs of flatbed trucks easier. Back in its day, it was a loading bay to the subterranean weapons storage area in the hillside behind it. It was only one of a number of repurposed military bunkers on Moorcock's property. After the Cold War ended, the federal government closed down more than 350 military installations and realigned many others to increase US Department of Defense efficiency. While many of the most remote decommissioned bases were taken over by the Bureau of Land Management and reinvented as state parks and nature reserves, others were sold off to private companies and landowners. In 1995 Eldon Moorcock purchased the defunct National Guard training encampment comprising of 840 acres in upstate New York, and set up home there. He was a man that did not believe that the peace accords would hold, only that the nation's enemies would change, and only those prepared and ready to protect themselves would survive the coming apocalypse. In time, Moorcock had drawn other patriots with a similar fear for the future of humanity to his fold. His community had expanded to over one hundred inhabitants now, with their ages ranging over several generations, and he'd been elevated to the status of ruler over his private fiefdom. He granted property and rights to his vassals in return for allegiance and service. He was about to call in a debt now.

He carried a key to the bunker. He left the huge steel doors shut for now, opening only a smaller door fitted into one of the larger doors. This door could allow easy access for people on foot. He was about to enter when he heard the rumble of tires and saw Darrell approaching in a GMC SUV, bristling with occupants. Moorcock waited until the SUV had disgorged its passengers. He rubbed at his bushy blond mustache as he evaluated those his son had chosen for the as yet unspoken task, and was happy. He clicked his fingers to usher them to him, then entered the bay through the door. He went across to a bank of switches on the wall and hit the lights. Overhead fluorescent tubes blinked to life, casting an ambient glow that didn't fully reach the corners. Darrell and the four other men trooped in and stood to a modicum of attention in front of Moorcock.

Without preamble he launched into what he expected of them. 'I've just had word from Caleb that he needs our help. Is there anything stopping any of you from giving him what he needs?'

His question was not asked to provoke a negative response. A couple of glances were exchanged between the men, but nobody refused.

Moorcock indicated one of the men. He was in his thirties, tall and square-shouldered with a laborer's thick forearms and wrists. 'What about you, Adam? You're about to become a father for the first time, your wife Julie is due to give birth, right?'

'She could go into labor at any time,' Adam Noble agreed, 'but she has her mother and sisters to take care of her till I get back. If Caleb needs me, helping him is never in question.'

A smile ghosted Moorcock's lips. Adam had given the correct answer, and it would serve to ensure the other men understood that they were not being given a choice to volunteer, that choice had been made for them.

Parked inside the bay there was a fleet of vehicles, most of them SUVs and pickup trucks, and a trio of vans. 'You're going to need one of the vans,' Moorcock told Darrell, because he was expected to assist his older brother too. 'Take the panel van, and have our boys here collect weapons from the arsenal. According to Caleb he isn't expecting trouble, but it's best to hope for the best but prepare for the worst.' He held out a keychain to Darrell, bristling with keys of various sizes and purposes. 'I'll have those back off you before you leave. Take some of the grab bags we prepared, and also food and water. It's a seven-hour drive, and I don't want any stopping except to take a leak. I'll have Caleb coordinate with you as you get closer, and have told him to expect you around about midnight tonight.'

Darrell checked his watch, then nodded at his instructions. It was a tight timescale, but achievable. None of this was a surprise to him, as he knew full well where his brother had gone and why. He'd been on stand-by to go help Caleb for days now, and was pumped for the mission. He clapped his hands to grab the attention of the others. 'You heard my pa. My big brother needs us. Let's hustle. Follow me to the armory room and let's get tooled up. It's a-ways to Portland and I don't want to waste any time before gettin' going.'

SIX

'I'm bored.'

'I'll switch on the TV for you.'

'I don't want to watch TV. I want to go outside. To walk. You said we could walk whenever we wanted, Mom, you said we'd be free to do whatever we pleased.'

'I did. We will. But right now we need to stay here. We need to get some rest before we move on tomorrow.' Taking Jacob out for some fresh air had been a rash move, but Elspeth was unable to keep the boy locked away all the time. They had both had more than enough of their lives being controlled and when she'd brought him with her it was with the promise that they would be free to do as they pleased. Earlier, against better sense, she'd caved in and taken him for ice cream and to see the boats and the ocean for the first time in his young life.

'I'm not tired.'

'I know, but we can't risk bumping into anyone else that recognizes me.' Elspeth sat down on the hotel bed alongside her son. She folded her hands on her knees. 'That man we met earlier, he's an old friend, but I can't trust him not to tell others he saw us. If he tells the wrong person . . .'

'Nobody here even knows my dad.'

'You'd be surprised who knows him,' said Elspeth, but didn't explain. She had first met her husband here in Portland and had followed him back to his home in New York State. This was before she discovered his true nature, and that the bucolic lifestyle he'd promised her had turned out to be a lie: instead of running barefoot through the wilderness, she'd spent most of the last decade behind concrete walls and locked doors. He had connections to people in many of the surrounding states of Vermont, New Hampshire, Massachusetts and here in Maine, criminal types. 'Tomorrow we'll get on a bus and go south, yeah? We'll go to Boston, or if you want, we'll head down to Manhattan.

You want to see the cities, right? We'll be able to hide in one of the bigger cities and never have to worry about your dad finding us again.'

'Can I use your cell phone?'

'What for? You're not going to—'

'I only wanna play a game on it, Mom!'

'I'd rather you didn't.' What Elspeth really meant was that she didn't want to risk handing over her phone in case Jacob had had second thoughts about running away and wanted to call his father. 'I'll put on the TV, and we'll call out for pizza. You like pizza, don't you?'

'I don't wanna watch the stupid TV, and I'm sick of stupid pizza.'

'Jacob, please listen to me . . .' She reached for him, but he turned away from her. He thumped down on the mattress and pulled one of the pillows over his head to muffle her words. His lean arms were exposed, the sleeves on his T-shirt riding up to expose the circular scars dotting his flesh.

A pang shot through her. Jacob's father liked to smoke cigars, and he liked to exert discipline; sometimes he'd enjoyed both pastimes together. Her own arms, her thighs, her breasts, they all were marred by similar scars, a reason why she favored long-sleeved blouses and billowing skirts. Her son's scars pained her more than hers did. Elspeth reached and touched the boy's scarred flesh, silently cursing herself for leaving it too late to protect her son from their abusive existence. He flinched from her touch, but she didn't relent. She wished to soothe him.

'It's like being in the cellar all over again,' Jacob groaned from under the pillow.

The room she'd taken was in a chain hotel, the cheapest she could find on offer. It was small, furnished with twin beds and a bathroom and little else, but it was clean and comfortable in a way that the cellar never had been. But Jacob was correct in a fashion: it consisted of four walls and a single locked door – kept barred out of necessity, granted – and the longer they were cooped up inside, the closer the walls seemed to loom.

'Did you fetch your hat?'

'Why would I need to wear a hat in here, Mom?'

She drew the pillow off his head, and ruffled his mane of dark hair. 'If we are going out I'd rather you covered this up. It makes you too distinctive.'

He twisted so he could peer spuriously at her mass of copper curls.

'Yeah, mine's too distinctive too. But I've a scarf I can cover mine with. What do you say, we'll be more careful this time and keep to ourselves. I'm sick of *stupid pizza* too' – they had mostly eaten take-out food for three days straight – 'and want to try some of those crab cakes they had on the pier. What do you say, Jacob?'

'I've got my hat, but I'm not eating crab. They look gross!'

'You can have anything you want,' she said, happy to find him off the bed and seeking his cap. 'Chicken? You want chicken? I'll get you chicken. Fries? You want fries? I'll get you—'

'I get *you*, Mom. I can have whatever I like!' Jacob grinned, showing white adult teeth slightly too large in his juvenile features. He yanked down a ball cap over his hair, shoving a few stray locks up under the brim. 'C'mon, Mom, where's your scarf? Let's get outta here.'

'I need to check I've enough cash . . .' She slapped her skirt pockets, then dug around, feeling for her billfold. It was more likely to be in her tote bag, but she checked for loose change: every spare cent was important. Her fingertips touched an unexpected item. She took out a laminated business card.

Where had the card come from? She read it and immediately understood. It carried a name: Teresa Grey, and the legend: Private Investigator, and her license number, plus her telephone and email contact details. After Elspeth turned down the offer of help from Nicolas Villere, and they'd hugged goodbye, he must have slipped the card into her pocket. She snapped the card against her opposite hand, in thought for a moment, before Jacob tossed her headscarf at her.

'C'mon, Mom, let's get outta here before I explode from boredom.'

'Just let me fix this,' Elspeth said, as she ducked in front of a mirror to wrap up her hair and tie the scarf. 'There, what do you think? Can you still tell who I am?'

Jacob snorted at her lame humor.

He headed for the door and began unlatching it.

Elspeth cast around, spotted her tote bag and grabbed it.

Distractedly she shoved Tess's business card back into her skirt pocket. She hurried over to help unlock the door before Jacob had it pulled off its hinges.

She shut the door behind her. Jacob was already halfway down the corridor towards the elevators. They had used the elevator only once during their stay: it was a new experience for her son, but not one he'd enjoyed. The small car was far too claustrophobic – and another throwback to the cellar – for comfort. He bypassed it and stood with a hand on the stairwell exit door.

'Wait for me,' she said, unwilling to let him out of her sight.

Jacob danced restlessly from foot to foot, and once she'd reached him he pushed open the door and began bounding down the stairs. Elspeth followed, almost as eager to reach open air. Leaving the hotel she kept her head down, glancing surreptitiously at other guests seated in the lobby and was relieved none had familiar faces. They spilled out onto Market Street. There were plenty eateries across the road from the hotel, but she'd put an idea into Jacob's head when mentioning the crab cakes she'd read about on a café menu on one of the piers. Jacob stepped out, heading across Fore Street towards the corner where she'd last seen Nicolas Villere.

She cast back her mind to how things with Nicolas had been, and how things might have turned out if she'd chosen him rather than the lies fed to her by her future husband and jailer. Her gaze went to Jacob as he sloped along the sidewalk, ungainly and awkward as he began entering puberty. What would life have been like for her son if he'd been raised here instead of that accursed commune? She grew misty-eyed, and regretful. She squeezed the bridge of her nose between her finger and thumb, then swept away the tears that had suddenly streamed down her cheeks: she didn't want Jacob to see her upset, she had to be strong for him. She was unaware of the man watching her from the doorway of a shop on the opposite sidewalk. If she'd spotted him, she would have recognized his face, because he made no attempt to hide it. He watched her continue towards the sea front, and once she had a block's lead he followed. He pulled out his cell phone as he walked.

SEVEN

'Well?' Po asked. 'What are you thinking, Tess?'

'I can't give you an answer,' Tess replied, 'because I don't know how I feel about it yet. I need some time to absorb the idea.'

'But what if he is my son?'

'You don't know if that's true or not, do you? Wait a minute, did Elspeth put that idea in your head?'

'Nope. I have eyes that can see, Tess.'

They were still on the porch swing, and evening had fallen. The breeze had dropped, and the air was still warm enough that Tess was yet to wrap up in a blanket. Unlike before, she had unfolded her legs from under her and settled her bare feet on the floor. She leaned forward and braced both palms on the front edge of the swing. By virtue of her posture, Po had been moved away a few inches along the seat. Their minor separation spoke volumes about their moods.

'Did you ask her about him?'

'Like I said, I only spoke with her for a coupla minutes, and didn't get chapter and verse. Only that she wasn't stickin' around, and that she was tryin' to avoid her abusive husband.'

'It's odd that she'd be so open about running away . . . and why.'

'Maybe she was reachin' out for help, after all. But she didn't know how to ask, and grew embarrassed when I offered it.'

'She seemed frightened?'

'Yeah. At first it was fear that I'd recognized her, then at what it might mean if I snitched.'

'Did you speak with the boy?'

'I said hi, but he was kinda tight-lipped. Looked me up and down like I was some kinda space alien from Mars. That was the extent of interest Jacob showed in me.'

'That's teenagers for you.'

'He ain't a teenager yet, he can't be more than nine, maybe ten at a push.'

'He was tall for his age.'

'Yeah,' Po agreed, forcing his original point home, 'so was I. He also has my coloring and my eyes.'

'His mother is tall, and, what about her eyes?'

'Green.'

'And Jacob's are turquoise, like yours?'

'Yup.'

'Doesn't mean a thing,' she said, and it must have sounded like total denial.

'Are you upset?'

'That you might be a father to a kid you've never met before?'

He didn't reply. The tilt of his head said, What else could I have meant?

'I'm not upset, Po,' she reassured him. 'What right have I got to be upset?'

'You're my fiancée.' He reached and placed his hand over hers. 'I thought maybe in the future, y'know, once we're wed, we'd try for babies of our own.'

'I do want kids . . . in the future.'

'It's just that we ain't gettin' any younger, Tess.'

She turned a sharp squint on him. Tess was in her mid-thirties, she might be pushing the envelope when it came to first-time motherhood, but she wasn't over the hill yet.

'Least, I am,' he corrected. 'The way things are going, I'm gonna be so old our kids might confuse me for their grandpa.'

Tess removed her hand, but only so she could nudge him with her elbow. 'Chill out, Methuselah, there's still some life in you yet.'

He ghosted a smile at the jibe, taking it for the endearment she intended.

'If he is my son . . .'

'Before you go any further with this you need to speak to Elspeth about him and find out for sure. After that, well, there's always a paternity test.'

'You'd support me if it came to it?'

Tess didn't answer. Really, there was no need.

Po fell silent.

Tess said, 'I'm not going to lie to you, Po. I'm a bit mixed up in my head, right now. But that isn't to say I'm upset, or mad, or anything else . . . I'm just, I don't know, *numb*. Like I said, I need to absorb this, but without any clarity I don't know exactly what to absorb.'

'So you think I should contact her and ask straight out?'

'Yeah. Yeah, I do.'

'You'd come with me?'

'If that's what you want.'

He took her hand again and squeezed.

'One problem,' he said.

'You don't know how to contact her? Then it's fortunate that your partner is a private investigator, isn't it?'

'How do you suggest we start looking?'

'So, she's on the run, and was trying to avoid anyone who knew her? That means she probably isn't staying with anyone local, so took a room at a hotel instead. What was her surname again?'

'Fuchs.'

'That's her married name?'

'Nope. That's what I knew her as. I don't know who she wed.'

'It's unlikely she used her married name when making a booking, would she have used her maiden name, though?' The question was rhetorical. 'Last you saw her she was walking off up Market Street, right? There's a hotel past the corner of Market and Fore.'

'Doesn't mean she's stayin' there. If she's on the run wouldn't she choose somewhere off the beaten path, and a bit less expensive?'

'By the same token, wouldn't she have avoided strolling about on the piers where it was likely she'd bump into somebody she knew?'

'Fair comment.'

'For somebody trying to hide she's making a poor job of it.'

'It's probably her first time,' Po reminded her. 'Running away from abuse isn't exactly somethin' you can become an expert at. You get away clean or you get caught, there's not much scope for fine-honing your skills.'

'Let me go fetch my cell phone and I'll make a start.' Tess stood from the swing, adjusting her shorts so they weren't riding so high. Po gave her rump an affectionate stroke. 'Behave yourself, I never said if I'd forgiven you for standing me up yet.'

He lounged back on the swing, watching her as she entered the house. She hobbled on her blistered feet, rubbing it in about her discomfort. He smiled at her daft antics. She was back within half a minute, walking perfectly normal this time. She frowned down at her cell phone.

'Whassup?' Po asked.

'My ringer was off. I've several missed calls, all from the same number.'

'Whose number?'

She squinted at him. 'Am I a psychic all of a sudden?'

'Maybe you should call her back.'

She turned the screen to him. 'Is this Elspeth's number?'

'I ain't psychic either, but I might've slipped her your business card when she hugged me goodbye. Y'know, just in case she had a change of mind.'

She shook her head, but admittedly his move with the business card could save her some trouble locating Elspeth. Her idea of calling the hotel on Market Street was only the first of many inquiries she could have to make before finding her. Shaking her head at him again, she brought up the number and hit the call button. She watched Po take a deep breath and hold it. The phone rang repeatedly.

'No answer,' she said, and Po finally exhaled; his face had grown several shades darker.

'Give it a minute and then try again,' he urged.

Tess was about to hit the call button. Instead her phone began ringing quietly, the volume still turned low and the reason they hadn't heard it ringing earlier. 'Same number.'

'You gonna answer it?'

She did. 'Hello, this is Tess Grey.'

'Is Nicolas there please?' The voice was an anxious whisper.

'Is this Elspeth Fuchs?' asked Tess, though the chance of it being anyone else verged on zero.

'Please, I need to speak with Nicolas.'

'Nicolas is with me,' Tess said, and held out the phone so that they could both hear and speak. 'Elspeth, is something the matter?'

'Please, I need your help,' Elspeth replied still at a fearful whisper. 'I'm being followed; I'm afraid they're going to take my son away. Nicolas said you could help.'

'Who's following you?' Po demanded.

Hearing him, Elspeth's words came out in a rush. 'I don't know, just some guy. I haven't had a good look at his face yet. But he followed us from the hotel and . . . I think he was watching for us leaving. He's on his cell, talking to somebody else. I think he's talking to Caleb. I think Caleb's coming for us. Please, Nicolas, you said you could help.'

Tess exchanged a glance with him, nodded, but he didn't require permission to answer for them both. 'We will help,' he said. 'Elspeth, where are you?'

'We're outside a chowder restaurant on Custom House Wharf.'

'This guy, can you see him?'

'Yes. He's further down the boardwalk pretending he's interested in the boats.'

'Is he aware that you've made him?'

'Yes. No. I don't know! He's watching us, but has been careful not to make eye contact; he's definitely after us. Everywhere we've been since we came out, he's been, and it isn't down to coincidence.'

They were already scrambling into action, Tess looking for shoes she could slip into, while Po was digging for his car keys. 'OK. Listen to me,' Po instructed. 'Don't give him any reason to approach or chase you. Carry on walking, take it easy, and stay near to other people. Go back to where we first laid eyes on each other this afternoon. You know where I mean, the Berlin Wall monument? Wait there in full view, so he can't get at you alone. If he does approach you, shout and scream, make as much noise and fuss as possible. We are about twenty minutes away, but we are comin', OK. Stay on the phone and don't hang up. I've a friend who might be much closer to you; if he's home he should be there within five minutes.'

Tess and Po raced to where his Mustang waited.

'How will I know your friend from another of Caleb's men?'

'He's called Pinky Leclerc,' said Po, as he clambered into the driving seat, 'and believe me, there's no mistakin' Pinky.'

EIGHT

Caleb Moorcock drove with his cell phone to his ear, taking things steady as he followed the traffic. It was dusk, and many of the daytime visitors had returned to their hotels or to restaurants for dinner. The streets were still busy though, with groups of drinkers making their first forays of the evening on the bars. It would do him no good to run over any of the young carousers who thought nothing of trotting out into the traffic without warning. His pickup, with its extended cab, was a huge vehicle and would turn a careless jaywalker into mulch beneath its tires. Not that he gave a shit for any of their lives, but he didn't want to attract the attention of the police while he was here in Portland. Unlike back home where his pa had most of the local sheriff's deputies on his payroll, the cops here were another story entirely. His intention was to leave Portland without anyone knowing he'd even been in town, his primary reason for not storming Elspeth's hotel already and dragging her and the boy kicking and screaming to his truck.

Days ago Caleb had traveled from the commune, dogging Elspeth's steps as she fled across the state lines to the town where she had grown up. When first she'd lit out, he had been unsure where she would flee, but with little experience of living anywhere but the commune it was likely she'd return somewhere familiar from her adolescence. He knew she'd no family here to speak of, both of her parents having passed, and her one surviving sister living in the Far East. Caleb had wondered if she had an old friend she planned running to, but it had been more than ten years since she had left Portland, and in that time he had not allowed her to keep in touch with anyone. The commune was secular, its regular inhabitants dissuaded from communicating with the outside world by the banning of cell phones, radios and computers. Only a select few had access to communication equipment, and the privilege did not extend to women or children. When Caleb had traveled here, it was with a companion. Jeremy Decker spoke to him on the phone, keeping him apprised of Elspeth's movements on the pier, guiding Caleb to his wife.

Earlier in the day, Caleb and Decker had both observed Elspeth and Jacob as they spoke briefly with a tall guy that Caleb was certain he had seen before. It was only when Elspeth initiated a hug that Caleb had recalled Po'boy's identity and caused his teeth to grind in anger. Po'boy was the damn Cajun Elspeth had been dallying with before Caleb arrived on the scene and swept her off her feet. As he watched them part, Elspeth blowing a kiss at her old sweetheart, Caleb had entertained the notion that Po'boy was her reason for returning here. But no. Further observation showed Elspeth rushing back to her hotel with Jacob in tow, almost as eager to escape Po'boy as from Caleb himself. Nominating Decker to stake out the hotel, Caleb had gone to another hotel from where he could strategize. He had used his cell phone to call his pa, and request some more guys to help him bring home his wife and son. His brother Darrell was en route now with four of the boys, and a vehicle in which the two runaways could be transported back to where they belonged. Worryingly, Decker had reported that Elspeth had seemingly gotten her hands on a cell phone and was talking to somebody, maybe making arrangements to move on. It wasn't an ideal scenario, but if the opportunity arose, Caleb would grab her and the boy and haul them away in his pickup first, and transfer them to the van once Darrell arrived.

According to Decker he could swing the pickup off the main strip onto the pier, and park perhaps outside one of the restaurants or boat hire shops there. If they could corral Elspeth and Jacob towards the truck, Caleb could step out once they were close and usher them onboard with little fuss. He felt for the gun on his hip, hidden for now under the tail of his jacket and thought showing it would be enough motivation to make them do as they were told. Their initial plan got scuppered though.

'They're on the move again,' Decker announced.

'Where to?'

'Coming back towards you. They're staying close to a bunch of local kids.'

'Has she spotted you, Jer?'

'I think we're still good, Caleb. She hasn't gotten a look at my face. If she had, she would've recognized me and made more of an attempt at escaping by now.'

'She still on her cell?'

'Carrying it, but isn't speaking. She was using it as a camera before, maybe that's why she's kept it out for now.' Decker's footsteps could be heard clopping along the sidewalk.

'I'm coming up on the parking lot we used earlier,' Caleb said, as he approached the public lot on Widgery Wharf. 'How far away are they?'

'A couple of blocks still.'

'OK,' said Caleb, making a quick right turn, 'I'm gonna park here. You keep me informed to where they go next.'

Keeping his cell line open, Caleb parked the truck and stepped out. He was near the front of the lot, with a view onto Commercial Street.

'Still heading your way,' Decker announced.

'Can't see them yet.'

'You will. No. Wait. They've veered off. Left onto another pier, I see a sign for Long Wharf. They're standing next to some graffiti-covered slabs of concrete.'

Caleb strode towards the main strip. It was more than a decade since he'd spent any length of time in Portland, but he still had a fair memory of its layout: a few businesses and store fronts had changed, but it was largely the same as when he used to conduct business here. He vaguely recalled there was some crappy monument to the fall of the Berlin Wall not too far away. He began moving towards it, but stalled after only a few steps. If Elspeth or Jacob spotted him he'd blow the plan to grab them quietly.

'I'm on hand for when things change,' he told Decker. 'For now, stick close to them and tell me when they move on.'

'Will do . . . uh, Caleb. We might have a problem.'

A spike of adrenalin shot through him. 'What kind of problem?'

'There's some big black guy just pulled in off the street and waved them over.'

'A black guy?'

'A black guy,' Decker confirmed, as if the newcomer's skin color was the determining factor of the perceived trouble. 'Maybe he's who Elspeth's been speaking with on her cell. What do you want me to do, Caleb?'

'I'm coming,' Caleb told him, 'on foot. Don't do anything. Just watch like I told you to.'

'You better be quick, it looks as if Elspeth and the boy are getting in the black dude's car.'

'Shit!' Caleb had been hopeful that the stranger had an innocent reason for calling over Elspeth; guys of his skin color were few and far between in Portland, and Caleb had hoped he was a tourist perhaps seeking directions. But no. Maybe Elspeth had hailed an Uber to take her elsewhere. If that were the case, then being on foot was not a good option for following. He span around and headed at a trot for his pickup. 'Jer, you keep your eyes on them. Tell me where they're going. I'm heading back for the truck.'

'Will do . . . uh, *damnit*, Caleb. The black guy's giving me the stink-eye.'

'Say what?'

'I think Elspeth might have made me, man.'

'Goddamnit!' Caleb piled into his pickup and got it started. 'OK, I'm moving. Keep outta the way for now, and don't say anything. Don't even look at them.'

'Yeah, I've backed off out of sight. The car's one of those big GMC suburbans, as black as its driver.'

'OK, yeah. I see it. It's back on the main strip heading back the way you just come. I'm three or four vehicles behind, so I don't think they're aware of me yet.'

'Pick me up,' said Decker.

'Can't take the chance they see me stopping for you, Jer. I'm gonna follow and see where they end up.'

'What do you want me to do, man?'

'I'll come back for you. Stay put or you can go on back to our hotel and wait there.'

'The hotel's miles away.'

'Use your head, Jer, and call a goddamn cab. Do I have to do all your thinking for you?'

Decker didn't answer. Caleb didn't have to do his thinking, no, but he rarely got to do what he wanted without Caleb's permission. Caleb ended the call. He concentrated on following the GMC, ignoring a plaintive look from Decker who he passed standing at roadside now. To give Decker his due, he made no indication towards the pickup. If those in the GMC had their eyes on its mirrors they'd have no idea Caleb's pickup was connected to the man they'd just given the slip.

The GMC headed out of town, took a left and followed the main thoroughfare to where it met the interstate highway. Caleb took precautions not to follow too closely onto the highway, allowing several more cars to get between them before he fell into line and crossed over the bridge at the mouth to Back Cove. Caleb expected the GMC to keep going but its flashers indicated a turn off the highway and before long he was only three cars back as the black guy took Elspeth and Jacob along the curving shoreline of the cove. Within another minute the GMC pulled into an asphalt parking lot at the entrance of a park. Caleb had nowhere to go but past, and he ensured he kept his face averted so he wasn't spotted. About fifty yards further on he caught a right turn giving vehicular access deeper into the park. With nothing else for it he drove another hundred yards or so along the road, then swung his pickup onto the grassy shoulder. Through the bushes at the edge of the park he could just see the black GMC's headlights, but little else. His vantage was no good. He pulled out again, and very shortly found another entrance into the memorial park, complete with plenty parking slots empty this late in the evening. Wasting no time he disembarked the vehicle and jogged down a footpath towards the front of the park. As he approached where he'd last seen the GMC's lights the scenario had changed: another vehicle had pulled into the lot alongside it. Several figures were standing around the cars. Caleb slunk off the path, and put his silhouette with his back to the trees; in the dimness he'd be nigh on indistinguishable from the foliage. With as much stealth as possible, he began approaching, hoping to hear what was being said. Back home he regularly stalked game in the woods surrounding the commune, so was confident he could stay hidden from these folks who'd have no possible reason to suspect they were being observed. Back there he was normally armed with a rifle. Out of habit, he drew his sidearm and held it down by his hip.

He got close, but their voices were a muffled babble.

It didn't matter if he could distinguish individual voices or not, he already had a fair idea what was going on. The backdrop of the cove helped him discern one figure from another: the city lights twinkled on the water, and he could easily determine one person from the next as they moved between the cars and the reflected lights. He counted four people in total, and guessed that Jacob had been instructed to stay inside the GMC while the adults conspired.

Elspeth's frame was tall and willowy, easily recognized. Decker had been correct in describing the black guy as big. In fact, if anything he'd underestimated him. The black guy was huge, both in height and girth, with most of the excess weight in his bottom half. There was another woman, whose hair looked fair even in the dimness, shorter and more rounded of limb than Elspeth. If Elspeth had a match that was her opposite sex it was with the final person. He was tall and slim too, but with wide shoulders and long arms he'd crossed at his chest.

'Goddamn, if it ain't Po'boy again,' Caleb growled under his breath.

Earlier, he'd decided that Elspeth's meeting with the Cajun had been random, unplanned. Now he was unconvinced. Maybe Elspeth hadn't spotted Decker at all, and this had always been the plan. Po'boy had arranged his black pal to pick up Elspeth and Jacob and meet him here to . . . then what?

Judging by their body language it was apparent that Po'boy and the blond were a couple, so surely this wasn't about Elspeth and the Cajun taking up where they'd last left off? He'd sooner walk on over there and blow both Po'boy's and Elspeth's brains out than allow her to go with another man. He had warned the bitch countless times; she belonged to him, and nobody could have her but *him*.

He was shivering in cold rage, his palm slick on the butt of his pistol, index finger jittery on the trigger. He chewed his bottom lip as he watched the four adults talking. Po'boy had unfolded his arms to gesticulate: his voice wasn't raised, but he damn well was making his point heard. Caleb wanted to hear more. He moved closer, using the hanging boughs of a tree as cover. He made no noise, kept his movements slow and controlled.

Po'boy snapped a look in his direction.

Caleb halted.

For a second he feared that the darkness wasn't deep enough to conceal him. He wondered if he had caught a reflection of the lights on him somehow and drawn the Cajun's attention. Po'boy stared at him intensely, and again Caleb stroked the trigger of his gun. The blond woman said something, and Po'boy's attention slipped from his hiding place as he turned to answer her. Caleb instantly retreated. He'd seen enough for now to understand there was nothing to be gained from getting this close. Rather than return to the path and jog back the way he'd come, he continued backing through the trees until he emerged onto the shoulder where he'd briefly stopped before. Out of sight of those on the parking lot he ran to get back to his pickup. Within a minute he was back, having driven with his headlamps doused. Through the trees he could still make out the glimmers of the GMC's and also the second vehicle's headlights, so they hadn't given him the slip. Through his open window he heard muffled voices, then the clunks of doors opening and closing. Both cars began to maneuver. Caleb waited. They passed the road end, the GMC followed by an old muscle car, and continued around the cove to his right. He allowed them ten seconds to gain some distance, then switched on his low beams and followed.

NINE

'We could rustle up some supper if you're hungry,' Tess offered.

'Not for me,' Elspeth said, 'I lost my appetite when I realized we were being followed.'

'What about your son? I bet he could eat something?'

'Boys are like puppies, they'll eat as much as you keep putting down for them.' Elspeth smiled at the imagery.

'I could do some eggs, bacon . . . whatever?'

'I think Jacob had his mind set on a cheeseburger and fries.'

'I can maybe have Po go out to the drive thru and—'

'Po,' said Elspeth. 'I've heard you call Nicolas by that name a few times now. He doesn't go by Po'boy anymore?'

'To hear him say it, he never did go by Po'boy. That was a snarky nickname given to him by some of the people hereabouts when they learned he hailed from way down south.' Tess laughed at a memory from the first time she'd met him in the grimy office of Charley's Autoshop. '"It was meant as a slur on my Acadian heritage. I showed them I was nobody's boy",' she mimicked him.

'Yeah, that sounds like him alright. He always was a proud man.'

Tess prickled at Elspeth's words, but hid her annoyance well. Another woman had no right speaking about her man with such familiarity. She moved away across the kitchen, to give herself a moment to compose a response that wouldn't make her sound jealous and insecure. 'He's gotten used to being called Po now; in fact it's what he tells his friends to call him. It's all I've ever known him as,' she said.

'So I should stop referring to him as Nicolas?'

'No, it's fine. Pinky still calls him Nicolas and he's his best friend of all.'

'You prefer Tess to Teresa?'

'Yep, Teresa's my professional name, or what my mother calls

me when I've supposedly done something wrong' – she chuckled
– 'which is usually every time we speak.'

'You're lucky to still have a mother who cares about you,'
Elspeth said morosely. 'My mom died when I was a child. Lord,
I miss her every day.'

Tess didn't know what to say. She wasn't going to offer fake
platitudes. 'At least Jacob still has his mom, right?'

'I'd die for that boy,' said Elspeth, and Tess believed her. She
had intended leading the conversation about Jacob, to perhaps
prompt Elspeth into revealing his parentage. It felt wrong though.
If there was going to be a conversation about Jacob's biological
father, it should be between Po and Elspeth first.

'Hopefully it won't come to that,' Tess said. She swirled a hand
in the air, as if to roll back the evening to when Elspeth realized
she was under observation before she was picked up and brought
back to Po's house.

'The man that was following you, you didn't get a clear look
at him?'

'He took care to hide his face. But there was plenty about him
I recognized. He was dressed differently than I've seen him before,
but I am positive it was a friend of my husband. I've had little to
do with him, but seen him around plenty of times, so I recognized
his general shape and his mannerisms. I can't be absolutely sure
without seeing his face, but I'd lay good money on him being
Jeremy Decker.'

'Is this Decker dangerous?'

'Not in the same way that Caleb and his brothers are,' Elspeth
said.

'What can we expect from Caleb if he does happen to be here
in Portland?'

Elspeth tussled with the question. 'There's only so much I can
tell you without endangering myself, and my son, more than we
already are. But here, I'll show you what kind of man Caleb
Moorcock is.'

Without warning, Elspeth hiked up her skirt to display her
long legs. Precariously close to her groin several scars marred
her. Most were puckered circles of risen tissue; a couple of the
obvious cigarette burns had eaten deep craters into her flesh. As
a sheriff's deputy Tess had witnessed some horrific sights, but

this demonstration of Caleb's cruelty had been totally unexpected and caused her to cringe. Elspeth nodded. 'I could show you more of these on my breasts. The burns are Caleb's way of ensuring no other man will ever find me desirable again.'

'Dear God,' Tess said, as Elspeth lowered her skirt, 'how long has this been going on?'

'Since the first time? Well, that would've been within days of me moving into his father's commune; it was Caleb's way of putting his stamp of ownership on me. These are my visible scars: you won't believe how many times I was beaten, but those bruises and welts have healed; up here' – she tapped her head – 'I still carry every one of them and they'll be with me for the rest of my life. But do you know something, Tess? These aren't the reason I finally built up the courage to run. It was because lately Caleb has turned his attention on Jacob.'

'He has been abusing the boy?'

'He has similar scars to mine on his arms and back.' Elspeth's eyes watered, and she shivered with poorly suppressed frustration. 'I tried to stop him, I really did, but he would just lock me up and then do whatever he wished to our boy.'

'We need to call the police—'

'No! Please don't.'

'Caleb can't be allowed to get away with what he's done to you both. We should—'

Again Elspeth cut her off; this time she lunged and grabbed the front of Tess's shirt. 'Please, Tess, don't tell the police.'

'Caleb should be held accountable.'

'He should, but he already warned me what will happen if I claimed he'd hurt us. He has dozens of witnesses that will swear I self-harmed, that I was the one that hurt Jacob. He said I'd be the one in trouble, and that I would have Jacob taken away from me and I'd never see him again. It's why I ran away, I had to get Jacob away from him, to protect him.'

'Once Jacob's testimony is heard and it backs up your version of events, Caleb won't have a leg to stand on.'

Elspeth released Tess and stood back. She lowered her voice, but it didn't lessen in emphasis. 'Caleb has already thought about that. He warned me how he'd smear my character with the help of the others in the commune; how they'd all swear I was a manipulative liar, and that I'd twisted everything about his dad in Jacob's mind. Tess, you don't know the hold the Moorcock family has over the others in the commune. They're all controlled to a lesser or greater degree than I was and will do and say anything they're instructed.'

'Other women and children are being abused? So this isn't only about Caleb being a lousy husband and father?'

'The commune has strict rules and they were made and are enforced by men.'

'Are the rules based on a particular religion?'

'Only where they suit my father-in-law's agenda. Mostly they're the gospel of Eldon Moorcock and that's all that is important to *him*.'

Tess's knowledge of community living was slim. What she knew she'd learned of through limited exposure to books or movies on the subject, and usually these were embroidered to fit the genre of the story. She was aware that hippie communes had been established in the US decades ago, and that some religious communities had flourished for decades too. Her main point of reference was what had occurred at the New Mount Carmel Center, outside Waco, Texas, with the fatal law enforcement siege of David Koresh's Branch Davidian compound. As a result she had a jaded view of cultists and commune leaders in general. From what she had already gathered from Elspeth, Eldon Moorcock's commune was more akin to a survivalist or prepper retreat, where her father-in-law had formed an armed militia prepared to protect their homes and property in the event of societal collapse, war or natural catastrophe. Eldon Moorcock had elevated himself to the commune's monarch, and by all accounts he ruled with an iron fist. Religion, in this case, was not the necessary ingredient of this half-baked tyrant; it was the cruelest form of misogyny.

'How does the commune sustain its lifestyle?' she asked.

'It was originally based upon the idea of income sharing. The members pooled their money in a collective pot, and it was apportioned out as and when it was needed. Ha! Well, that was the original idea. The Moorcock family never goes without, whereas the rest of us, we live off the scraps that Eldon throws to us.'

'A place ran like that sounds unsustainable. Surely its inhabitants are unhappy with the arrangement, and I doubt they'd attract new members willing to hand over their savings.'

'Fear is a strong motivator. It ensures obedience, cooperation and silence. New members are few and far between, but Eldon doesn't rely on fresh donors these days, he has built other "avenues of revenue".'

'In what way?'

Elspeth shook her head. 'I said earlier there's only so much I can tell you. I've already endangered us by running away with Jacob, and can expect to be punished if we're caught, but if Eldon suspects I've given away any of his secrets, it risks our lives.'

'These avenues are obviously criminal?'

Tess's question was rhetorical and didn't require an answer. Elspeth waved it off though. 'I can't say.'

'You're still allowing your fear of him to control you,' Tess warned.

'If you were in *my* shoes?'

'You're right, and I won't push you for more. You've barely met me, and I have no right expecting you to fully trust me yet. But I hope once you think about it you'll tell me everything. I want to help you and Jacob, Elspeth. I also want to help the others being held under Eldon's control. Don't you think they also deserve help?'

'Right now I'm only interested in protecting my son.' Elspeth abruptly spun around, realizing that she had not kept her eye glued on her boy, perhaps for the first time since they'd fled the commune. 'Jacob? Jacob!'

'It's OK, Elspeth,' said Tess, 'he's through in the family room with Po and Pinky. He's perfectly safe with them.'

Elspeth shivered with indecision: it was easy to tell she had formed a poor opinion of men, but considering what she'd gone through for years it was unsurprising.

'They're both the best of men,' Tess reassured her. 'Totally the opposite of the monsters you've been controlled by.'

'Is Pinky . . .?'

Tess guessed where the unfinished question was heading. 'Is Pinky gay?'

Elspeth made a face.

Pinky probably was gay, by anyone's definition but his. He was more asexual – or he wasn't defined by a single sexuality – and as far as Tess was aware was not sexually active. Once she'd believed he suffered a hang up over his medical condition that often caused a painful bloating of his lower limbs, and for that reason refrained from romantic dalliances. However, as she'd grown to know him better, she had come to understand that love of the heart and mind trumped the physical act for Pinky. One thing that he was not was any danger to little boys and Tess was about to defend him. There was no need.

'I was about to ask if he's a little *strange*,' Elspeth corrected her. 'He has a very odd way with words. He's very eccentric, he's . . . *flamboyant*.'

'He is indeed. He has an odd way of expressing himself, but no, he isn't odd or strange in any other way. He's a lovely person, the best friend you could ask for, and like I said the best of men.'

'By his very existence, Caleb and his family would hate him. He embodies everything they despise in men.'

'The more I hear about your in-laws the more I think they need to be muzzled like slathering beasts.'

'I wish I'd known the truth ten years ago. Things would have been so different, so much better.'

Tess nibbled her bottom lip. It was best that she didn't answer directly, because if Elspeth hadn't followed Caleb back to New York, then who knew how Elspeth's relationship with Po might have progressed. She loved Po and couldn't countenance her life without him in it now. 'We can all be wise in hindsight,' she finally said.

'Speaking of which, I need to make arrangements to move on.'

'You and Jacob are welcome to stay here a few days, until you can—'

'Thanks, Tess, but no. We'll stay the night, but in the morning we're moving on. Now we know that Caleb has found us here we can't stay. I might ask that you take us back to our hotel in the morning, to collect our things, and then maybe wait until we get on a bus.'

'Then what? You just keep on running? You disappear?'

'That's the plan.'

Tess again fell silent. More than ever it was imperative that Po talked with Elspeth before she was allowed to vanish with Jacob.

But then what? What if it transpired that he was Jacob's biological father? One thing that Tess was positive about: if Jacob was his child, and he discovered how Caleb had abused him, then woe betide the consequences.

TEN

Stalking alert prey is difficult, and Caleb was under no illusion: Po'boy was more alert to his surroundings than most. Following the convoy of two vehicles back to this neighborhood north of Portland hadn't been the issue. He'd managed to stay back far enough to avoid being picked out from other road users as the muscle car led the way to this secluded spot. Caleb was unfamiliar with this part of town, but once they'd gotten into a series of winding suburban streets he'd had the sense to fall back. There could only be a few destinations where Po'boy was heading to, because Caleb had taken note of signage stating that the streets ahead were 'no thru roads'. He guessed there was some feature of the landscape that constrained the neighborhood, and was unsurprised when they'd come upon a river. Caleb had prowled the streets after that until he followed a twisting route and discovered the Mustang and GMC parked in the yard of a ranch-style property abutting the woods adjacent to the riverbank. Caleb had driven away to a safer spot and left his pickup, returning on foot to observe from the ranch's perimeter. Trees and underbrush gave him plenty of hiding places.

There were neighboring houses, but none close enough that he risked discovery. He secreted himself in a drainage ditch, currently dried out, and watched the ranch through a screen of grass and bushes left to grow wild at the edge of the property. There was not much to see. Several rooms were lighted, but the drapes were drawn at most of the windows. He occasionally spotted a shadow cast upon the drapes as somebody moved about inside the house. A light burned on the porch above the front door too, but the door was shut for the most part. However, Po'boy had come outside twice while Caleb hid in the ditch, each time sparking up a cigarette and standing out in the yard. This was where Caleb gained the impression that the Cajun was more in tune with his surroundings than most other people. Po'boy smoked, but did so at a slow prowl around his front yard. He moved languidly, but with his ears cocked to the slightest sound and his eyes were on swivels.

The first time he'd come outside to smoke, Caleb had shifted. He barely heard the brush of his clothing against the grass, but Po'boy's head snapped around. How had he heard the slight sounds he'd made when the burble of the nearby river filled the night with white noise? Caleb couldn't be seen in the dark, but he lowered down nevertheless, peering out between the grasses as Po'boy stared back at him. He watched the tall man take a couple of steps forward, and Caleb drew his firearm. Shooting Po'boy wasn't in his initial plan, but if it came to him being discovered he would pull the trigger. After that he would be forced to storm the house and take his chances with the black dude and the blonde woman, and drag his wife and boy away at gunpoint. It was a crazy, rash response to consider, but that was Caleb Moorcock's nature.

As it were Mother Nature conspired to assist Caleb. A bird roosting in the trees a few yards away made an abrupt squawk, and then it clattered through the branches as it took flight. It only made a short-lived swoop before it found a perch on the next tree. It squawked again. Po'boy rather than Caleb had disturbed its roost. The Cajun relaxed, the sudden tightness going out of his frame, and he dropped his cigarette and ground it underfoot. He returned to the house.

The immediate danger of discovery over, Caleb holstered his pistol. He was jittery, feeling the effects of a spike of adrenalin as he realized how close he'd come to spoiling everything. If he murdered Po'boy here, stormed the house and killed its occupants before taking Elspeth and Jacob hostage, he would have called down the entire law enforcement community on his head, and there would be no way of breaching the police cordons between here and New York state. Instead of allowing his tripwire nature to control him, he must think things through and act only when the abduction could be successful. He checked his wristwatch: it was still hours until Darrell and the other reinforcements were due to arrive. His only other asset for now was Jeremy Decker, and he had proven next to useless. If Caleb summoned him here, and made him stake out the house, he'd probably give the game away next time its owner came out to smoke. As much as he found squatting in the ditch undesirable and uncomfortable, Caleb still deemed himself the best man for the job.

Because Po'boy's attention had already been focused on this spot, it was time to move. He scooted away, came up to a crouch and then stalked along the fence line to a spot nearer the yard's entrance. From the fresh vantage his view was slightly limited, but it gave him better access to retreat should Po'boy decide to investigate a suspicious sound next time. Besides, everyone was inside, and if and when his targets left, it would probably be in either one of the vehicles parked out front. Before they were done boarding, Caleb could slip away, get in his pickup and be waiting for when they passed him. It was still not too late for her rescuers to return Elspeth and Jacob back to their hotel, but Caleb doubted it would happen: they'd probably be given shelter in the ranch for the night. He wondered what entreaties Elspeth had made of her hosts, and worse, what secrets she had spilled in the meantime. Once he had them back in his hands, he'd learn the entire truth, and it might be that storming Po'boy's house would be in the cards, because the Moorcocks assiduously protected their secrets. As and when Caleb chose to return, it would be gang-handed and unexpected. They'd be in and out again with little fuss or noise, and be back in the commune long before Po'boy's corpse, and those of his girl and nigger pal, was discovered.

Caleb entertained himself with thoughts of slaying his adversaries. It passed the time swiftly, and then the door opened and Po'boy stepped outside again. He sat on the porch swing, thought better of it, and then came down the steps to stand once more in the yard. He gave a slow, measured perusal of his surroundings, then dug in his shirt pocket and pulled out a pack of cigarettes. He moved between the parked cars while lighting up and taking a deep draw of smoke into his lungs. In the wash of light from the porch light, the smoke wreathed around his head like a halo. Caleb drew his pistol again, resting his thumb on the hammer: he was still entertaining murderous thoughts.

Po'boy emerged from between the cars, and Caleb wasn't surprised when the man's attention went towards his previous hiding place. Po'boy came to a halt, and stood, watching. Finally, his suspicion appeased for now, he allowed his attention to roam. Caleb remained stock-still, even holding his breath while the man's gaze alighted momentarily on his new hiding place. He was invisible in the darkness, fully concealed by brush, but for an insane moment he worried that Po'boy's senses were so heightened he could pierce the night and pick him out where he crouched. Po'boy put his cigarette to his lips and inhaled. He blew out a plume of smoke that dissipated on the breeze. His eyes never left Caleb's position. Caleb adjusted his pistol, aiming at Po'boy's broad chest.

The front door squeaked open and the big black guy came out on the porch. It broke the moment, and Po'boy turned away to regard his pal. Caleb lowered his gun. He studied the newcomer, watching as the big man danced down the steps and joined his friend in the yard. He was huge, with legs like felled lumber, and yet he moved with the grace of a gazelle; he flicked his hands as he spoke, and defined points with a pursed mouth or roll of his shaven head. Caleb hated him passionately. He reconsidered his decision to put off storming the house, because he sure would enjoy putting down that black sonofabitch.

'What are you doing out here, you?' asked the black man as he joined Po'boy.

Po'boy held up his cigarette. 'She doesn't say it, but I know Tess doesn't like me smokin' indoors.'

'You're just looking for an excuse to put things off, you.'

'No, I'm just takin' a smoke, Pinky.'

Pinky? What kind of fuckin' name is that? Caleb shook his head at the ridiculousness of it: big, black motherfucker like that and he goes by Pinky! But then he supposed, the name kind of explained his flapping hands and mellifluous voice. Caleb had hated him on sight; he hated him even more now. This flounce was the man that'd put fear into Jeremy Decker at a glance? Decker needed to man the fuck up!

'C'mon, Nicolas, you can fool a fool, but I ain't nobody's fool, me.'

Nicolas. Caleb had forgotten the Cajun's given name. But it came back to him now: Nicolas *Villere*. When first he'd gotten together with Elspeth she'd mentioned dating Villere to him a few times, until jealousy had gotten the better of him and he'd forbade her from mentioning his goddamn name again.

'I ain't tryin' to fool ya, just tryin' to enjoy a smoke.' To punctuate his point, Villere – Caleb thought of him only as Villere now – took another long drag on his cigarette, before he aimed the glowing ember at where Caleb had previously taken cover. 'Also wanted to check a thing or two out.'

'Like what?'

'Ever got the feelin' you were bein' watched?'

'Nicolas, I'd be upset if I thought people weren't payin' me attention.'

Villere ignored Pinky's assertion. Instead he gestured again at where Caleb had been hidden. 'Thought I heard somethin' from over there, but it was nothin', just a bird lettin' itself be heard. But still, I got that creepy feelin' where the hair stands up on the back of your neck.'

'Maybe it was a ghost.' Even at a distance, Caleb saw the flash of Pinky's sclera as he rolled his eyes. 'I used to think the bayous back home were spooky; they have nothing on these creepy-assed Maine woods at night.'

'Maybe I'm lettin' paranoia get ahold of me. But if Elspeth was right and that guy was followin' her back at the pier, it pays to stay vigilant.'

'Elspeth's a stunning-looking woman, Nicolas, maybe that guy fancied himself as a suitor, him, and was just trying to build up his courage to make his move.'

'Elspeth told Tess she thought she knew him from back home, she even gave him a name: Decker.'

'She didn't get a good look at his face, her, and couldn't be sure. I put the vibe on him and he scuttled off like a rodent. Don't think we need worry about him bothering her again.'

'It still pays to keep an eye out. If that was Decker, Elspeth said his only reason for being here is on her asshole husband's behalf. He might show up yet.'

'You think? Way I see it, me, he's a punk-assed wife-beater with teeny-tiny *cajones*. I don't think we need shed any sweat over him, Nicolas.'

'He doesn't sweat me,' Villere said, 'in fact, I'm out here prayin' the son of a bitch does show up so's I can knock his damn ass into the dirt. D'you see those burns on Jacob's arms? Well, I'm guessin' that boy didn't put those there.'

'Poor kid,' said Pinky. 'Even if he was responsible, which I doubt, he'd have to have some reason for hurting himself like that, and my guess is his home life was shit. And from what I've seen, he loves his momma, him, so I'm guessing Daddy's the real bad guy.'

'That piece of crap doesn't deserve to be called a daddy.'

Caleb had listened to the discourse with growing rage. In the space of a minute he'd been derided left, right and center, called everything from a coward down to a eunuch and back again. He had been threatened with violence by a backwater redneck and a goddamn nigger faggot! But the thing that got his goat most was Villere's final summation. He rose up an inch or two, gripping his gun tightly with the intention of blowing both those bastards apart, before sense grabbed him and gave him a mental shake. Now was not the right time, he cautioned. Wait, be patient, your time will come. Then they'll see what kind of man you really are.

He turned and crawled until he was far enough away. Once he was out of their line of sight he gained his feet, and then back-tracked to where he'd left his pickup. Nobody was going anywhere tonight, he'd concluded, but he'd be back in the small hours for his wife and son, and there was going to be a hellacious reckoning with those boys.

ELEVEN

T he women had moved into the family room by the time Po and Pinky returned inside. Tess had offered the spare room she used as an office, wherein Elspeth and Jacob could bed down for the night, but Elspeth had politely refused. After he'd eaten the supper Tess had cooked up, Jacob had nodded off. Elspeth had sat beside him on a couch, and pulled him in to rest his head on her lap. She teased his locks through her fingers. He was probably a bit old for mollycoddling like a toddler, but under the circumstances Tess thought that comforting him was the right thing to do. He was also old enough to follow the various adult conversations and understand the desperate situation they were in, so her gentle motherly touch was the perfect medicine.

Tess eyed Po as he stalked the room. He was still to raise the subject of Jacob's parentage with Elspeth, and with the boy in the room it wasn't ideal. The kid was confused enough without overhearing what could prove to be a mind-blowing denouement if Po was his father. The subject should be privately discussed between Po and his mother, and the outcome later explained to Jacob if necessary. If Po's suspicion was wrong, it would be best for the boy that he never knew his heritage had been in contention.

Pinky settled into Po's recliner, stretching out his legs and steepling his fingers on his belly. His feet stuck up like a couple of tombstones. Pinky always made himself at home when visiting, and usually disproved the adage that three's a crowd. For the first time, Tess wondered if the maxim was true. But no, it wasn't the case. She and Po had gotten little opportunity to talk things through yet, but it didn't escape her that there were probably things that Po might never be able to comfortably share with her, but he might with his best pal. It was right that Pinky was here to support Po through what must be a confusing and worrying time for her man. Pinky could probably offer a logical and wise response to his concerns, whereas Tess's would more likely be based on emotion. She'd told Po earlier she wasn't angry, and it was true, but if it also proved true that he was Jacob's dad, then it would impact their lives together whichever way she looked at it. At that time, it was difficult imagining her future with a stepson in it.

Admittedly the boy did resemble Po. He had the same intense coloration of his eyes and raven hair, but more so, a similar shape to his beetling brow and strong nose, and several times Tess had caught him frowning and he was how she imagined Po must have looked as a brooding adolescent. After Po's mother deserted him, and his father was murdered, Po's next stint at life was as an inmate at Angola, otherwise known as the Louisiana State Penitentiary. His family home had been sold off, and with it any belongings left behind; as a result, all records of his childhood had been disposed of or lost, so there wasn't a photograph available that Tess could compare Jacob to. Then again, he had fuller lips and a more rounded chin, and they didn't appear to have been passed down through his mother's genes, and could probably be from Caleb Moorcock.

Tess said, 'He's a handsome boy.'

Immediately Po's glance flicked from her to Elspeth, studying the woman's response.

'Yeah, he takes after me,' Elspeth replied, which as an answer was no help whatsoever.

'Does he have anything of his father in him?' Tess asked.

Po scowled so hard he was in danger of forever altering the contours of his features.

Elspeth looked down at her son. The muscles of his face were lax, softened in sleep. 'For his sake, I sure hope not.'

Her answer turned Po away, and he went through into the kitchen. The sound of gushing water followed, and he must have gulped down a glassful. He returned, dashing his lips dry with the back of a wrist. He exchanged a look with Tess, and she answered his unspoken question with a barely perceptible shrug: in her opinion, Elspeth had been referring to Caleb, but that didn't confirm who the boy's biological father was. Her gentle probing for an answer was getting them nowhere.

However, Pinky put things more bluntly. 'Y'know, Nicolas, that boy has a look of you. If I didn't know otherwise I'd say—'

Tess's glare stalled him.

'Uh, what did I say, me?' he asked innocently.

But it was too late to backtrack, and besides, Elspeth had stiffened at his proclamation. Her shoulders rounded as she wrapped her son in both arms and pulled him into a tighter embrace. Jacob stirred and peered up at her but she was unaware. Her eyes darted between Tess and Po, her head shaking as if she was feverish. 'What's this about?' she demanded at a croak.

'I think you know what must be going through all our minds,' said Tess, 'but if it's something you'd rather discuss without Jacob here you could put him to bed in our room.'

'I'm not letting *my son* out of my sight,' Elspeth said, and the croak had become a bitter hiss.

Tess looked to Po for support and he stepped up to the mark. He had obviously concluded that tiptoeing around the subject would get them nowhere. 'Well, Elspeth, you left me what, near to eleven years ago . . . were you pregnant with Jacob at the time?'

'What?' Elspeth struggled to stand, but had to juggle Jacob around first. The boy blinked in confusion, and not a little fear at the sudden change of tone. 'Are you kidding me?' Elspeth demanded as she shot to her feet. She darted looks at all three of her accusers, the darkest of all at Tess. 'Is this coming from *you*? What's wrong, Tess, does our being here threaten your relationship with Nicolas?'

Initially Tess was too stunned to reply.

Po said, 'It's a valid question.'

He was not referring to Elspeth's but his own.

'I took one look at him and thought—'

'Thought what?'

'You heard what Pinky said a moment ago,' Po said.

'Jacob.' Elspeth bent and shook some life into him. The boy was still curled on the couch, blinking, mouth open at the rapid-fire questions, slowly understanding that he was the subject of discussion.

'Mom, what's going on? What are they saying?'

'Never mind *them*. C'mon, get up. We are leaving.'

'Wait,' said Tess, moving in to try to calm Elspeth.

Elspeth swiped an arm at her. 'Get away. We're leaving. I knew expecting to get help from you was too good to be true!'

'Elspeth, wait, calm down. Let's talk things through—' Tess again had to dodge a swipe of Elspeth's hand.

'No, we're leaving. You can't make us stay!' Elspeth dragged Jacob into her embrace, while seeking where she'd left her tote bag.

Po stepped in close and took her elbow in his hand.

Elspeth went from naught to sixty in an instant. She screeched as she tried to wrench free. Po hopped back, both hands held up in surrender. Perhaps taking hold of a woman who'd been subjected to years of misogynistic abuse was not his finest idea. Tess got between Po and Elspeth, holding out her palms, trying to calm the woman. However, Elspeth was in panic mode. She dodged around Tess, drawing Jacob along with her, and then raced to where she'd put down her bag on arrival.

Tess followed, trying to get Elspeth to listen, but she was having none of it. Elspeth grabbed her bag and steamed for the exit door.

'Hold up,' Po said, 'it's miles back to town. Stay here and—'

Jacob broke free of his mother and flung himself bodily at Po.

'Leave my mom alone!' he shrieked as he thrust his hands at Po's chest. Po turned aside, and the boy went after him.

Po caught him by his shoulders and spun him around. 'Don't be stupid, boy. Best you just go with your mother.'

'Jacob! Come on.' Elspeth already had the door open.

Tears streamed from the boy's eyes. He chewed his lips in frustration. He ran to Elspeth, but aimed another command at everyone to leave her alone.

They fled the house, running down the steps into the yard.

Tess and Po both followed to the threshold, but halted there.

Pinky sat where he was, goggle-eyed at the dramatics.

'Geez, that wasn't how I hoped things would go,' said Po.

Elspeth and Jacob were halfway across the yard, heading for the gate.

Tess and Po stepped out onto the porch.

Spotting them Elspeth urged more speed from her son, as if they would pursue them and drag them back inside. Tess got the feeling that Po was entertaining doing just that. She fed her hand into his and held onto him, and felt him rocking back and forth on his heels.

'You'll only make matters worse if you chase them,' she cautioned. 'It's better if we let them calm down and think before we try talking to them again.'

Mother and son had disappeared beyond the ranch's boundary, hidden now by the darkness as they fled down the adjoining road.

'It's one hell of a walk back to their hotel,' Po said, and moved as if he was going to get in the Mustang and give chase. Tess held onto his hand, anchoring him. He looked down at her, at a loss at how to proceed.

'Elspeth has a cell phone, she'll probably phone a cab once she calms down a bit.'

'Man, I feel like a complete heel now, me!' Pinky had joined them on the porch. His usually jovial features were clouded by his perceived wrongdoing. 'Why'd I have to go and open my big yap like that?'

'You only said what was preying on your mind,' Po told him, 'and exactly what was on mine too.'

'I guess you guys hoped to handle the subject more diplomatically though, eh?'

'Whichever way we approached the subject, I don't think Elspeth would've reacted any differently,' said Tess.

'She's frightened,' Po said, in defense of the woman's histrionics.

Tess nodded in agreement, and then added a summation of her own. 'I'd say she's terrified.'

'We can't just let her disappear like this, not before we get an honest answer,' said Po.

'You want me to go after her?' Pinky offered. 'I could take her back to the hotel, give you guys some private time to talk things through.'

Tess said, 'The way she's acting, she'll probably scream blue murder if you go after her, Pinky. Somebody might get the wrong idea, and we don't want you getting in trouble with the cops.'

'Tess's right,' said Po. 'We need to let her cool down first. Let's just let them go for now, and we can go to their hotel first thing. Hopefully by then she'll be calmer and more amenable to our questions.'

'What if that Decker guy's still hanging around?' Pinky asked.

'I'm not convinced he was who she thought he was,' said Po. 'You saw how she reacted just now . . . I think Elspeth's grown so paranoid she's gotten unhinged.'

'She did act a bit irrational,' Tess agreed, 'but it's hardly surprising under the circumstances. Maybe she just felt trapped by us just now and her response was to run rather than face up to the truth.'

'That's the problem, we're no closer to the truth than we were before,' said Po. He stared. As if Elspeth might have second thoughts and lead her boy back to the ranch. 'And whether I'm unconvinced about this Decker guy isn't important. Elspeth believed it was him and it might force her into runnin' before we can get to her in the morning. Tess. What do you say we go after her, we pick her up and take her back to her hotel?'

'Isn't that what I just offered to do, Nicolas?' asked Pinky.

'Yeah. My thoughts are bouncin', right now. Gotta admit, I don't know what the right thing to do is.'

'Then let me decide for myself. If she kicks and screams I won't force the issue, me. I'll back off to a safe distance and keep an eye on them till they're safely in their hotel. If somebody calls the cops about me, you might have to pull a few strings with your bro, Tess.'

He was talking about pulling a favor from Alex Grey. Her older brother had recently been promoted to patrol sergeant with the Portland PD, and was also in a romantic relationship with Tess's employer Emma Clancy. Occasionally Tess used the familial strands they'd knit through their work to assist her. She didn't believe Pinky would need Alex's intervention if he was given a chance to explain why a black guy was trying to coax a frightened white woman and child into his car this late in the evening; however, it was a sad fact that even two decades into the twenty-first century there were still some cops with eighteenth-century mentalities when it came to skin color. If he met the wrong officer Pinky would probably find himself face down on the sidewalk with a service pistol aimed at his head.

'I think I should be the one to go after her,' Tess said. 'There's less risk, and besides, she might say more to me, woman to woman.'

'She could turn on you too. She already accused you of jealousy,' Po reminded her.

'From what I've seen of Elspeth, I've nothing to be envious about.'

Po's mouth formed a thin slit as he appraised her.

Pinky dangled the keys to his GMC. 'Take my ride, pretty Tess. If she spots Nicolas's Mustang coming she'll probably hide in a bush, her.'

TWELVE

Falling leaves pattered on the windshield and hood of Caleb's pickup. The breeze had gotten stiffer than before, and the stirred boughs overhead sifted debris down on his sparkling paintwork. He had parked the big truck out of sight at the edge of a small copse of red spruce, maple and white pine. Being a woodsman he could identify the trees, not that they'd crossed his mind since his return to the cab.

Once he was inside, the first thing he did was call Decker on his cell phone.

'Were you asleep?' he asked gruffly.

'Nah, Caleb,' Decker obviously lied. 'I just had my feet up for a few minutes, that's all. You want me?'

'Are you back at the hotel?'

It was a pointless question: where else would Decker have chosen to rest?

'Uh, yeah, you said I should—'

'Listen up. You must have gotten a cab back there, right?'

'Well, yeah, you said—'

'I don't need reminding, Jer. You've still got the number for that cab, you hang up and punch it in now. I want you here with me.'

'Uh, yeah, sure.' Decker's fumbling with the cell phone, not to mention his words, was getting on Caleb's nerves.

'Actually,' he growled, 'do remind me why I chose you to come with me to Portland? Stop fucking around, Jer! I need you on your goddamn A-game.'

'Yeah, sorry, man. Where is it you need me?'

Caleb had memorized a nearby street name, and he repeated it to Decker. 'Don't keep me waiting,' he warned and hung up.

That was about twenty minutes ago, so Decker shouldn't be too far away now.

Caleb was still undecided on what his next move should entail. He was leaning more towards a home invasion, but he'd prefer to have the numbers to ensure that everyone inside could be contained, and permanently shut up, so he wanted every man available on the job. Darrell and his reinforcements were still about an hour from arriving in Portland, and it would take another hour to formulate and execute a plan of attack. It was fortunate that Villere's nearest neighbors were a fair distance away, so they should be able to invade the ranch, grab Elspeth and Jacob and put the others down without attracting attention. Darrell and the guys were coming heavily armed, but their weapons should be used only to threaten and coerce Villere and his friends; once subdued they could be killed silently with a sharp knife or blunt instrument. His wife and kid could go in the van for the swift return to the commune. It could be days before the corpses were found, and by then he and his people would be back several states away, safely within the compound. He trusted that nobody had raised the issue of his presence in town except between themselves, so there was no way that Caleb could be tied to the home invasion. The booking made at his hotel was under false details; yes, both his and Decker's images would undoubtedly have been captured on CCTV, but unless the cops knew who to look for there was no reason to interrogate a random hotel security system for random guests. The same could be said for Elspeth and Jacob; his runaway wife would have used false details when booking their room downtown, and paid in cash. He supposed she must have gotten her hands on a cell phone since running away, but she wasn't the holder of any type of credit or bankcards: he'd ensured that she was totally reliant on his generosity in order to eat and clothe her and the boy, so there would be no digital trail of their presence here. Her escape attempt had been solely financed up until now by the cash the ungrateful bitch had stolen from him.

Caleb and his brothers had become experts at control and manipulation of those under their thrall at the commune, but he'd be the first to admit that assaulting the occupants of a house, and staging a kidnapping, was beyond his usual remit. But never mind that. There was a first time for everything, and you couldn't gain expertise without hands-on experience. On his return to the pickup he'd seethed with rage at what he had overheard from Villere and Pinky, but the more he thought about it, the more excited he grew at the possibility of putting them in their place. Caleb had killed before. In fact, he had several murders under his belt. He didn't balk at the murderous plan hatching in his mind, if anything he was eager to get things moving.

Supposedly patience was a virtue; well it wasn't a commodity he held in abundance, but then he had never considered himself virtuous. He knew what he wanted and was not the type to wait. What wasn't given he took and lord help the man or woman that tried to deny him.

His cell phone rang.

'It'ℨ me. Jer.'

'Where the hell are you?' Caleb checked all around for any sign of the man.

'I got a cab like you told me to, but I got to thinking. If we're going to snatch your kin like you want, it was unwise of me – a stranger – getting dropped too near where you are. If things come to light with the cops, I didn't want a suspicious cabbie recalling where he'd dropped me off when it would lead them back to the hotel he'd picked me up from. If they checked who I was and found I was booked in under false details, it'd give them reason to dig deeper. I didn't want this coming back on you or your pa.'

Decker was not the fool Caleb often took him for. But he hadn't been asked to think. He was supposed to get here as quickly as possible.

'Where the hell are you?' Caleb demanded again.

'Not far.' He read off a road sign that meant nothing to Caleb. Decker had gotten dropped off on one of the other dead-end streets hemmed in by the river. 'I mapped it before I set off, so's I could tell the cabbie my destination. I'm only a couple minutes from where you're at.'

'Good. Wait there. I'll come fetch you.'

'You heard from Darrell yet?'

'No, but he can't be too far off now. Sit tight, Jer, don't make me waste time looking for you.'

Caleb started the truck and backed out from under the trees onto a single-track lane. He had parked with convenience in mind, so was pointed in the right direction. He found an intersecting road and took it, heading for Decker's location. He stopped the truck. Stared through the windshield at the figures that had emerged from another intersection to hurry down the road a hundred yards ahead.

He took out his cell and returned Decker's call.

'Change of plan, Jer. Start walking towards me.'

'Sure, I'll—'

'You'll do nothing but what I tell you to do. Listen up. Do you know what serendipity is?'

'Coincidence?'

'More like one of those happy accidents that happens because of other random shit, when you're almost convinced somebody up there really is looking after you. If you had done what I asked in the first place, I wouldn't have been forced to come fetch your ass. But then this wouldn't have happened.'

'Yeah? What's happened, Caleb?'

'We've just been given an advantage, and we're going to make the most of it. You ain't going to believe who's walking towards you, man.'

Actually, it didn't take too much imagination for Decker to guess.

'You've got eyes on Elspeth and Jacob?'

'I don't know how they come to be here, but it's them. Once you reach the through road you'll see them. In fact, stay back so's they don't see you till I'm ready. We'll time it so we pinch them between us. You grab ahold of Jacob, I'll take Elspeth into hand.'

'I'm unarmed,' said Decker.

'You need a gun to control a ten-year-old kid? He gets vocal, bust his goddamn lip.'

Decker didn't answer.

'Don't fuck this up, Jer. This is a golden opportunity we can't waste.'

'You can rely on me, Caleb.'

'Good. Now I'm rolling, you get ready.'

Caleb started the pickup crawling along the street with his main beams doused. The truck was big, with a gutsy engine, but it was also practically brand new, so it purred rather than grumbled. Elspeth was intent on gaining distance between her and whatever she was fleeing, and was verging on a trot as she dragged Jacob along. She was so wrapped up in her thoughts that she was unaware of the pickup gaining on her. It was Jacob who happened to look back first, but to him the unfamiliar pickup meant nothing, and he wasn't alarmed. Within the darkened cab Caleb was unrecognizable too. His mother tugged Jacob on.

Caleb checked for possible witnesses. This was a quiet, leafy suburb, where people expected peace and quiet: homes were set back from the roads on private plots of land. There was nobody in sight, and Caleb hadn't seen another vehicle on the road since first following Villere and the others back here. The circumstances had stacked in his favor, and he was now a believer that the concept of serendipity was the real deal.

'You at the road yet?' Caleb asked.

'Right here,' Decker confirmed.

'They're almost on you.'

'You want me to block their path.'

'Wait . . . wait . . . wait . . . *do it now*!'

Caleb hit the gas one second and the brake the next, sweeping in to lock Elspeth and Jacob on the sidewalk. He was aware of Decker lunging out from the next corner and spreading his arms wide like a goalkeeper, but there was still a gap between the pickup and him. Caleb dumped his cell phone and threw open the door. He pounced out and grabbed Elspeth even as she back-pedaled in horror from Decker. Caleb grasped her thick hair and tugged her off balance. Jacob was wrenched out of her grasp. Caleb clamped his hand over Elspeth's open mouth, while Jacob dithered. The boy's mind was in flux, unsure what to do. He wanted to protect his mom, but this was his dad, and he knew what he'd got whenever he had tried to man up in the past. Under Caleb's palm, Elspeth shrieked. Before Jacob could do anything, Decker grabbed him around his waist and buried him under his bulk as he steered the boy towards the pickup. Jacob struggled, and he let out a plaintive yell.

'Shut him up before he wakes the goddamn neighborhood,' Caleb snarled.

Decker slapped a hand over Jacob's mouth. Instantly he let go, with a curse and a shake of his fingers. 'The little shit bit me.'

'Then do what I told you and bust his goddamn lip. Disobedient little shits need shown their rightful place.'

Hearing his proclamation, Elspeth struggled against Caleb. She flopped and kicked to try saving her son. Rather than beat the boy, Decker jammed his palm over his mouth a second time, this time grinding the edge of his hand down to mash Jacob's lips against his teeth.

Caleb shook his head in disbelief. Sometimes action was a better example over words. He twisted Elspeth's hair, craning her head around. 'Want to get mouthy with me, bitch?' he snarled into her ear. 'This is what you get.'

He slammed her face so hard it was wondrous her jaw wasn't broken. Her eyelids squeezed shut, and she moaned at her core: she verged on unconsciousness, and that suited Caleb. He jostled her to the cab, yanked open the rear door and threw her headfirst inside. He grabbed her legs and forced her knees to bend, and gave her another heave so she was forced across the bench seat. Decker was beside him with the boy. 'Throw him in on top of her, then you get in. Here' – Caleb drew his pistol and held it out to Decker – 'keep them out of sight and keep them quiet till I can get us outta here.'

Decker threw Jacob on Elspeth's back. He took the gun gingerly, but without argument. Then he squeezed inside the extended cab, wagging the gun at Jacob, an index finger to his lips. He sat on Elspeth's legs, and drew shut the door. Elspeth couldn't get up, but she tried. Decker shoved the gun's muzzle in the small of her back. 'Don't make me hurt you,' he warned.

'If she shouts, screams, does anything, you have my permission to hurt Jacob,' said Caleb as he slid back into the driving position. 'D'you hear that in the back? I'm talking to y'all.'

Jacob had scrunched down so he was between his mother and the back of the front seats. He folded over her, as if to shield her. Decker prodded him with the gun. Jacob cast a tearful glare at him, and Decker grimaced at the sheer hatred aimed at him. He said, 'We ain't going to get any trouble from them, Caleb.'

'Good. You keep things that way till we meet with Darrell.'

Caleb checked all around. The abduction had been swift and mostly without fuss; nobody had witnessed it. He set the pickup moving again, with a plan to circumnavigate and cut Darrell off before the van reached the city limits. He grinned at his fortune; yes, somebody up there certainly liked him. The only downside was that Villere and Pinky's comeuppances would have to happen another time and at another place.

He drove sensibly, taking it easy as he wended their way out of the neighborhood. He had made a couple of turns before Tess Grey drove Pinky Leclerc's GMC down the same road where the abduction had taken place. By then there was no hint whatsoever that anything untoward had happened.

THIRTEEN

There was probably little rationality for Elspeth in choosing her direction of travel. Familiar with Po's neighborhood, Tess knew the most direct ways out towards the major routes into Portland whereas Elspeth could have little inkling. Elspeth had last resided in Portland more than a decade ago, and as far as Tess was aware it wasn't out here in the burbs: she doubted she knew her way back through these winding streets. Trying to avoid the mindset of a motorist, Tess put her mind on foot, and tried to imagine the twists and turns that Elspeth might follow, being mindful she was accompanied by a young boy. There were lanes and cut-through paths inaccessible by car, but unless Elspeth knew they existed, and to where they led, she'd be unlikely to follow them. Trying to think like a frightened mother, Tess stuck to the open roads, ranging further out each time she made a sweep of the neighborhood. The further she traveled, the less confident she was of picking up Elspeth's trail.

She checked the clock on the car's dashboard. It was a quarter of an hour at least since Elspeth had dragged Jacob away from the ranch. How far could the two have walked in fifteen minutes? Tess thought that she would have caught up to them by now if they had stuck to the streets. The options for their complete disappearance were few: Elspeth had hailed a cab or they were currently hiding somewhere behind Tess and she'd missed them during her search.

Pulling the GMC to the curb, Tess rethought her strategy, deciding it was time to work her way back towards the ranch in the hope of coming across them. Another thought struck her: Elspeth had rung her cell phone earlier. If only she had access to the same locator app she'd used when tracking Po that afternoon, her search would be over in minutes. But there was hopefully another way of locating Elspeth and Jacob, and that was by asking. She dug out her cell phone from her back pocket and brought up the received calls log. She found Elspeth's number and hit the call button.

The ringtone rang out a number of times, then fell silent.

Tess hit the call button again.

This time the ringtone only sounded once before it cut off.

She wasn't for giving in so easily. If she was persistent she might get an angry response from Elspeth, but it would be a response, and from there she could hope to draw the woman into a negotiation. She hit the call button again. This time she received an automated message informing her that her call couldn't be connected. Elspeth must have switched off her phone.

'Damnit!' She shouldn't have been so persistent after all, and spaced out her attempts to allow Elspeth time to think and maybe respond differently. She set her phone on the passenger seat, for easy access to it should Elspeth have second thoughts and return her call. She turned the GMC in the street and began a reverse search towards home.

The closer she approached the ranch the guiltier she grew. There was a part of her that was relieved that Elspeth had given her the slip. Already Elspeth had accused her of being envious over her previous relationship with Po, and it irked to admit that she wasn't totally wrong. There was also the issue that Po might be the biological father of Jacob, and despite her denials given to Po about her feelings towards the issue, there was also part of her that wished to have his baby, and it to be a unique soul brought into the world by them. She felt no ill towards Jacob, but she wanted any baby of Po's to also be hers. Why had Elspeth shown up now and brought this dilemma with her? Why hadn't she run elsewhere instead of to Portland where there was always the chance of running into her past? Things would be so much simpler for them all if she had never left that damn commune!

Tess braked hard.

She sat gripping the steering wheel, breathing heavily, her eyes prickling. She felt guilty before, now she felt ashamed. It was not in her nature to think like that. Instead of wishing Po had never laid eyes on them that afternoon, she must accept that he had and the clock couldn't be turned back. Elspeth and Jacob needed help. They were both fleeing horrible abuse at the hands of the person who should rightly be the one to protect them: Caleb Moorcock had failed them terribly, so they needed somebody else to stand up for them. When she had encouraged Po to speak to Elspeth, she had not only aligned to support her man, but also had extended the hand of protection to the woman and her son. Broaching the subject of Jacob's parentage had been perhaps too soon for any of them to handle with anything except emotion, as such it had been a blunt approach guaranteed to receive a blunt response. Supposedly in a safe environment for the first time in how many years, Elspeth must have felt attacked, cornered by them, felt threatened as she had numerous times by her abusive husband. It was little wonder she'd taken Jacob and fled. Now they were both out there, unprotected, afraid and probably with no idea where to turn to next.

Tess rubbed her eyes with her thumb and index finger, then pinched the bridge of her nose. Her cheeks were damp. She dabbed at them with the pad of her thumb, then checked her reflection in the rearview mirror. Her eyes were glassy, the sclera pink. 'Get a grip, Tess,' she warned aloud, 'you're helping nobody sitting here like this.'

She shifted her backside in the seat, steeling herself. Then she reached for the cell phone again. Perhaps there'd been a glitch in the service earlier and that was why her last call had been unable to go through. She tried Elspeth again, but with the same result as before: her call couldn't be connected. She was disappointed but unsurprised; Elspeth's phone had been switched off.

Po and Pinky were on the porch when she returned home. Pinky was on the swing seat, his elbows on his knees, feet braced on the floor to keep it from moving. Po stalked back and forth, smoking in sharp inhalations. The cigarette burned down as rapidly as the fuse on a stick of dynamite. As she drew the GMC to a halt in the yard, he flicked aside the burning stump and practically jumped down the steps to greet her. He craned to see if she had any passengers. She shook her head at him and his shoulders drooped. She gathered her phone, got out of the car and Po embraced her.

'What's wrong?' he asked.

'I'm fine,' she lied.

'You don't look fine. Have you been crying?'

'No, of course not.' She turned aside and contorted her face a little, feeling dried tears crack apart on her cheeks.

'You didn't find them then?'

'I drove out as far as Pine Grove Park, and checked all points between, but there was no sign of them. I doubt they'd have been able to walk further than that. Elspeth must have called a cab to take them back to the hotel.'

'That's right! She called your phone—'

Tess held up a hand, stopping him. 'I tried ringing and after a few attempts she switched off her phone.'

He thought for a moment. 'Did you try ringing the hotel to check they got back safely?'

'Not yet. Do you want me to do that?'

'Our decision to wait till the mornin', I've been thinking about it. By morning Elspeth might have gathered her things and left already.'

'I'll ring,' she offered.

'I'd prefer it if we went there.'

Tess looked over at Pinky. He only offered a tight smile. The men had obviously talked things through while she had been searching, and come up with a plan of action should she return empty-handed.

'I don't want her to skip town before I get the honest truth about Jacob,' Po said. 'If we call the hotel it might push Elspeth into running immediately, and who knows when we'll see or hear from her again?'

'If that's what you want,' she said, and dangled the GMC's keys in Pinky's direction. 'Is it OK with you if I go with Po?'

'It's important that you do go, you,' said Pinky.

'We should have somebody wait here, incase Elspeth has a change of mind and comes back.'

'I'm comfortable right where I'm at, me.' He sat back to emphasize his point, lifted his heels off the deck and let the swing go.

Po headed for the Mustang.

Tess underhanded the GMC's keys to Pinky and he snatched them out of the air, then she mouthed a thank-you for giving them some privacy as they worked through the issue.

Po drove them at a slower pace than was common for him, and Tess joined him in visually scouring the side streets they passed for any sightings. Once they were beyond the three-ways intersection of Auburn Street and Allen and Washington Avenues, he deemed there were too many alternative routes Elspeth might have taken back to town, so he hit the gas and made haste for the hotel.

Unfortunately, when they arrived, mother and child were not there. Begging a favor from the night clerk, and twenty dollars slipped to him by Po, a brief 'welfare check' of Elspeth's room found some soiled clothing and a few bare essentials left behind: the room had apparently been abandoned, but this in itself was not an uncommon occurrence they were told. To Tess and Po it was very worrisome indeed.

FOURTEEN

It had grown too chilly for wearing a T-shirt and shorts by the time they arrived back at the house. Tess shivered as she left the warmth of the Mustang and trotted up the steps onto the porch, her arms crossed over her breasts: goose pimples were raised on her forearms. Pinky was still on the swing seat, though it was doubtful he had assumed that position the entire length of time they'd been gone. Hearing via a call from Tess that they were heading back, he must have come out to welcome them home.

'No luck, eh?'

'I'm going to put on something a bit warmer,' Tess announced and went inside. She returned less than two minutes later, having shucked off her shorts in favor of full-length jeans, and she'd pulled on a sweatshirt emblazoned with the Cumberland County Sheriff's department logo. She still shivered, partly from the chill of the early hours, partly through the disruption of her circadian rhythm: she should have been tucked up in bed, nice and warm, asleep for several hours by now. Po had joined Pinky on the porch. He braced one arm on the rail, his other hand held a cigarette he'd lit. His eyebrows formed a V as he scowled out into the darkness.

'Shift up,' Tess said, and then snuggled in alongside Pinky, pulling her feet up under her backside. His warmth was very welcome.

Po turned, resting his backside against the rail. He dragged in smoke then averted his face to blow it out again. For now, he nipped off the ember and dropped it over the rail. He set the unsmoked end on the rail itself. Tess knew he was in need of his nicotine crutch, but he would forego it on her behalf. 'Light up again,' she urged him, 'the smoke doesn't bother me.'

Actually, if she was to be honest with him, she would kill for a cigarette. It was years ago that she gave up the habit, but there were occasions where she still craved the hot hit at the center of her chest, followed by the cold wash of adrenalin. She resisted the temptation to hold out her hand for a pull on his cigarette.

'I'm good for now,' he said. 'Got more on my mind.'

'They just dropped off the face of the earth, them?' Pinky asked.

'When we discovered they hadn't returned to the hotel we checked out a few of the obvious places, but there was no sign of them,' Tess explained. 'We checked the train and coach stations, and also some bus stops in the town center and over in South Portland.' They'd crossed the Casco Bay Bridge and checked the bus transit hub there on the off-chance Elspeth had taken a taxi across the water to put some distance between them. There was no sign of Elspeth or Jacob, and when Tess described them to a ticketing clerk she'd drawn a blank. She looked earnestly at Po as she added, 'I'm going to ring around the local taxi firms and ask if any of them picked them up and where they took them.'

'I fear you might be wastin' your time,' said Po.

'Perhaps, but we have to cover our bases.'

'I think we should face reality.'

Tess set her teeth and breathed out the corners of her mouth, knowing exactly where he was going with this.

Po nodded regretfully at what was in his mind. 'We should've taken Elspeth more seriously when she claimed she was being followed. We writ off that Decker guy and thought we'd left him in our dust. What if we missed another watcher and they followed us back here?'

'What're the chances?' Tess challenged.

'When I was out here earlier, I had the feelin' I was being watched from over at those bushes. I should've trusted my damn instincts and checked things out.'

'I'm relieved that you didn't. Who knows what might've happened if you'd found somebody.'

Po subconsciously curled his fists, proving Tess's point.

'You could've walked into an ambush, you,' Pinky added.

'Maybe, maybe not. Whoever was out there we allowed Elspeth and Jacob to walk right into their arms.'

'We can't say that's what happened,' Tess asserted. 'Besides, we didn't *allow* anything. It wasn't for us to stop Elspeth doing what she wanted, and couldn't stop her leaving.'

'F'sure,' said Po, 'but she wouldn't have left knowing they were out here.'

Tess nibbled at a hangnail on her thumb. With the offending

sliver of skin excised, she said, 'Before we assume they were abducted I should still check with the taxi companies. We don't want to jump to conclusions.'

'You don't suppose a Good Samaritan saw them, a woman and child out alone in the dark, and offered them a ride?' asked Pinky.

'It isn't beyond the realm of possibility,' Tess said, 'but it's doubtful Elspeth would accept a ride from a stranger. She's on edge, paranoid with fear . . .'

'Rightly so by the look of things,' said Po

'So?' Pinky posed the question also on their minds. 'Do we call the cops, us?'

'And tell them what?' Tess had no intention of being contentious. She used to be a cop. A regular part of her job was following up on missing person enquiries, but in general they were as a result of genuine concerns for the person's welfare. They had no proof whatsoever that Elspeth and Jacob had been abducted and in imminent danger. Elspeth was a grown woman, and mother to Jacob: she had the liberty and freedom to decide where and when they went if she chose. They could of course report to the police what Elspeth had told them about the abuse they'd both suffered at the hands of her husband and his family, and that others were allegedly being similarly abused over at the Moorcock family's commune, but Elspeth had pleaded with Tess not to. In so many words she had intimated that if the police were involved, she could expect to be defamed, have her child taken from her, or – ultimately – silenced completely. Reading between the lines, Tess had concluded that murder had taken place on the Moorcock property, and that would be Elspeth's fate if law enforcement got too nosey because of her. They'd talked about how Eldon Moorcock had 'avenues of revenue', meaning the ill-gotten gains of crime, and how he would react if his income lines were threatened. 'I'll speak to Alex about things, but respecting Elspeth's wishes it'll have to be off the record for now. She pleaded with me not to involve the police.'

'What can Alex help with if it ain't made official?' Po asked.

Tess rocked her head. There were routes of inquiry blocked to her that Alex could access. Plus, it would be good to have someone in law enforcement in their camp if her suspicion about what Po wanted to do happened. Instead she told them about the burn wounds inflicted on Elspeth and her son by Caleb, and how she feared they were the lesser punishment she could expect if the police came sniffing around the Moorcocks. Pinky was disgusted, Po on the other hand seethed with cold rage.

'Maybe you should keep this from your brother for now,' he suggested. 'Telling him makes him duty-bound to do somethin'. I'd rather we dug into this first before we get shut out of the investigation by the cops.'

'What you really mean is you want to deal with Caleb and his family before the cops can intervene and protect them?' Tess laughed at the fatality of his plan.

'You make me sound like some kinda crazy vigilante,' he said, and offered a tight-lipped smile.

No, she thought, *you sound like a protective father doing what's right to protect your kid.*

'Road trip?' Pinky asked hopefully.

Tess squeezed one of his large knees. 'I've some calls to make, and then we all need to get some rest.'

'Then we're going on a road trip, us?'

Tess looked up at Po, and he nodded, as it was already a given fact he was going to upstate New York.

FIFTEEN

He was itching to teach Elspeth a much-needed lesson, but for the purposes of transporting her and Jacob silently over state lines, Caleb had held off for the time being. Half an hour after grabbing his hostages, he'd rendezvoused with Darrell on the deserted lot of an amusement park a few miles north of Saco, having taken Route 1 out of Portland to avoid the tollbooths on the Maine Turnpike. They'd parked their vehicles distant enough from the park to avoid cameras and the attention of security patrols, and their hostages were quickly transferred from the pickup to the van. Behind them a fiber glass polar bear clutched an inflatable dinghy as it stood astride a faux mountain, as if about to launch itself down one of the park's water flumes. Such a sight would ordinarily attract the wonder of a ten-year-old boy, but as they were quickly manhandled from one vehicle to the other, Jacob's eyes had alighted only on his dad. Caleb had expected to see fear, a plea for pity, but instead Jacob only glared defiance at him. The kid had spunk, Caleb decided, normally an admirable trait, but not when directed at him. The boy's open defiance was disrespectful, and Caleb wouldn't usually entertain disrespect. Once they were back at the commune he'd show how easily defiance could be knocked out of him. For now he must refrain from anything that might attract undue attention.

Caleb intended riding home with Darrell, but the van was too cramped to accommodate him alongside the five men and their hostages. Instead he told Jeremy Decker to join those in the van, and he invited Darrell to ride with him in his pickup. Decker had enjoyed some rest, those in the van had been on the road for hours, and therefore Decker was designated as the driver. For the same reason, Caleb would allow Darrell to get some shut-eye on the journey back. He was still buzzing with satisfaction at recapturing his wayward wife, so was fully alert and ready to put hundreds of miles under his tires. Before hitting the road, he stood a moment at the open door in the side of the van: Elspeth and Jacob had been allowed to huddle between three of the guys from the commune. Eager to impress Caleb, the three young men aimed weapons at their hostages, a needless threat, when all it would take was a few words from him to guarantee compliance. 'Don't make me have to stop and beat some sense into you,' he growled directly at his wife.

Elspeth wouldn't meet his gaze. She cuddled the boy.

'What the fuck is that?'

There was the faint jangle of a ringtone coming from under Elspeth's clothes.

'She's got a cell phone. Goddamnit, didn't anyone have the sense to search her?' He was shedding the blame; he knew from when Elspeth was down at the pier that she'd summoned help via a cell phone. But why take the blame when it could be directed at some-body else?

One of the young men quickly jumped to it, pulling and tugging at Elspeth's skirt, and he came out with a phone in his hand. He held it out to Caleb. Caleb grabbed it and inspected the screen. The cell was a cheap pay-as-you-go model. The number on the screen gave no hint of who was calling. Caleb declined the call. Within a few seconds the phone rang again: same number. He declined the call again, then dropped the phone on the floor and stamped on it several times until it was a broken mess of component parts.

'Who was that calling you?' he snapped at Elspeth.

She didn't reply, only buried her face in Jacob's shoulder.

'What are the rules about having a cell phone?' Caleb clenched a fist, and it was all he could do to stop from climbing in the van and beating an answer out of her.

Her silence didn't matter; he'd punish her later for her disobedience.

He also suspected who was at the other end of that call: fucking Villere.

'Did you really think Po'boy could protect you?' he said, smirking at how easily he'd shown that notion to be untrue.

'Who the fuck is Po'boy?' asked Darrell over his shoulder.

'He's some old flame of Elspeth's. From what I recall, he was supposed to be some kinda badass ex-con from down south. They go way back. Maybe it was Elspeth's plan to run back to him, open her legs and take up where they left off last time.'

'Damn whore,' Darrell growled.

'Yeah, well, apparently Po'boy isn't interested in you, is he?' he asked, again directing his words at his wife. 'He's got himself a pretty young blonde, he wants no piece of a dried-up bitch like you. You're mine, Elspeth, and you should be goddamn grateful you've got a man to look after you.'

He eyed her but again got no response.

'You,' he said to the young man who'd found the phone. 'Check her bag and make sure there are no other surprises in there.'

The man set to as instructed.

'OK,' Caleb said, 'we've wasted enough time here. Let's get these two runaways back where they belong.'

He shut the sliding door, and went to the pickup with Darrell.

They set off, with the pickup leading a few hundred feet ahead of the van. Caleb looked for a route home that would avoid the major highways, despite it meaning more time behind the wheel. Darrell told him how he'd followed a half circle passing around Albany, through Massachusetts to Boston, then he'd cut up to Portland through New Hampshire. Darrell's was the fastest route despite adding on many miles. Caleb had it in mind to cut a more direct swathe home, through Concord, Brattleboro and then hit New York nearer to Saratoga Springs.

'Everything good back home?' he asked Darrell when they were about an hour into the drive.

Darrell had fallen asleep, his head bouncing softly on his chest.

Caleb shoved him.

Darrell blinked awake. 'Uh, whassup?'

'I asked if everything was good back home.'

'Yeah, everything's in hand, man. Day or two ago we had to deal with a trespasser. Some A-hole thought he could come onto our land and shoot himself a buck or two.'

'Hunter?'

'Poacher.' He grunted in mirth at the memory. He mimed ramming a blade upward. 'To teach him a lesson, Pa had me open up his gut sack.'

Caleb jerked his head in reaction.

'Then he had Randy put him outta his misery. Our kid bro shot him through the heart with his own arrow. Ha!'

Caleb sneered over at him. 'You're one bloodthirsty son of a gun, Darrell.'

'Just exercising our God-given right to protect what's ours, Caleb. Same as I drove all the way across country to help you do the same.'

Caleb reached out and gave his brother's knee an affectionate squeeze.

Mid-journey they made a stop at a turn-off at the head of Harriman Reservoir in Vermont. There was a marina and boat hire shop, both still closed and deserted due to the early hour, but Caleb led the van down a dirt track hidden from view by stands of trees, towards the lakeside. There, they all graciously disembarked to empty their bladders and stretch their legs: Caleb allowed his prisoners to relieve themselves too, but under the constant guard of two of the men holding weapons. Elspeth found peeing difficult with AR-15 assault rifles aimed at her. Caleb enjoyed her distress.

'Hike up that skirt,' he ordered her, 'so's I can see you ain't just stalling and wasting my time.'

Mortified, she tried to stand. She'd rather suffer the discomfort of a full bladder than be paraded before the lascivious gazes of her audience. She saw one of them darting a tongue over his lips, his eyes glassy as he stared intently at her. Caleb thumped a fist into the man's arm, but not in punishment. 'Hey! You're making her uneasy,' Caleb laughed.

He wasn't laughing when he strode forward and grabbed Elspeth's hair and twisted it, forcing her to crouch. He growled close to her ear for emphasis. 'You do it here, or you don't get to do it at all, y'hear? I swear I'll fetch a hot iron and seal you up completely. See if you can open your legs for fucking Po'boy Villere after I do that to you. Now piss.'

'I . . . I *can't.*'

'Then get the fuck back in the van.' He threw her and she sprawled in the dirt. Her skirt rucked up around her waist.

'Stop ogling her skinny ass, goddamnit,' he now snapped at the leering men, 'and get her back inside. Everybody done? Good. Let's move, we've still aways to go.'

As the leering man moved to pick up Elspeth, Jacob intervened. He had stood silently, fearful and embarrassed for his mother, but seeing her debased, lying half-naked in the dirt, he threw himself

at the man, swinging wildly for his face. His knuckles found the
man's eye socket, and then his mouth. The man grimaced in pain,
but fired a quick glance at Caleb for permission before grabbing
Jacob by the throat and holding him at arm's length. Jacob kicked
the man between the legs, and broke free as the man sank to his
knees. The other gunman rammed the butt of his rifle in Jacob's
gut to drop him wheezing alongside his mother.

'OK,' said Caleb, 'the fun's over. Do what I said and get them
back in the van.'

The men were none too gentle about following their order.
Elspeth and Jacob were bundled into the panel van, and several
harsh curses were cast at them before Jacob began weeping loudly.

'You've raised a real firecracker there, Caleb,' Darrell laughed.

'Yup,' Caleb grinned, 'I'll make a man out of the little crybaby
yet. One day he'll be proud to call himself a Moorcock.'

They drove through the rest of the night and the first hour of
dawn. Life in the commune began early, but there were few of its
residents around when the pickup and van pulled up on the area
once utilized as a parade ground by the National Guard. Some of
the original barracks had survived, long, low buildings that had
been transformed into a communal mess hall, a school and a
laundry. Other military buildings had been converted into family
dwellings. The parade ground acted as a village square would to
the residents of any other small town.

Caleb got out of the pickup. By now he'd been awake for almost
twenty-four hours, and was feeling every missing minute of sleep.
His eyes felt gritty, his brain wrapped in cotton wool. He lacked
the energy for anger, or for doling out immediate punishment. 'I
can't deal with them right now,' he grumbled as Elspeth and Jacob
were manhandled out of the van. All the menfolk looked pale and
fatigued. 'Put them in the cellar, then get some rest.'

SIXTEEN

The vintage Ford Mustang was Po's preferred method of travel, but he acquiesced to Tess and Pinky in taking the bigger GMC for the trip. The Mustang was never designed to accommodate a person of Pinky's girth, and besides, taking Pinky's car there wouldn't be an issue when it came to dividing up their time behind the wheel. Tess wouldn't say that Po was overly protective of his muscle car, but there was no other way to say it: if they used it, he'd elect to drive all the way to upstate New York rather than vacate the driving seat. He parked it on the sloping drive outside Pinky's place on Cumberland Avenue. Tess smiled at the notion she'd accused Po of being too precious over his car when it was still difficult for her to shake the idea that Pinky was living in her house. The upper story apartment, perched atop a curios and antiques shop, had been home to Tess for several years before she moved into Po's ranch. She still occasionally missed her old place, and the chats she'd had with Anne Ridgeway, the elderly but formidable owner of the antiques shop. Mrs Ridgeway was inside the shop, looking after a customer, when Tess and Po transferred their bags to the GMC at curbside. Pinky had already locked up, and was raring to go. He grinned at Po from behind the steering wheel.

Po didn't share his enthusiasm. He was eager to get the journey started but he had fretted all night that they might be too late to help. It had taken some firm reasoning from Tess to convince him to let her follow up some necessary enquiries before they set off across the country for a showdown with Caleb Moorcock. She had used the connections she had made both as a cop and then as a private investigator to confirm none of the local taxi firms had picked up a fare in their neighborhood last night. One company admitted they had dropped a man a few blocks away from Po's ranch, but she couldn't figure how he was connected to Elspeth's subsequent disappearance. She had rung several hotels and B&Bs in town but none had welcomed a mother and

son last night. Also she'd inquired with some of the local social
care services and homeless shelters on the off chance that Elspeth
had sought help from them, but had equally struck out. Po understood they had to cover all their bases but each minute that passed
had been a minute they should have been on the road in his
mind.

'Let's do this, podna,' he said as he commandeered the front
passenger seat.

'Just waiting for you to get your bony ass settled, me,' Pinky
replied with a wicked smile.

Tess climbed in the back, happy for now to be relegated to the
cheap seats, as they had a long journey ahead and she fully intended
stretching out. Last night it had been late before she had gone to
bed, but Po's tossing and turning had kept her hovering in the
lightest of sleep modes, then she was up bright and early to conduct
her telephone calls. She felt as if a solid eight hours of deep sleep
wouldn't go amiss, pretty much a similar amount of time they would
be driving, but it was doubtful she'd even snooze. She had brought
her cell phone, tablet, and even a lightweight laptop computer
equipped with a mobile Wi-Fi dongle along to keep her mind busy
during the ride.

Before they were beyond the city limits she had brought up
the schematic map of the decommissioned National Guard
training encampment sold to Eldon Moorcock, and alongside it
a satellite view of how the camp appeared recently. She wished
that she had access to real-time satellite footage, where she
fancied she would be able to zoom right down to where Elspeth
and her son were being held, to see the tears on their cheeks, and
somehow imbue through the satellite's beam that they needn't
despair as help was coming. Juxtaposing the satellite imagery
over the schematics, it was apparent that some of the old military
installations had disappeared, or that they had been reconstructed
for other uses, their arrangements added to or adjusted. A number
of new buildings had been erected, and she assumed that these
were the private dwellings of the community's elite. A parade
ground served as a town square and parking lot. Acres of land
had been tilled and sown with crops, and an orchard took up
land that was once a firing range. On the schematic map, she
noted several dotted lines, and thought they must be designated

trails through the woods to outlying structures, but most must have fallen out of use because there was nothing that corresponded with them on the aerial view.

Something else that was apparent: there was no way of identifying the individual properties to who lived there, so they couldn't determine Caleb's house from any of the rest. Neither was there an obvious location where Elspeth and Jacob could be held as the choice was too wide. There were domiciles, hangars and huts, even something that looked as if it might be a subterranean bunker capable of withstanding a nuclear blast. At a loss, she stretched the satellite view to get a better idea of the terrain and possible approach routes. A river and one of its tributaries contained most of the commune's northern and eastern borders. To the west the ground swept up to a series of forested hills at the hinterland of the High Peaks Wilderness. Access from the south was denied by a long, narrow lake called Booger Pond. She pinched and zoomed the view along the river and found a single bridge, the only way in or out of the commune by road. A few miles to the northeast a small town named Muller Falls was the commune's nearest neighboring settlement.

'Did either of you guys pack your gumboots?' she asked.

'What's that about gumboots?' Po turned to see her.

'From what I can make out we are either going to get wet or we're going to have to learn how to scale mountains.' She indicated the map on her laptop, and Po frowned at her for clarity. 'There's one way in, across a river bridge, and if they're the secretive bunch Elspeth told us about, the Moorcocks will probably have it guarded. A lake and some rugged mountains protect the community's other borders.'

'You're all for us making an incursion of the commune?' Po asked, surprised.

'Tell me there's anything else on your mind other than sneaking in and I'll suspect you're lying,' she said.

'You don't think it's a good idea?'

'I think we could do with some evidence that Elspeth and Jacob were taken back there before we do *anything*.'

'How do you suggest we get the evidence without sneaking in?'

'Yeah, that's the dilemma.' She placed her laptop down on the seat beside her, reached between the seats and grasped Po's arm.

She squeezed gently. 'Promise me you won't go charging in until we at least have some idea where Elspeth and Jacob are.'

'It won't pay us to rush in blind,' he admitted. 'Especially if we've just waded across a river.'

'Getting a little wet doesn't deter Pinky Leclerc,' Pinky interjected. 'Y'all know, I can swim like a fish, me!'

'No disrespect, bra, but if there's any sneakin' inside to be done I think it should be done by me.'

'You doubt my skills, Nicolas? I can move like a ninja, me, as stealthy as a shadow and as deadly as a cottonmouth. *Wassa!*' He emitted the Bruce Lee-style war cry and chopped the air with the side of a hand.

Po grunted in mirth. It was Pinky's desired response. But then he wasn't totally kidding either, and from past experience he'd shown his abilities in several life-or-death situations they'd gotten into together.

'Don't laugh, or I'll be forced to hit you with the one finger of death!' Pinky rolled all but his middle finger into his palm, and flipped Po the bird.

'Put that away, will ya, I don't know where it's been,' said Po, and had to avert his face when Pinky aimed the wiggling tip of his finger at his mouth. Po play-chopped it aside with his hand. The men laughed like a couple of schoolboys. 'Keep your eyes on the road, and your hands on the wheel, whydon'tcha?'

Tess shook her head at their antics. 'The priority is getting Elspeth and Jacob safely away from her husband. If we can do that silently then that's best for all of us; if there's any karate chopping to be done it's best saved for afterwards.'

'Anywhere on those maps that give a clue where they could be?' Po asked.

'There are too many hiding spots to pinpoint one.'

'How's that trick going with the cell phone signal?'

'It isn't.'

Ordinarily Tess could access a program via Emma Clancy's computers, through which she could triangulate a cell phone's location. This time she had not been granted access because she hadn't enquired. Agreeing to Elspeth's plea that the police weren't informed of her plight, Tess couldn't take the problem to her soon-to-be sister-in-law. Emma Clancy's specialist inquiry firm was not only Tess's frequent employer, but its manager was also her brother Alex's fiancée. Tess could have asked Emma to keep their search for Elspeth and Jacob between them for now, but that would compromise not only their relationship, but also Emma's with Alex. Also, through her position serving the Portland district attorney's office, Emma was as equally duty-bound to report the suspicions regarding the Moorcock family's criminal activities as Alex was as a cop.

'I tried ringing her cell a few more times this morning,' Tess explained, 'and got the same recorded message as before. It has been switched off, perhaps broken in pieces. I think that Elspeth ditched her phone not long after she left our house.'

'More like it was smashed by Caleb after he took her.'

'Who can say?'

Minutes later they had passed through Scarborough and followed the highway towards Saco, passing the amusement park where Caleb had indeed found and destroyed Elspeth's only life-line to rescue. Earlier the tinkling remnants of her cell phone had been crushed under the tires of some of the first customers to arrive at the park. It was still early in the day as they drove past, but the park had thrown open its gates and already kids were riding the water flumes and other attractions, whooping and screaming in delight as they made the most of the late-summer warmth. None of them could suspect how close they had come to where the prisoners had been transferred to the van for the long journey to the commune, and as it were, their chosen paths wouldn't cross again for most of the day: Pinky got off US-1 at the next turnpike, taking them overland to join the Maine Turnpike for a faster, smoother ride.

Pinky drove the first leg of the journey, and handed over the reins at Lebanon, near the state lines of New Hampshire and Vermont. Po took the next stint, holding on until they were north of Saratoga Springs, where he pulled into a gas station at a small town on the shore of Lake George, where they refueled the vehicle and also purchased snacks and coffee at the adjoining convenience store. He drove the short distance to the lakeside and they sat beside the water to eat and drink.

'I'm still good for the rest of the way,' Po announced as they prepared to get under way once more, but Tess had grown bored and antsy in the back. She held out her hand for the keys and he reluctantly handed them over.

'We should arrive in Muller Falls within the next hour or two,' Tess announced to her companions. 'It's going to be late afternoon by then, so I took the liberty of booking us rooms at a hotel in town.'

'We should go direct to the commune,' Po said.

'And do what? Rattle the gates and demand that they bring out Elspeth and Jacob? How do you think that will go?'

'The longer they're in there, the longer they have to endure whatever that sadistic son of a bitch puts them through,' Po replied.

'I know, but we have to plan how we're going to approach this, Po. We can't just try sneaking in and hoping for the best. Eldon Moorcock has built a private militia, and they're supposedly keen on expressing their second amendment rights. Catching us sneaking in they might choose to shoot first and ask questions later.'

'Do they have a castle doctrine in New York State?' he asked.

'I'm unsure.' He was referring to an individual's right to defend their person and property, permissible in some US states. In Maine there was a duty to retreat from using lethal force when one could do so with absolute safety; Tess was unsure if the same rule applied in New York. Of course, persons engaged in criminal activity didn't usually abide by rules. It was more likely that Moorcock's people would shoot them, dispose of their bodies and then close ranks, so the legality of their shootings would never come into question. 'If it's OK with you I'd rather not put it to the test.'

'Are you armed, y'know, should things grow a bit hot?'

'No.' Tess was licensed to carry a firearm, but was loathe doing so. Her grandfather's old service pistol was in a secure lockbox back at the ranch. Po didn't carry a gun, but she'd bet his knife was tucked in the concealed pouch in his high-topped boots; this was not simply a weapon, he'd claimed, but a multi-purpose tool. In the past he had used it in both ways.

Pinky was unusually tight-lipped.

'You packing, podna?' Po asked.

'I gave up the illegal arms trade,' he reminded them, then flashed a sly grin, and thumbed towards the trunk, 'but I might have held onto a couple of keepsakes, me.'

'You know it's illegal to transport certain types of weapons over state lines, yeah?' said Tess.

'I won't tell if you don't,' said Pinky with a grandiose wink.

'Your secret's safe with me, bra,' said Po.

Tess groaned into her palms, her fingertips digging into her forehead. 'You guys . . .'

'Face it, Tess,' said Po, 'it's inevitable we're gonna come into conflict with the Moorcocks before we're done, and if they're packin' heat we should be too.'

'Or we keep our sensible heads on, treat this as an evidence-gathering mission, then hand it over to law enforcement to act upon.'

'Didn't you say that Eldon Moorcock has most of the local cops on his payroll?'

'I said no such thing. Elspeth might've mentioned something along those lines, but who's to say she's right? Some people have a dim view of the police, and think they're all corrupt bullies out to get them. It might be true of a few bad apples, but the majority of law enforcement officers are good people trying to do their best to serve. I don't believe Eldon Moorcock has an entire police force doing his bidding, and besides, if we uncover something *big* then I'll hand over the evidence to the feds.'

'It's unsurprising that you'd have a different view of the cops,' said Po.

'I thought by now your perception would've changed,' she challenged.

Pinky rocked his head, 'Must say, I get stop-checked by Portland PD more than your average citizen does.'

'Pinky, you've changed your ways, but it stands to reason the cops were a bit suspicious about your relocation to Maine and have checked out your rap sheet. When Nicolas first moved north, he was treated similarly.' She switched her attention to Po. 'Can you say the same now?'

'Nope. The local cops know me now, and it has helped keep the heat off me by havin' you as my partner. But *this*' – he wagged a finger between him and Tess – 'won't mean a damn thing to some hick cops out in the sticks.'

Tess couldn't really argue. Not when she had no proof one way or the other about the integrity of Muller Falls PD. It was possible that Eldon was paying off a dirty cop to turn a blind eye to his activities, but an entire police department? She recalled her fears for Pinky last night, when imagining how some of her ex-colleagues might've perceived things if they came across him trying to coax a frightened woman and child into his car, and how he might end up face down on the sidewalk with guns pointed at his head, or worse. Perceptions could be wrong, and fed by bias, and even otherwise good people could make terrible mistakes. Po was probably right, and the MFPD avoided as best they could

As they returned to the GMC, Po called shotgun. Pinky was happy with the arrangement, and settled himself across the expansive back seat, hands steepled on his midriff, ankles crossed in the footwell, and his head propped against the opposite side window. He smiled indolently, reminiscent of a big friendly bear in a kids' cartoon show. 'So, pretty Tess, what you said back there, you . . . does that mean I've attained a level of fame, seeing as my reputation precedes me?'

'A level of infamy, more like,' said Po.

'Aah, so that's why I keep getting pulled over, they've all got it *infamy*?'

'Geez, Pinky,' Tess chuckled. 'It's more like they're after you because of your crimes against comedy. That joke was old back in the 1960s.'

SEVENTEEN

L ined of face, and bent through years of manual labor, Ellie-May Moorcock looked a decade older than her actual sixty-five years, but she was still a formidable woman. The commune was run under the patriarchy of her husband, but her house was her domain, and she its matriarch. Of all the chambers in the large house, the kitchen was her throne room, and she presided over it with surly dominance, and with an archaic pipe nipped between her teeth. By all appearances she looked a century out of date, but then so was her husband's ways when it came to raising his family, both his blood kin and those within the wider community. Eldon was seated at the head of the table, but that was a matter of opinion when she sat opposite him. Her adult sons occupied three of the other chairs, while a fourth sat empty, once designated for when Jacob came of age, but now his position in the family's hierarchy was in question. Darrell and Randolph sat shoulder to shoulder, while Caleb, the eldest son, sat opposite them. The table was heaped with food that Ellie-May had prepared, and it displeased her that it was being ignored by the menfolk as they bragged and bickered. Ellie-May puffed vigorously on her pipe, caring less that her smoke polluted the atmosphere; worse to her was the bad language seeping from the menfolk. Had they forgotten that she didn't tolerate cursing in *her* kitchen?

She thumped a fist on the table, making the crockery rattle. All eyes turned on her. 'Soup's going cold,' she growled. 'Get eating, unless you want me to say grace first?'

Randolph, the youngest of her brood, grabbed for his spoon and began ladling soup to his mouth. The others weren't as fast to take the hint – they had more to talk and disagree about considering they were directly involved with Caleb's jaunt to Maine, whereas Randy had been kept out of the loop. She thumped the table again, and this time caught her husband's eye.

'I didn't stand over that kettle for hours for you to let my food

go cold,' she said. 'Can't you keep this discussion for later and
let our boys eat?'

Eldon stroked his long white mustache, pinching and tugging
it, while he returned her look. Finally his eyes crinkled, and he
offered her a smile. 'We can eat and talk,' he said, enforcing his
control over his decision, but also to please Ellie-May. 'C'mon
boys, eat up.'

'And no more cussing,' Ellie-May added.

'Sorry, Ma,' said Caleb, 'I've been away for a few days and
had to fit in with outsiders. I shouldn't carry their bad language
back here.'

'Speak however you want, son, just not in my hearing.' She
puffed on her pipe, as if in defiance of her own wish they'd eat.

Caleb supped down two spoonfuls of thick vegetable soup. Then
he pointed his spoon at Darrell and said, 'What you waitin' for?'

Darrell ignored the food; he spoke directly to his father. 'Caleb
isn't concerned but I think we should prepare for a visit from the
cops. Those people that sheltered Elspeth, a business card was
found in Elspeth's pocket and it turns out the woman's a private
investigator.'

'Yeah, and Po'boy Villere's a convicted killer,' Caleb countered.
'So what? They have no idea what happened to Elspeth last night,
and as far as they know she hopped on a Greyhound bus and left
Portland in its rearview mirror. They've no reason to believe I
grabbed her and fetched her home. Hell, if Elspeth has any sense,
she won't have told them where home is.'

'You attracted unwanted attention,' Eldon stated.

'That's not true, Pa,' Caleb replied. He aimed his spoon across
the table at Darrell and sighted down it as if it was a gun. 'They
had no idea I was in town. I got within twenty feet of Po'boy and
he hadn't a clue I was this close to killing him. Pow!'

'You could've killed him but didn't.' Eldon settled a stern look
on Caleb for an uncomfortable length of time. 'Maybe there's still
an ounce of sense in that hot head of yours after all, Caleb. Shooting
this guy would've ensured a murder inquiry and a manhunt that'd
lead right back to our door. Well done for restraining your urge.'

'I'd've killed the others too. There wouldn't have been anyone
left alive to point their finger here.'

'Do you actually hear yourself, Caleb? Pa was being sarcastic just now.' Darrell shook his head in disbelief and knuckled the side of his head. 'You called me a bloodthirsty son of a gun, but you're the one with something wrong up here.'

Eldon cocked his head at his middle son. 'You suggesting Caleb hasn't the right to level things with those who've wronged him?'

'No, Pa, I'm not saying that at all. I'm just saying that with Elspeth disappearing so suddenly it might pique the interest of this private eye, and she might start digging into what's going on here. It was important that Caleb got his kin back, sure, but at what expense?'

'You've changed your tune since last night,' Caleb grumbled. 'You sound now as if you didn't mean it when you were supposedly happy to come to Maine to help me get Elspeth back.'

'I was happy. Man, Caleb, you know I'd do anything for you. It's just I've had some time to reflect on how things went down and don't think it was our best play. We should've waited. We had the van and the manpower to do it quietly and at a different time and place. I only think that with Elspeth and Jacob disappearing like that, it's going to guarantee a reaction from a nosey private detective.'

'When was the last you heard of a private eye doing *pro bono* work? That shit's just for the movies.' Caleb began digging into the last few chunks of vegetable left in his bowl. 'Uh, sorry about using the S-word, Ma.'

Ellie-May snorted. Her pipe finished with, she set it aside and reached for the pan she'd set upon a trivet at the center of the table. Randolph scuttled to assist her, lifting the pan in reach, and she ladled soup into her own bowl. Then she added a ladleful into Caleb's emptied bowl. 'Darrell's speaking sense,' she announced. 'Y'all should listen to him. All of you.'

'As usual your ma is right,' said Eldon. 'What with dealing with Orson Burdon and now this, we should take some extra care. Now isn't the time to have anybody come poking around our business let alone a nosey private eye. Randy, are you listening to me, boy?'

'Sure am, Pa,' said Randolph without raising his head from his food. He'd moved on from the soup to the main course.

'Good. I want you to double the guard on the perimeter, and have the barrier manned at the bridge. Nobody comes in or out of here without my permission. Y'hear?'

'Loud and clear.'

'Darrell. Your ma's right. You do speak sense, but don't be getting smart-mouthed with your brother again. I was being sarcastic, but that was between me and Caleb and he didn't need you pointing it out to him. Caleb's no idiot.'

'If that's what it sounded like I was saying, I'm sorry, Pa.'

'It's not me you should be apologizing to.'

'Caleb,' Darrell said, sounding sincere, 'I'm sorry I insinuated that there was something wrong with your head. I only meant that you weren't thinking straight, right now. And it's understandable, brother. It was important that you brought your kin home, and, yeah, in your shoes I'd have done the exact same thing. I wasn't criticizing, just saying we should maybe best get ready for trouble, should it head our way.'

Caleb shrugged off the apology. 'Seems I should put your mind at rest, Darrell. I'll go and speak with Elspeth. I'll get it out of her if she had anything bad to say about us to anyone.' He sat back, nudging aside his empty second bowl of soup. 'Ma, you've done it again and served up a terrific meal, but I'm full. May I be excused from the table?'

'It's about time you showed Elspeth who's boss,' Ellie-May said, 'and could have saved us all this bickering had you taken her in hand before now and gotten the truth out of her. You want, you can take my stick and beat some obedience into her.'

Caleb glanced at her walking stick. He'd never known his mother to rely on it to help walk before; the stick had been a disciplinary tool, and he recalled times when it had cracked across his shoulders, his backside, and occasionally round his head hard enough to leave it ringing for days afterwards. He raised an open hand; his palms were calloused and as tough as sun-dried leather. 'Thanks, Ma, but this will do just fine.'

'Suit yourself,' said Ellie-May. 'You're excused.'

EIGHTEEN

So much for avoiding the local cops, Tess thought as she sat down at the table. Po took the bench alongside her, while Pinky jostled the table a few times until he was settled on the opposite side. He reached for the stack of folded menus, and began perusing the treats on offer: partly to avoid meeting the dour gaze of the police officers sitting on stools at the counter. Po wasn't as shy; he met each cop's eyes with a nod of acknowledgment, but received no reply.

The instant they entered the café all eyes in the place had turned on them. Tess felt like a gunslinger in a western movie, pushing in through the saloon's swing doors only for the pianist to fall silent. Necks craned over shoulders so that they could be studied in full, and more eyebrows than those of the cops' beetled at their appearance. Perhaps they struck an unusual trio to people whose stock fashion appeared to be plaid shirts and denim jeans. The way in which some of those people discarded her as interesting, and fixated on Pinky, made her wonder if people of color were in the minority around here; but no, that wasn't it, because several of the faces in the room were brown. Even one of the cops was a black man.

As they moved to a vacant table, she decided that strangers per se were in the minority, and it partially stood to reason. Muller Falls was off the beaten track, on a road that petered to nothing a few miles into the forested hills. It was not one of the towns that had sprung up round one of the major north/south routes further to the east, or those that had grown to accommodate vacationers making their way into the Wild Peaks Wilderness. By all appearances the town had existed here since frontiersmen first began taming the land in upper New York before there was such a thing as a state line marked on a map. There were no surviving structures of that vintage she'd seen, but some were more than a century old, and probably built on the foundations of much earlier buildings. Most of the homes were American craftsman-style built with wood, stone and brick, with low-pitched roofs and wide front porches, but several were more ornate Victorian-era homes with turrets, bay windows and wraparound balconies, decorated with metal filigree. The hotel in which she'd booked rooms for their stay was one of the latter, and as they'd arrived Tess had briefly imagined Norman Bates' mother waving in greeting from an uppermost window. The café was a relatively modern construct though, and resembled most others she'd ever eaten in. It had a red-and-white checkered floor, white Formica tables arranged in individual booths, with red faux leather on the bench seats. The serving counter was clad in stainless steel, and dully reflected the color scheme. The fry cook wielded a spatula directly beyond the counter, where a sign claimed that every meat dish was freshly cooked to order.

Pinky became absorbed in the menu.

Po rested his elbows on the table and cupped his hands as he finally disregarded the cops and allowed his attention to travel around the other faces blinking back at him. Slowly people returned to their meals, and the low buzz of conversation filled the place. The police officers returned to their coffees and sandwiches.

'Awkward,' Tess stage-whispered out the side of her mouth.

'Fuck 'em,' said Po, uncharacteristically coarse for him.

Unfortunately his voice traveled to the ears of the cops at the counter. Tess noticed the tightening of the black cop's back, while the other man, a freckle-faced redhead with a small mouth, turned and eyeballed Po anew. Tess grabbed and shoved a menu towards Po, averting a confrontation they could do without. Po studied the menu dispassionately and the cop sneered but lost interest.

'Try not to have us run out of town the minute after we've got here,' Tess whispered.

'Just wondering if those two are on Eldon Moorcock's payroll,' said Po, but this time sotto voce. 'That sour-mouthed sumbitch strikes me as the type that'd take the back of his hand to a woman.'

'Let's not make any unfounded assumptions,' Tess warned.

'How can I not when everybody in the place looked at us as if we just trod dog shit all over their clean floor?'

Again Po's surly behavior was uncharacteristic, except she knew why. In his mind he thought they were wasting precious time coming to the diner, when they could already have snuck into the Moorcocks' commune and located Elspeth and Jacob.

The freckle-faced cop was drawing his ire towards Caleb by proxy. Thankfully the cop hadn't chosen to challenge Po's language, otherwise Tess thought things could end badly, and their rescue attempt thwarted before it had even begun.

A server approached, and she seemed friendly enough, though her ebullience could be well practiced. She had short-cropped graying hair, twinkling green eyes set in plump cheeks atop a stick-slim body at odds with her round head. She wore black leggings and a white T-shirt tucked into a short apron. The name of the café was emblazoned on the shirt, a faded screen-printed motif that said: Annabel's Pantry, Est. 1972. Tess wondered if the woman was Annabel, and if the fry cook was her husband. There was no other member of staff she could see.

Her assumption was dispelled immediately.

'Hi, I'm Jenny and I'll be your server,' the woman announced with a smile. She took out a cloth from her apron pocket, and swiped the table clean. 'Can I get you started on some drinks while you finish off checking the menus?'

'Coffees all round?' Tess asked, with a quick check for affirmation from the others.

'Sure. I'll get those going for you momentarily.' Jenny tidied the condiments briskly. 'Say, are you folks visiting relatives in town or something? It's just we don't get too many out-of-towners calling in, 'specially not late on a mid-week afternoon like this.'

'That'd explain the puzzled looks we just got,' said Tess, and tempered her comment with a smile. 'No, we don't have any family in town, we're just passing through.'

'Oh, where are you on your way to?' The question was loaded, and this time Jenny's smile was definitely faked.

'Just wherever the road takes us,' Tess lied. 'We're taking a few days out from a hectic schedule to clear our heads and see parts of the country we've never been before. We're staying the night at a hotel up the road from here, but will be moving on tomorrow. Are you local, Jenny? By that I mean, are there any beauty spots hereabouts you'd recommend us seeing before we leave, ones that tourists might otherwise miss? What about the waterfall the town's named for?'

Tess had offered enough of an explanation to appease the server's inquisitiveness, and hopefully Jenny would report back to the cops and anyone else suspicious of their arrival in town, and they'd be left alone afterwards. Except Jenny chewed her inner cheek at mention of Muller Falls, and she couldn't hide the glance she darted at the cops. She leaned in to make her words heard, 'Sorry, hon, the waterfall's out of bounds, I'm afraid. It's on private property, y'see, and intruders aren't welcomed.'

'Oh, that's such a shame,' said Tess. 'Is there anywhere else we should be wary of trespassing?'

'The private land's posted. Stay to the south of town and you should be fine. That's the road you must've come in on, and the one that takes you back out to the highway.' Jenny eyed Tess steadily, silently importing a warning. Then she abruptly switched her attention to the men, her voice jovial and louder than before. 'Had time to choose yet? No? I'll give you a minute and go get those coffees started for y'all.'

As Jenny headed away, the black cop reached and caught her by the wrist. He leaned in to speak to her, and the freckled cop again peered over at them. Jenny shrugged her shoulders, and gave a noncommittal reply, before she gently pulled free and went around the other side of the counter. As she filled mugs and set them on a tray, the fry cook said something to the cops that had all three men laughing.

'You might've just set the cat among the pigeons, Tess,' Po said.

'Sounded as if our server was giving us a friendly warning, her,' said Pinky.

Tess thought the same. But Jenny wasn't warning her about the cops, she was telling her to steer clear of the private property, with enough emphasis that she suggested they hightail it back to the highway to ensure they avoided its tenants. 'Sounds to me as if it's common knowledge what's going on out at the commune, but people are too fearful of speaking about it.'

Po aimed a flick of his hand at the cops. 'Tells me if they aren't doin' anythin' about it, then they must be complicit in what's going on. Dirty cops are the worst kind of scum.'

'More the reason you don't attract their attention,' Tess warned. 'Let's just eat up, keep ourselves to ourselves, then go back to the hotel. Once we're there we can plan our next move.'

Po didn't reply directly. He only offered a greeting to Jenny as the woman bustled towards them wielding a tray stacked with rattling crockery and utensils. She set down the tray and began doling out the mugs of steaming black coffee. 'There's cream and sugar,' she said, and transferred a small jug and a ceramic pot jammed with sachets between them. She tucked the now empty tray under her left armpit and stood poised with a pen over an order book. 'Did you give what you want any thought yet?'

'Were those cops asking about us?' Po said.

She darted a glance at the officers again, then offered the tiniest of nods. 'They asked where you were from, and I told them I didn't know. I only said you plan on moving on tomorrow.'

'And that was good enough for them?'

'Shouldn't it be?'

'I'll have the daily special,' Po said.

Pinky and Tess gave their orders. Before long Jenny was back with their dishes, but she ensured they didn't converse too deeply this time, other than uttering a few pleasantries and to wish them an enjoyable meal. When they were partly through eating, Po stopped, his fork poised in the air as he watched the cops stand up from the counter and say their goodbyes. The cops left without looking at them, and Tess thought that she'd diverted attention off them with her tale about being on a journey of discovery. She began eating, this time enjoying the flavors of fried chicken, mashed potatoes and gravy.

Po set down his cutlery, leaning to see past Tess through the window. 'Apparently it wasn't enough to put them off our scent.'

Out front, the freckled cop was standing alongside Pinky's GMC talking into his radio. The black cop moved around the suburban, kicking the tires and checking in through each window. Whatever notification the freckled cop received he hailed his partner, and the black cop frowned, then stared directly back at them through the café's window.

'Me and my damn reputation preceding me again,' Pinky muttered.

'Let's hope they don't order you to open the trunk,' Tess said, genuinely concerned.

'You don't need worry about that, Tess. They're leaving.'

Po was correct. The cops walked away, probably to where they'd left their cruiser parked out of sight while they enjoyed their break.

'Hopefully that's the last we'll see of them,' Tess said.

'Yeah,' said Po, sounding as if he didn't hold out any hope of that.

After they were fed and their caffeine quota sated, Po picked up the tab and added a generous tip. Jenny thanked him graciously, and as an afterthought she added a reminder. 'What I said earlier about that private property? There are some unwelcoming people out there, you want nothing to do with any of them.'

'We'll make sure we don't run into any of them,' said Po, and the double meaning of his words weren't lost on her.

Outside the café, Po lit a Marlboro. While he smoked, he scanned the street. Muller Falls was what was sometimes referred to as a wide space in the road. Homes and businesses were strung out on alternating plots of land along the main strip, probably for a distance of more than a quarter mile. Midway along a couple of cross streets had been added and several local businesses had sprung up to accommodate the townsfolk. There was also the ubiquitous lumber yard and also a steel fabricator's workshop and also a RV site they'd passed on the drive in that to all intents looked as if its customers were permanent. Their hotel was one of the few in town, and sat off the main road just beyond the hub. Yet Muller Falls was still large enough to have its own police department; even if the duo of cops amounted to the entire manpower, they must also serve the outlying region otherwise they'd go insane with boredom. A couple of hundred yards away, a dog barked, but it was the only hint of life beyond the café.

Po ground his cigarette under his sole, then picked up the crushed stump and flicked it into a trashcan. Tess and Pinky took it as a sign they were moving, and went to the GMC. Po was a half-minute behind them after they'd settled into their seats. Po had again taken over the driving duty. He slid into the driver's seat. 'The cops are waiting for us,' he announced.

'Yeah,' said Pinky from the back, 'I see them now.'

The hood of the marked MFPD cruiser nosed out of the entrance to the steel fabricator's workshop.

'Maybe it's just their usual hang-out spot, where they sit and digest their dinners,' said Tess, playing devil's advocate, except she was in agreement with her male companions. The cops were positioned so that they could pull out behind them as they returned to their hotel.

'What say I drive out of town the other way and leave them wondering what the hell became of us?' asked Po.

'Let's not be assholes,' Tess warned. 'If you start pissing them off it'll make them more determined to give us a hard time. Let's just return to the hotel and give them no reason to pull us over.'

Po started the engine, and he turned the big suburban on the hardpack that served as the café's parking lot. He pulled out on the main street and drove, a mile or two below the speed limit, for the hotel. The three of them ensured they didn't stare as they passed the cops. They had progressed another fifty yards before the cruiser pulled out and followed.

'What exactly have you hidden in the back?' Tess asked.

'Don't get all twisted outta shape, pretty Tess,' said Pinky, 'it's only a couple of pistols; I don't have a heavy machine gun tucked in my trunk, me. Plus, they'll have to be pretty determined to find them.'

'They're keeping their distance,' Po announced.

The cops had made no attempt at closing in on them. Seconds later, Po hit the flashers and pulled into the hotel's adjoining parking lot. By the time he parked the GMC, the cruiser was on its way past the entrance. It traveled slow and steady, and again both cops' faces turned towards them, but that was the extent of interest they showed.

'Let's get inside,' Tess suggested. 'They were probably checking out our story about staying here, and might come back to satisfy themselves we didn't pull in here as a ruse.'

They all disembarked, and were strolling for the entrance door when the cruiser crawled past again, this time heading back towards the fabrication shop. Once they were another ten yards on the driver hit the gas and the cruiser sped away.

'Hopefully that's the last time we're troubled by them,' said Tess, and immediately wished she had bitten her tongue: her words, she feared, probably tempted fate.

NINETEEN

F ear fought with anger, despondency warred with frustration. She was at first a weeping mess and next Elspeth was hammering at the steel door until the heels of her hands became bruised. Several times she'd alternated between victim and protector, but neither had helped. The steel door remained resolutely locked. Their brief experience of freedom made their recapture all the more bitter to Elspeth. It would have been better for them if she had not taken Jacob away from his father, because now she had condemned them both to lives worse than even they'd endured before. Had she run away alone, and somehow found a way to free her son from Caleb's clutches in the future, neither of them would now be suffering at her husband's hands.

During the trip back to the commune in the back of the van – except for when Caleb had tried humiliating her at the lakeside, by trying to force her to urinate under the scrutiny of his goons – they had been mostly treated with indifference. Billy Grayson, whose eye Jacob blackened, had even cooled down, and before their arrival at the commune, he had shown a hint at reconciliation when he'd offered Jacob a chocolate bar from the men's stash of travel snacks. As soon as they were back and under the baleful eyes of the Moorcock elders, Elspeth and the boy had known only surly attitudes, and shoves and thumps to enforce compliance. They had been prodded into one of the surviving military huts at the edge of the parade ground, and forced downstairs into a subterranean network of tunnels invisible from above ground. Back during its military usage the room had stored equipment beyond Elspeth's ken, if not weapons then something else controlled, which required keeping under lock and key. She couldn't think of the room in any other fashion than how Jacob had dubbed it. It was the cellar. The room was perhaps ten feet deep and only six wide, with walls of chipped concrete. Reaching overhead Elspeth could place her palms flat on the concrete ceiling. A single vent at the base of the steel door was the only source of oxygen – the room was never designed for human confinement – and of the meagre glow that sent dim fingers across the floor. The cell was under-ground, with no windows, so had no natural source of light. A pallet had been raised at the back end of the room, on which were piled some blankets, and a plastic bucket with a lid was their only toilet. Most of the time mother and son huddled together on the pallet, or Elspeth beat at the door. Part of her was fearful of when her knocking would be answered, because then who knew what fresh torment would follow?

She was full of regret. Not least at ever succumbing to Caleb's charms, but also at more recent events. Yesterday evening she had panicked when challenged over Jacob's parentage, and as she had from the challenge presented by her husband, she had sought to flee. If she'd stayed with Nicolas and Tess, they would both be safe now, instead of being again locked up and waiting for the inevitable punishment Caleb dreamed up. If only she had leant on the support that Nicolas and Tess had promised, her son would be safe now. She had always planned on leaving Portland in the morning, but they would have been delivered safely to the bus or train station for their onward journey, and Caleb would have been left far behind. All that Nicolas wanted in return was an answer, and she could see how it must be important to him, but she had panicked. By turning down their help, dragging Jacob out into the night, she had delivered them into Caleb's hands; it was entirely her fault that they were back in the cellar.

The cellar wasn't soundproofed. From a distance there came a squeak of door hinges. The ringing of boot heels on the concrete floor followed. Elspeth reached for Jacob, and she eased him down behind her as she stood and faced the door. As the footsteps neared the glow through the vent became brighter. Behind her Jacob muttered angrily under his breath: he had transcended fear now and having gotten a taste for defending her he was about to try again.

'Please Jacob, don't do or say anything to anger him.'

'It's not fair, Mom. It shouldn't be allowed . . .'

Nothing that Caleb did to punish them was allowed in a civilized world, but that was a different world to the one that existed within the confines of the Moorcock commune.

'Just please don't make him angry with *you* . . . whatever happens.'

The footsteps halted outside the door. The bars of light through the vent danced as the person outside shifted to unlock the bolts.

'Step away from the door,' Caleb ordered. It was his first instruction whenever he entered the cellar, and before Elspeth had always believed it was so that they couldn't rush out past him as soon as the door was open. Now she understood that it was because he was conscious of his vulnerability should his wife and son decide to fight back. Elspeth was tempted to go for his eyes the instant he showed his face. She didn't. She did as commanded, moving back further so that her heels came up against the pallet, on which Jacob crouched out of sight. Her obedience was testament to how far Caleb had programmed the desired response from her. She silently cursed her cowardice.

The door opened outwards.

Caleb stood limned by the dim glow from a bulkhead lamp on the wall to his right. Alone it would've been enough to make her blink at the intrusion of light into the darkness, but Caleb had also fetched a flashlight. He aimed its beam directly at her face, and she screwed her eyelids, and cringed away as if burned.

Caleb ignored her.

'Where are you, son?'

It was obvious that Jacob was concealed behind Elspeth, but he wanted – he demanded – an answer.

'Jacob,' he went on, 'come out and let me see you.'

'Leave him be,' Elspeth said. 'If you're going to punish anyone, punish me.'

Caleb aimed the flashlight at her face a second time. 'You'd better believe you're going to be punished. But I've been thinking and don't think Jacob deserves the same. I don't think Jacob would ever have run away, not of his own accord, and must have been pressed into it by you. Come on out, son, there's nothing to be afraid of.'

Jacob shivered behind his mother.

'Please, Caleb, just leave him alone,' Elspeth said.

'Stand aside.'

'Caleb, just—'

'I won't repeat myself. Let me see my son.'

Elspeth stood defiant.

Caleb hit her without warning, driving the butt of the flashlight into her abdomen. Being struck was a regular occurrence, but this time the blow had come at an unexpected angle and she had no defense against it. Her wind gusted from her lungs and she folded to her knees, cupping her stomach with one arm while still ineffectively trying to protect Jacob with the other. Caleb swiped her aside and she fell against the cellar wall.

'Aah, there you are, son,' Caleb crowed.

Jacob still crouched, but he had tensed, ready to leap to his mother's aid.

'Don't, Jacob,' Elspeth croaked. 'Remember what I said—'

'You don't need to listen to her,' Caleb cut in quickly. 'I'm the only one you should obey. Stand up and let me see you. I've missed you, son.'

'I hate you,' Jacob snarled.

'That's your mother speaking,' Caleb said. 'She has put those words in your mouth. She has poisoned you against me, son. But don't worry; from here on in, you don't have to listen to her lies anymore. Come on out of there, come and join me.'

Jacob looked at the hand his father held out to him as if it was the venomous head of a serpent.

'You can trust me, son. There's nothing to be afraid of. Come on, take my hand and you won't ever have to be locked in this room again.'

'Go with him, Jacob.'

Elspeth's instruction came as a surprise even to her. The last she wanted was for Jacob to be taken from her, but less so she wanted him to suffer on her behalf. They had been locked there in the darkness for many hours already and she could expect many more of confinement: she knew how much claustrophobia affected her son. Above ground, Jacob would still be a prisoner, but at least he'd see daylight and he'd be able to breathe. When weighed against the opposite, then it would be cruel of her to want him locked in the cellar beside her.

'I'm not leaving you, Mom,' said Jacob.

'It's OK. You must go with your dad.'

Caleb hadn't lowered his hand. His mouth twitched in triumph each time Elspeth coaxed their son to obey.

'I'm staying here with you,' Jacob reiterated.

'Listen to your mother, Jacob,' Caleb said.

'You told me I should only listen to you! You said my mother tells lies. You're the liar!'

Caleb grinned at him. As Darrell pointed out earlier, he'd raised a firecracker. He said, 'I have never lied to you, son. Has there ever been a time when you didn't know exactly what I expected from you? If I was ever unclear I soon cleared things up by spanking you, right? Since when did a spanking ever harm anyone, huh? You should've been me when I was a kid. I've still got the stripes on my back from Grandma's stick, but d'you ever hear me complaining? See, Jacob. I never got a beating that I didn't deserve, and the same goes for you and your mom. Maybe you think I've been too hard on you both, but I only ever hit either of you to teach you a lesson, to make you better people. To help you fit in here.'

'I don't want to fit in here. I hate it here. I hate you!'

'When I was your age, I felt the same. But I learned to embrace my life here, and understood that it was my duty to protect our way of life. Your grandpa won't live forever son, and when it comes time, I'll take over as the leader. Guess who gets that honor when my time is done?' Caleb pointed at the boy. 'Yeah, one of these days all of this is going to be yours, Jacob, and it's high time you started enjoying some of the benefits befitting its future leader.'

'I don't want to be the leader. I hate it here. I want to leave and never come back.'

'Again, those are poisonous words your mother has put in your head. You only hate *this*.' Caleb indicated the cellar by shining the torch beam on the walls and ceiling. 'Like I said though, come with me and you won't *ever* have to be locked in here again.'

'Let Mom come out too,' said Jacob.

'Not yet.'

'I'm not coming yet then.'

Elspeth feared what would happen next if Jacob didn't obey. She had righted herself while Caleb tried cajoling the boy, and had got her back braced against the wall. She looked up at where Jacob still stood on the pallet like an animal poised to leap for Caleb's throat. 'Son, if you want to help me, just do as your father asks.'

Jacob sneered, and it hurt that he was equally nasty towards her. 'That's the thing, Mom. After what I overheard, I'm not sure *Caleb* is my daddy anymore.'

Jacob was trying to sting his father with a hateful barb; he couldn't understand how hurtful his words were, or how much peril he'd just placed them both in. Her guts tied in a knot, as Elspeth blinked up at Caleb.

'What did you just say?' Caleb scowled.

'You aren't my dad.'

'What the hell's that supposed to mean? I'm not your dad?' Caleb dropped pretense at being amiable; he lunged and grabbed Jacob by the front of his shirt. 'If I'm not your father, who is then?'

Jacob squirmed, tried to pull free, but Caleb's grip was relentless. He picked the boy off his feet and held him one-handed while demanding an answer. He snapped a glare on Elspeth, then again fixed on Jacob. 'You heard your mom say I wasn't your father?'

Elspeth tried answering for him. 'Caleb, he overheard nothing of the sort, he's gotten things mixed up.'

Caleb threw Jacob down as if he was a bundle of rags. Jacob hit the pallet – the blankets saved him from serious injury, but the impact still hurt and knocked the wind out of him. Elspeth reached for her son with a cry. Caleb grabbed her by her hair and wrenched her head back. He snarled directly into her face. 'Not my son, huh? Not my *goddamn* son? Well, he can stay the hell here while I find out who you betrayed me with.'

'No, Caleb, please. Listen to me. Jacob has gotten things all wrong.'

'Lying bitch! I know exactly who he thinks his daddy is. And I damn well know who put that idea in his head too!'

'No, I didn't . . . Caleb, I didn't.'

Caleb hauled her out of the cellar. She clamped her hands over his so that her hair wasn't torn out of the scalp, while trying desperately to get her feet under her. Her legs windmilled, her heels skidded on the concrete floor: she couldn't take her eyes off Jacob. The boy squirmed in pain as he tried to get up off the pallet. He finally made it to his hands and knees, and he knelt there, his mouth wide in a shout of terror as he anticipated what was coming. Elspeth cried out for him, even as Caleb kicked the steel door shut, muffling Jacob's answering wail of terror. Caleb dumped her a moment on the floor; he required both hands to juggle the flashlight and also to throw the bolts. Elspeth tried to scramble away, but he was fired up. He kicked her savagely in the rump, and sent her to her belly on the floor as white-hot agony writhed through her. Finished locking the door, he knelt over her, feeding his fingers through her thick hair again. He yanked her head up, arching her spine, to place his lips alongside her ear. 'The sooner you tell me the truth, the sooner you'll be back here and be reunited with your little bastard.'

Caleb dragged her along the corridor.

TWENTY

'**B**e careful,' Tess whispered needlessly before backing away. Po was aware of the rush of water below but ignored its proximity. He concentrated on the view across the river. An iron bridge spanned the river at a choke point between massive boulders, closed off at the nearside by sawhorses, while at its far end a counterweighted barrier completely blocked the road beyond to traffic. There were 'No Entry' signs on both ends of the bridge, bolstered by other signs shouting in lurid fonts 'Private Property' and 'No Trespassing'. The lettering was visible due to the wash of headlights from a pickup truck parked cater-corner to the bridge. It had arrived after Tess, Po and Pinky had set up across the river, joining a car already in attendance. Several figures stood between the two vehicles, talking and smoking. They were unaware they were being observed. After a few minutes one figure returned to the car and drove away, disappearing in seconds into the darkness. One of those from the car had stayed behind, pairing up with the man from the pickup to guard the bridge. Po assumed they were armed, but for now their weapons were out of sight. The two men were lax about their duties, standing with their backs to the river, their cigarettes protected from the breeze. Po thought he could cross the bridge and take them both out before they were aware he was there. But this was not about assaulting the guards. Their mission was to infiltrate the commune and leave again without alerting anyone to their presence, and knocking out the guards was not the way to go.

Po made his way over the boulders, then hopped up onto the riverbank alongside the road. Tess and Pinky were hidden from the bridge guards by way of a kink in the road. It followed the contours of the twisting river, and huge rocks and boulders similar to those at the riverside dotted the terrain. The GMC was tucked into a ravine between two towering boulders crowned by shrubs.

'There's no crossing the bridge,' Po reported. 'But I might've spotted another way in.'

'How?' Tess asked.

'Upriver towards the falls there's a spot where the banks of the river almost meet. With a run, I think I can jump the gap.'

'What about us?'

'I'd rather neither of you risk it,' said Po.

'But I've to let you risk it?' Tess countered.

'No disrespect intended, but I think the jump's outta your reach, guys,' said Po. 'Besides, this incursion's only about recon, we don't all need to get inside, not yet. Things will be different once we come back, but for now I only need to sneak in, take a look around and find out where they're keepin' Elspeth and Jacob.'

'Letting you go alone was never part of the plan,' Tess argued.

'We've got to face reality, us,' Pinky said, siding with Po's logic, 'if we can't make the jump, we aren't getting in. Not without getting wet, and I thought you were only joking when you said we'd need gumboots.'

'I'm unhappy about you going in alone, Po,' Tess said.

'I'll be fine. You needn't worry about me. I'll be in and out in no time, and those guys in there will be none the wiser.' It wasn't an idle boast; Po had proven his ability at moving with stealth on previous occasions. If the others within the commune were as inattentive as the bridge guards were, then he'd have no trouble whatsoever.

'I still think you should have a gun with you,' Pinky said. Earlier, after their close call with the local PD, they had removed his weapons from the trunk of the GMC and hidden them in their hotel room. As Po had pointed out already, this mission was about gaining intelligence, not about launching a rescue attempt. Carrying a gun was unnecessary, and risked arrest or worse if they ran into the cops again.

He raised his right heel and tapped the side of his boot. 'I've got all I need right here.'

He caught a tremor of concern in Tess's eyes. 'Promise me you won't use it unless it becomes absolutely necessary,' she said.

'I might need to force a lock, or cut a fence wire,' he said, explaining why he might need his knife. 'Don't you fret, Tess, I'm not goin' in there lookin' for a fight.'

'Po, I think I know you well enough by now. You might not go in looking for a fight, but you won't turn one down if it finds you.'

'This is about rescuing a mother and child,' he said, 'not about getting my kicks. I'll behave, I promise.'

'You'd better.' She kissed him briefly. Then she held him by the front of his jacket. 'You have your cell phone on, right? Yeah? Make sure the ringer's off, but keep it on vibrate, in case I need to reach you.'

'Sure thing,' he said.

'Whatever happens in there, whether you find them or not, I want you to come back here within two hours. If you don't, and we don't hear from you, I'll have Pinky take me back to the hotel, we're getting those guns and we're following you in.'

'I hear you.' He took out his cell, and set it up as instructed. He frowned at the screen. 'Signal strength's kinda poor, Tess.'

'There should still be enough to send a text,' she said.

He wondered if there would be enough for her to plot his course on the locator app she'd had them install on their phones, her real reason for having him keep his switched on. He didn't mind being spied upon; in truth, it made sense that he should make things easier to find him should his mission go sideways. He bumped fists with Pinky. Then he gave Tess another reassuring peck on the cheek. 'See you in no time,' he promised, and immediately turned away and loped off towards the riverside.

He was hidden in darkness from those guarding the bridge. He took a moment to check them out and noted that they were still engaged in conversation. Really, they didn't need to be hyper-alert. Anyone approaching the bridge would normally arrive by car and be denied crossing by the sawhorses. If anyone attempted pushing aside the blockade, the guards would have plenty of time to retrieve their guns from the car before they could proceed across the bridge. Po had to also consider that their lack of attention was due to the commune having other forms of covert security in place. There was no sign of CCTV at the perimeter fence, but that wasn't to say it didn't exist. He must be warier than first thought.

Upriver the Muller waterfall was situated on the Moorcocks' land, but the river below the falls extended out of the property, then ran adjacent to it for several miles. Some smaller waterfalls were features of the river as it dropped in elevation out of the foothills. In places the river cut through high-sided canyons between massive boulders tumbled there by raging flashfloods during epochs gone by. As he closed in on the point where the river foamed between the rocks, Po thought he might have overestimated his athleticism, that or the rocks were further apart than his earlier vantage point had suggested. The gap between the two gnarly rocks was at least nine feet. On the flat, taking a running jump into a sandpit, it would be no problem for him, but these were not ideal circumstances. His take-off would be after a short run, and his landing onto jagged stone; waiting below was tumultuous white water that would thrash him downstream, throwing him mercilessly against more ragged boulders should he slip and fall. He was a strong swimmer, but there'd be no fighting against the river's power, and he'd drown and be pounded to chuck against the rocks.

'So don't fall in, lunkhead,' he said.

Pep talk over, he clambered up the nearest of the boulders, and crouched there a moment as he scanned downstream towards the bridge. It was barely visible in the dark, plus the contours of the land blocked most of his view of it. He was confident the guards wouldn't observe his jump. He next checked upriver, where there was no sign of observers or any surveillance equipment. Lastly he gauged the distance he must leap: yeah, at least nine feet, and worse still, the rock opposite was taller than the one on which he was perched. The jump would be a son of a bitch to make, but Po wasn't for turning back. He checked his pockets, securing everything down, and lastly dipped to his boot and ensured his knife was secure in its sheath. He backed to the furthest edge of the boulder, and rose up and down on the balls of his feet as he figured out his best approach for the leap. Three steps and he'd be at the edge, and then there'd be nowhere to go but into space.

'Don't fall,' he commanded again, and before he could allow doubt to set in, he sprang forward, legs pumping.

He hurtled into the air.

His boots hit rock, but at a sharp angle, and he churned his feet for purchase. At the same time his palms slapped down on the top of the boulder, followed a second later by his chest. His wind was knocked out of him in a long pained exhalation. Gravity grabbed him and tried to peel him backwards off the boulder. He dug in with his fingertips, seeking fissures and protrusions, and finally caught himself. His fingernails felt as if they'd been prized from at least two of his fingers, and his palms were barked raw. Using the discomfort to galvanize him, he scrambled for footholds and pushed up and heaved his body on top of the boulder. He lay there for a moment, catching his wind, before gathering his feet under him and standing. His instinct was to check back to the place he'd jumped from, and he saw that returning that way might not be any easier, but for now it was his single escape route. Next he checked downstream: there was no indication that the guards at the bridge had heard or seen him scrambling for his life. He was, however, too prominent atop the boulder, presenting too much of his figure against the night sky. He quickly clambered from the perch and onto the riverbank on the commune's side of the river. Thick, untamed woodland encroached on the riverbank. The terrain suited him. Po dug out his cell phone and rapidly typed a text message to Tess. It surprised him that she hadn't accompanied him to the river crossing, but he was glad she hadn't. She'd have been mortified witnessing how close he'd come to disaster. He kept his message short and sweet, so there was less chance of worrying her: *I'M IN.*

BE CAREFUL, she replied needlessly.

TWENTY-ONE

P o entered the woods. Earlier he had studied the maps and schematics of the commune that Tess had found, so he had a fair idea of its layout and the direction he must travel to get there. However, he had no idea of the kinds of challenges the terrain might present before he reached the buildings. A few contour lines on a map didn't do full justice to the ruggedness of the actual hills. He immediately discovered that traversing the woods was going to be incredibly tough in the dark: the trees were ancient; many of them had fallen over and become entangled, causing deep impenetrable thickets. Large crags rose from the ground and exposed limestone ridges snaked between the thickest copses of trees. Tess had given him a two-hour window before threatening to come in with guns blazing; there was no possible way he could forge a path through the woodlands and back in that time. He backtracked to the riverbank. His best approach would be to avoid the guards at the bridge, circumvent them and follow the road in towards the commune. The going would be much easier, and also, he was more likely to spot somebody approaching when they'd use lights to pick their way along the road.

A wire fence close to the riverbank indicated he was approaching the private land. There were signs posted every hundred yards or so, and without paying them much attention, Po understood they'd been there since when this was a military base. He reached a spot where a game trail converged with the riverbank and found that the wire had been pushed down, giving him easy access. He stepped over it and stuck to the beaten path, following it obliquely behind the position of the bridge to where it met the road. Po waited a moment. If his transgression onto the private property had been discovered by electronic means, an alert would be sent to the bridge guards and they'd begin searching for him. For now they were still engaged in conversation, seemingly unconcerned about interlopers. He allowed another few minutes in case a search party was dispatched from the commune, and was reasonably assured his presence had gone undetected when the road stayed empty ahead. He began a steady tread along the edge of the road, staying to the shoulder – if there were pressure pads installed they would more likely be buried in the road than under thick grasses. He was alert to the possibility of motion sensors attached to the trees but spotted nothing suspicious. About four hundred yards into the private land he came upon a taller fence, and gates secured against entry. Before approaching the gates he checked either side for CCTV. He saw none. He padded up to the gate and found it locked with a combination padlock; he could spring a normal lock but perhaps not a coded one.

The communal dwellings around the central square were perhaps a quarter of a mile from the gate, hidden from his view by the woods. If he'd any hope of discovering where Elspeth and Jacob were he must get inside. The gates were about eight feet tall and again emblazoned with 'Keep Out' and 'No Entry' signs. Barbed wire was strung across the top. The fence appeared to be an original feature from when this was a military encampment. It was also eight feet tall, sturdy and strung with coils of razor wire. The uppermost two feet of the fence angled outward to make scaling it even more difficult. The fence didn't perturb him much. It was well maintained each side of the gate, but he'd bet things would be different deeper into the woods. He was about to test his theory when he spotted lights approaching. He ducked out of sight, concealing his body behind a tree stump at the edge of the shoulder, and watched the headlights grow brighter.

Within seconds a vehicle rattled to a stop at the gate and a young man disembarked from the passenger side. He reached through the gate, seized the lock and deftly input the code. The lock dropped open and he pushed the gates open. He waited while the car, an SUV this time, was driven through, then jogged over to get back inside. As was often the case, security measures were as fallible as those relying on them. Rather than relock the gate, the new arrivals had left it open for what they probably anticipated would be a swift return. The SUV drove off, heading for the bridge. The instant they were out of sight, Po rose up from hiding and jogged through the gate. Once inside the inner cordon, he again went to the shoulder of the road and began walking at a faster, though equally wary, clip. A few minutes later and the SUV came bouncing along the road behind him, those inside having returned from their trip to the bridge, and Po again hid in the woods until they passed. Behind him, he must assume that the lock had been reset on the gate, but he wasn't perturbed: scaling the fence from this side wouldn't prove as difficult when it was designed to keep people out not in.

His expectations were shattered on his arrival at the edge of the commune. Elspeth had warned that Eldon Moorcock had formed an armed militia and ruled the commune like a tinpot dictator. He'd conjured images in his mind's eye of fortified walls, machinegun towers, and perhaps crucified skeletons placed as warnings against transgressors. At the very least he expected to find armed guards patrolling, and maybe an indicator of what served as a jail. The reality was that he spied out over a peaceful encampment of small neat houses and gardens, some larger sheds, and also some buildings that had once undoubtedly been hangars and equipment storage huts. Most of the dwellings were set around an expanse of decaying concrete, on which several vehicles were parked. Further north, the houses were larger and appeared to have been purposefully erected in a semi-circle that encompassed the far end of 'town'. Po caught no hint of anyone that could be described as a threat. There were lights on in several of the houses, and he could hear the faint strains of music coming from nearby – he was unsure if it was over a radio, or if the musician was playing live. It'd be easy to be lulled into a false sense of security.

He considered making his way along the edge of town to where the bigger houses were arranged around a green area and turning circle. From there he supposed Eldon Moorcock watched over his domain. It made sense that one of those houses would belong to his eldest son, Caleb, and where he and Elspeth had raised Jacob the past ten years. If Caleb had snatched them, and returned with them here, it would be to his house, surely? Elspeth had feared punishment, but surely not every person within the community was a sadistic misogynist who'd turn a blind eye to the open abuse of a woman and child? It didn't have to be the case. Po had spent time behind bars in one of the most violent prisons in the US; he knew how a dominant figure could control those around him through the application of fear or reward. Some here might not approve of Caleb's behavior but they'd know enough to keep their opinions to themselves. But Po doubted that Caleb would hurt her when her cries might be deemed a noisy inconvenience to his nearest neighbors, his family. He would take her elsewhere where he could force as much noise from her as it pleased him.

He looked for an applicable location but nothing jumped out. A deep ditch had recently been excavated, but it wouldn't serve to hold prisoners. On the far side of the old parade ground a squat structure drew his gaze. Not because it stood out, or that there was anything unique about it, only that he had seen a woman emerge from a door at its side and hurry across the square towards one of the smaller houses. She was dressed not unlike Elspeth had been in a flowing blouse and long skirt. Was it the prevalent female fashion? Possibly the men here demanded that their wives be covered up demurely. Po waited until she'd disappeared inside the house, then settled once more on the building she had exited. He considered checking it but discarded it in the next few seconds when he saw another woman emerge, this one carrying a pile of folded garments in her arms. He was looking at some kind of communal laundry; not somewhere he'd expect to find prisoners.

He began a slow circumvention of the town, heading in the opposite direction to the largest houses. Now he was clear of the forest, his night vision had sharpened and he could define most buildings clearly by way of starlight and moonbeams. Other shapes began to form further back inside the opposite tree line, and he recalled from Tess's maps that disused bunkers nestled among the trees. If Caleb wished to hold Elspeth and Jacob prisoner somewhere, where better than inside a secure bunker? His mind made up, Po slipped out from between the trees and took a more direct route across the bottom end of town. He used the sheds dotted at the end of the parade ground as concealment as he cut towards an old crumbling road that led into the woods.

'Who is that?'

The voice came from Po's right.

In his haste to check the nearest bunker, he'd allowed his guard to drop. As he had passed behind what he took to be an uninhabited shed, a man seated on a felled log had been invisible to him. As Po heard the words, he ensured he didn't alter his gait and give the man reason to be suspicious. He held up a hand in greeting and replied with an innocuous mutter, 'It's only me.'

Often, his response would be enough. It might leave an observer scratching their head at which of their neighbors had strode past, on some errand or other, and they would have brushed the incident off as unimportant. However, this time, Po's lackadaisical response begged to be challenged.

'And who are *you* supposed to be?' the man called, louder than before. Po glanced back and saw that he had stood up from his perch, and worryingly he held a rifle slanted across his middle. For now, the rifle wasn't aimed at Po.

Po turned back, began walking directly towards the man, hands held out amiably from his sides. The moon was behind him, his face in shadow. 'It's only me,' he repeated, and offered a name that should be familiar to the guard, 'Jeremy. Jeremy Decker? You don't recognize me?'

Po stood four or five inches taller than Decker, and his frame was built differently, but as he walked towards the guard, shrouded in darkness, there was enough doubt cast into the man's mind to ensure that he took a harder look. While he was still trying to figure out if he was being lied to, Po had crossed the distance and was within a few yards of him. By then, Po's charade could not be maintained.

'Hold on a minute, you aren't—'

Whether the guard was about to call him out on his lie, or whether he was still trying to make sense of Po's appearance, it didn't matter. Po stepped in without warning, clamping one hand down on the rifle barrel, even as he snapped his forehead into the man's face.

The man sagged, stunned, but Po had tempered his blow somewhat. He didn't know the man from Adam, and had no idea of his temperament or nature: he didn't wish to needlessly harm a guy given a crappy job. However, weighed against his risk of discovery, he had to make another play when the man tried to grapple for the rifle. Po spun it out of the man's grasp and rammed the butt into his forehead. This time the man fell like a cut tree and Po stood over him a few seconds, listening for signs their struggle had been overheard. All remained quiet.

The man was out, but his unconscious state wouldn't last. It would be minutes at most before the alarm was raised. Po had no option except retreat and hope he could scale the fence before a search party cornered him. Even if he escaped pursuit, the Moorcocks would have been alerted to a trespasser on their property, and in future they might tighten things down so there'd be no hope of returning.

His reconnaissance mission was effectively over.

No, there were other ways to approach the problem.

He could slit the guard's throat, drag him out in the woods and have done. That way no alarm would be raised and the Moorcocks kept oblivious to his incursion until the corpse was discovered. Po smiled down at the sleeping man grimly. 'Fortunately for you I'm a better man than that, bra,' he said.

Po set aside the rifle. He got behind the man, grabbed under his armpits and dragged him towards the nearest hut. An unlocked door led into a storage shed full of gardening equipment. There, he crouched and unlaced the man's boots, and used the laces to bind his wrists and ankles together. Next he pulled off the man's belt and one of his socks and improvised a gag. Finally, Po found a length of electrical wire and he secured the sleeping man to the chassis of a sit-on-and-ride lawnmower. When he woke up, the man would have some freedom of movement, and the gag wouldn't wholly smother his shouts, but he would be slowed down from raising the alarm. Po had won back a few minutes' grace.

'So get movin' goddamnit,' he muttered.

Outside the shed again he retrieved the rifle and took it with him as he hurried towards the nearest bunker.

TWENTY-TWO

'These are going to be the longest two hours of my life,' Tess admitted. She was seated alongside him in the front of Pinky's GMC. The large SUV was still tucked back off the road between the twin hulking boulders, facing the road and the river beyond.

Pinky nodded his agreement. 'How long has he had?'

Tess had set a countdown running on her cell phone. 'He's already been gone fifty-two minutes. That surprises me. It feels like minutes since he left us, but at the same time an eternity ago.'

'He'll be fine, him,' said Pinky, waving off any concern, as much for his own peace of mind. 'He's got skills has Nicolas Villere.'

'Agreed. But he also has an impulsive streak a mile wide. If he spots Jacob or Elspeth, do you really believe he won't try rescuing them single-handed?'

'He promised he wouldn't.'

'I suspect he had his fingers crossed behind his back,' said Tess.

'Yeah, like that stunt he pulled up in Bangor where he allowed himself to be taken hostage? It was not his wisest idea.'

'And that wasn't the first crazy stunt he has pulled, either.'

'Yet he always manages to pull off a good result, him,' Pinky said, with admiration in his tone.

'He has been lucky before. But fortune won't be on his side every time. This is bad now, waiting for him to return, knowing he might do something reckless and I'll never see him again.'

'He'll be fine, him,' Pinky repeated, but with less certainty than before. 'Uh, do you think maybe we should go get those weapons and be ready in case he doesn't show?'

'We daren't leave yet. If he comes out and we're gone, how's he going to know where we are?'

'Drop him a text. Tell him what we are doing, us, and that we'll be right back.'

'The signal strength on my cell has fallen off. I've had no

service for the past twenty minutes. I'm betting the signal's even weaker where Po is by now.'

'That tracker app's useless out here?' he asked.

'Oh, Po mentioned that did he?'

'It would be neat if you could see where he is.' Pinky turned a rheumy gaze on her. It was obvious that she was torn by indecision, but her desire to be there to greet him when Po returned was greatest. 'We'll wait, us,' he assured her. Then he flicked a hand in the direction of the bridge. 'If the worst happens and Nicolas doesn't show, I swear I'll ram those barricades outta the way, and get us some weapons off those punks standing guard.'

Tess flashed a smile at his bravado. Except Pinky wasn't kidding. He was a big cuddly teddy bear of a man . . . until riled. In defense of his loved ones, Pinky could become a remorseless and nigh on unstoppable force. She had no doubt whatsoever that he'd fulfill his promise if it came to it. Hopefully Po would return soon and Pinky's oath wouldn't be tested.

'There's another vehicle approaching,' Tess said, sitting up straighter in the passenger seat.

On the far side of the river, headlights flickered between the boles of the trees, heading towards the bridge. They had to both get out the GMC to get a clear look at what was going on. They moved together and stood at the edge of the road.

'It doesn't look as if they're coming across the bridge,' said Tess. The newly arrived vehicle had stopped and its occupants had gotten out. They mingled with the guards, their voices raised in mirth as the quartet of friends met. A box was transferred from the newcomers' vehicle onto the flatbed of the pickup truck and more distant laughter rang out. The sound was innocuous and in contention with the concern Tess had for Po. But, on the contrary, the laughter was a good sign, as it meant that those inside the commune were relaxed: Po's incursion on their land had not been discovered yet.

The two newcomers got back in their vehicle and returned the way they'd come from. As soon as they were out of sight, the guards delved in the box. They pulled out what Tess took to be wrapped sandwiches, or something edible like them. One of the men took out a flask and poured from it: fresh coffee, most likely.

'Looks as if they've been supplied by their buddies for a long

night spent under the stars,' Pinky observed. 'Don't know about
you, Tess, but I sure could drink a coffee or two right now.'

Tess's mouth was as dry as chalk too. But she was under no
illusion; if she tried drinking or eating the tiniest morsel she
wouldn't be able to keep it down, not until after Po had returned
safely. They backed from the roadside, about to return to the GMC.

'Y'hear that, you?' Pinky asked.

She could hear what had caught his attention. It was the sound
of another vehicle approaching, but this time from the road out of
the town of Muller Falls. There wasn't a curfew on road traffic in
or out of town, but this was the first time another vehicle had
approached while they'd been parked there. For all they knew it
could be somebody returning from town to the commune, and
therefore they didn't want to be spotted. She caught at Pinky's wrist
and urged him back into the darkness. They stood alongside the
GMC, listening as the vehicle drew closer, and then passed by.

'It was those cops from town,' Pinky said.

The cruiser was slowing as the driver anticipated the turn onto
the bridge. Except the maneuver was not completed. The driver
braked before reaching the bridge, and the reverse light flashed on.

'Damnit,' Tess wheezed, 'they must've spotted us.'

'So how do we play this, pretty Tess? You going to come clean
with them?'

'Not yet.' She bit her bottom lip, came to a decision. 'How do
you feel about kissing girls, Pinky?'

'Well, I'm no virgin, if that's what's worrying you.'

'Get in.'

They both clambered inside the GMC and embraced and not a
moment too soon. The police cruiser came to a halt, blocking the
fissure between the boulders and their route back to the road.
The driver turned a flashlight on them, and as if caught in an illicit
tongue-lock, Tess and Pinky reared apart, blinking and shielding
their faces at the sudden intrusion of light.

'Think we fooled them?' Pinky stage-whispered.

'We'll see,' said Tess, as she pretended to straighten her
clothes. 'Act guilty.'

'I *feel* guilty. Nicolas might take me to task for kissing you like
that.'

'He'll understand it was just an act.'

'An act I probably enjoyed more than I should've, me,' said Pinky with a shit-eating grin. 'I enjoyed it so much I want to do it again, just as an act, you understand?'

Tess elbowed him playfully.

The driver didn't immediately get out of the police car, but his partner did. The black officer approached the GMC, a penlight of his own now flicking over the windshield as he checked them out. His other hand hovered over his service pistol. 'You in the car,' he barked, 'let me see your hands.'

Pinky lowered their windows and they both showed their hands were empty. Pinky called out, 'Is there a problem, officer?'

'Are we going to have a problem? Get out the vehicle, let me see you.'

'We are unarmed, officer.'

'Get out of the vehicle. Both of you.' The cop had drawn his pistol. Also, his freckle-faced partner had gotten out of the cruiser and was also approaching with his service weapon drawn.

'We are getting out. We are unarmed. We are doing as you command,' Tess called out, and then popped the lock open on her door. To Pinky she hissed, 'Don't give them a reason to shoot us.'

'Sometimes being this color is reason enough.' Pinky got out, holding both his hands aloft and showing zero inclination to cause trouble. He ensured he had the full attention of the black cop, engaging him brother to brother. Tess showed her hands to the white cop now approaching on the opposite side. He was alert, looking for Po, no doubt.

'There are just the two of us,' Tess assured him.

The cop still ducked around her, bobbed a look in the back of the GMC, before calling to his partner, 'Don't know what became of the cowboy.'

'Where's your friend?' asked the black cop. His name badge read Wilson.

'Man,' Pinky responded, with a roll of his eyes at Tess. 'Don't you know that three's a crowd?'

The white cop squinted at Tess. 'You two are partners?'

'Is there a reason why we shouldn't be?' she responded.

'When we saw you in the café earlier, I took it you and the cowboy were a couple.'

'He's gay,' said Pinky.

The cops exchanged glimpses.

'Let us see some ID,' said the white cop, whose badge identified him as Rossiter.

They had already checked out the GMC earlier, and probably had Pinky's name and address from the DMV.

'Got my license and insurance right here,' said Pinky, pointing at his jacket front. 'Is it OK for me to reach for it?'

'Go ahead,' said Officer Wilson, but he kept his gun aimed at Pinky

Pinky handed over his documents. Tess also presented ID, but she avoided anything showing that she was a private investigator.

'Jerome Leclerc,' the cop read aloud. Wilson used his penlight to illuminate Pinky's face and compared it with the photo on his license. 'Got any fines or warrants outstanding?'

'I'm one of the good guys, me,' said Pinky. 'Go ahead. Check and you'll see, bra.'

'I'll take your word for it.' Officer Wilson wasn't fooling them, it was apparent he'd already checked Pinky's details out after enquiring about the GMC's ownership earlier. Currently, Pinky's sheet was clean. The cop handed him back his documents.

'That isn't a Maine accent. You're from way down south. What brings you north?'

Pinky nodded over at Tess. 'I'm a sucker for love. My girl lives in Maine, stands to reason I'd want to join her.'

'So what you doing in Muller Falls?' asked Officer Rossiter, still acting surly even after confirming Tess's details with her picture.

'Sightseeing,' she said, as it was the story she'd given the server in the café, and who'd passed it on to the cops at the time. 'We're on a road trip. Us and our friend Nicolas.'

'That's the cowboy's name, huh? Nicolas?'

'Nicolas Villere,' she said, because to lie would only court trouble.

Rossiter slid away his gun and clipped the strap down on his holster. 'So you left him back at the hotel and thought you'd have a romantic drive out here.' He glanced over at Pinky. 'Just the two of you?'

'He's our buddy but three's a crowd,' Pinky repeated. 'We have separate rooms, but that hotel has such thin walls, y'know?'

'Have we done something unlawful?' Tess asked, feigning naivety.

'Not yet,' said Rossiter. His small mouth twisted up at one side. 'You weren't perhaps thinking about trying to cross the river, were you? See I'd strongly advise against it. Everything you see on the other side is private property, and the owners aren't the most welcoming types.'

'We had hoped to see the waterfalls while we were in town,' Tess admitted, 'but Jenny, our server back at the café, told us it was out of bounds. So no, we don't intend trying to cross the river. We parked here where we can see and hear it, and that's good enough. Officers, we tucked our car back here out of the way so we weren't causing an impediment to other road users. Sorry if we gave you cause to find our actions suspicious.'

The officers weren't stupid, and Tess momentarily regretted laying on the act too thick. She expected them to dig deeper, perhaps decide to search the car for evidence of what they were really up to, and Tess didn't want them to see what was in her computer's search history. They wouldn't need a warrant to search while they had guns and she and Pinky at their mercy. But it seemed that her opinion of them had been partly shaped by Po's and Pinky's distrust of backwoods police departments. Officer Rossiter shrugged and said, 'No problem, ma'am. This has been the highlight of an otherwise uneventful night for us.'

Tess was dying to press the cops for information on the Moorcock family, to gauge their suspicions about what was happening beyond that barricaded bridge, but she fought the urge. She only wanted them to leave and for Po to return. Hopefully the latter wouldn't occur before the cops had left; otherwise they would have some awkward questions to answer.

The cops walked to their cruiser, but before getting inside Officer Rossiter turned back to them. 'Maybe y'all should take yourselves on back to town now, in case you draw some unwelcome attention. Some of those backwards folks don't take too kindly to mixed-race relationships and might make their feelings felt.'

Tess followed his subtle nod towards the bridge. The police activity would have drawn the attention of the guards. Once the cruiser left the scene, the guards might decide to investigate what the police had been up to and discover their hiding spot. Tess

doubted that the following discussion would be resolved so peace-
fully, especially if the guards suspected they were being spied
upon, or worse, that they were waiting on somebody already
trespassing on their land.

'Our hand has been forced, Pinky,' Tess announced as they
returned to the GMC. 'We're going to have to leave for now, so
we may as well kill two birds with one stone.'

'I should've planned this better,' Pinky opined. 'You should text
Nicolas, and hope it goes through to him.'

'I will.' She checked the timer counting down and saw they
were now well into the two hours timescale she'd allotted. If it
took half an hour to drive to the hotel, grab the weapons and
return, it should be approaching the deadline they'd planned for
his return.

Pinky drove them away. In the rearview mirror Tess watched
the police cruiser's blinkers come on and it took a right onto the
bridge and pulled up at the sawhorse barricade. Hopefully the cops
made regular stops to speak with the guards there, and this time
was not out of the ordinary. Officer Rossiter had cautioned them
about drawing attention from those within the commune, she
doubted he'd therefore tell the guards about finding them hiding
back there in the ravine. The GMC took a bend in the road and
the bridge was concealed from view.

'I hated lying to those cops like that,' said Tess, 'and maybe it
showed. Do you think they believed anything we told them?'

'What? You don't think I make fine boyfriend material, me?'

'I promised Elspeth I wouldn't involve the police, but downright
lying to them goes against my grain. What did you make of those
cops? Do you think we can trust them or do you still think they're
on Eldon Moorcock's payroll?'

'It's hard to say. Once they'd put away their guns they treated
us with respect, but what if theirs was an act too. What if they
keep an eye on the outer perimeter of the commune, and they see
off any nosey people like us with what just sounds like a friendly
warning? How'd you think they would've reacted if you'd came
clean and told them we are looking for an abducted woman and
kid? Do you think they'd have been polite and respectful then, or
would they have arrested us for being accessories after the event,
or would they have run us off at gunpoint?' As was often the case

when Pinky grew emphatic, he dropped the strange, affected speech pattern he was known for. 'They came across as stand-up guys, but I still don't trust them, Tess. For all we know they've joined their buddies on the bridge and are laughing about how they caught us in a compromised position and chased us back to our hotel.'

'It's probably best to err on the side of caution for now,' she concurred, although she couldn't shake the feeling that she was making the totally wrong judgment on this. If they went to the police with their suspicions and the law enforcement community was mobilized to help with the search for Elspeth and Jacob, then none of this would be necessary. 'Let's get this done as quickly as possible. Who knows what might happen next?'

TWENTY-THREE

He could sense the mass of the hillside looming above him as Po went deeper inside the bunker. At first he'd entered a cavernous space decked out like a loading bay at a large logistics hub. There were several vehicles parked in the area, and Po had wondered if any of them had been used during the abduction of Elspeth and Jacob. A panel van with its rear windows blacked out was a contender, he thought. He had tried checking the van for any clues but it was locked and the tinted windows foiled his view inside; he could have forced the locks with his knife but to what end? Up on the raised loading platform he discovered prints of several distinct pairs of boots and shoes in the dust and had followed them further into the bowels of the bunker. He had hoped to discover where Elspeth and her boy were being held, but the footprints had petered out and since then he'd found no visual clue to where he should try next in the maze of tunnels.

The first chambers he checked turned out to be storage rooms, some of them holding dry goods, others held perishable foods and fruit and vegetables, and one of them had been converted to a butcher's workshop and cold storage, complete with industrial-sized fridges and freezers. It stood to reason that a community of this size would require stocking up on food, drink and other necessities. Many prepper communities kept similar caches in preparation for the day when society collapsed. It didn't surprise him when an adjacent storeroom contained all manner of small arms and ammunition. He was tempted to add to his weaponry with a handgun he could tuck into his belt, but in the end he left well enough alone. A gunfight should be avoided at all cost, and besides, if it came to shooting it would be preferable at the distance the rifle already afforded him.

The first bunker was a dead end for his search. He checked his watch and saw that barely thirty minutes of the time Tess had allotted remained. It would take him a quarter hour to get back to the river unimpeded. The man he'd knocked out and tied up would have wakened by now: had he already attempted to free himself, and perhaps raised the alarm? Po got no hint that a hunting party was on his heels. He backtracked through the dimly lit tunnels, and was approaching the room containing the guns once more when he noticed a door he'd missed the first time. A large figure '9' was stenciled on the door but there was no other signage. He tried the handle and found it stiff but unlocked. He pulled the door open and peered into a narrow passage that led as straight as an arrow shot into the darkness. By his reckoning, the passage must extend beyond the hill in which the bunker had been built. He recalled the dotted lines on Tess's maps of the compound, and understood they were indications of a subterranean network of pathways throughout the camp. He was tempted to enter the passage and follow wherever it may lead, but he was on the clock and every second was precious.

He closed the door and moved back towards the loading bay.

Voices filtered to him from beyond the huge steel shutters.

Po had gained entry through a smaller door in the shutter, the padlock securing it proving no impediment to his knife. The problem was he had left the opened lock hanging on its hook, the latch swinging loose, so he had an escape route. From what he could make of the voices, the open lock had been discovered. He ducked back out of sight just as the door squealed open and a face peered into the cavernous loading bay. Luckily for him, it appeared the man he'd knocked out was yet to be found, so the open padlock was the only cause for alarm: for now it provoked only surprise and mild concern from the duo of men that'd discovered it.

The two men entered the loading dock tentatively, calling out, 'Eldon? Are you in here?'

It made sense to Po that Eldon held the keys to the storage bunker, being as he supposedly controlled all aspects of life in the commune. The men expected to find their leader inside, and when he didn't reply it gave them pause. Would they enter further, when it was apparent to Po they had no right to be there unsupervised?

The two men debated.

Po listened, gauging their movements from the scuffs of feet on concrete and their brief mutterings.

He should do something other than stand there with his back
to a wall, because he had a horrible idea about what might come
next.

The men gave up, and deciding that they'd overstayed their
welcome, they retreated from the bunker. Po exhaled in frustration as he heard the latch being fixed in place. The padlock was
about to be fastened securely. The duo must have concluded that
leaving the padlock undone was an oversight from Eldon's last
visit, and they chose only to rectify his mistake. If it were locked
from the outside, it sealed Po inside the bunker with no hope of
returning to Tess and Pinky in the agreed time. Concerned by
his non-appearance they would enter the commune seeking him,
and needlessly place themselves in danger. He couldn't allow
that to happen.

Without further thought, Po stepped around the corner, and hurled
an oath at the door. He ran along the loading dock and jumped
down between the parked vehicles, slamming his palm repeatedly
on the side of the panel van. The racket was heard, and he was
relieved to hear that the padlock had not yet been clasped shut.
Confused by whom they were about to lock inside the bunker, and
probably afraid that they had unduly raised the ire of their leader,
the duo rapidly worked the latch off its hook and yanked open the
door again. They peered in from the open portal, but Po needed
them inside with him.

'Over here,' he croaked, 'help me.'

'What's wrong?' asked one of the men. Happily, he hadn't
enquired who had begged for help. At this moment they'd no
reason to suspect that a stranger had infiltrated the commune let
alone made it inside the usually secure bunker. The first man
stepped inside.

'Help me, I'm hurt,' Po wheezed. 'I fell and busted my ankle.'

'Where are you?'

'I'm here.'

'Who is it?'

'It's me, Jeremy Decker.'

The two men debated a few seconds, and then the second man
entered too. They approached, one of them pulling a flashlight out
of a pouch on his belt and flicking it on. The beam danced over
the parked vehicles and landed on Po. He faced them with the

rifle braced against his shoulder. 'Make one damn sound and I'll shoot you dead,' Po warned.

These men, like others living under Eldon Moorcock's thrall, were not necessarily bad men. Po felt no personal ire towards either man, except for a couple of brief facts: right then they stood between him and his quest to find Elspeth and Jacob, and to return safely to Tess's side.

'Get over here,' he ordered, jerking the rifle barrel towards the van for clarity. 'And take that damn flashlight outta my eyes.'

The men were younger than he first thought, neither of them older than their mid-twenties. Sometimes the rashness of youth can cause an illogical response to a threat, where they believed testosterone made them immune to bullets, but it seemed that these men had been systematically conditioned into taking orders from their elders. They both stumbled forward and the guy with the flashlight lowered it as commanded.

'Kneel,' Po instructed.

Perhaps it was the wrong signal to send out. A hostage was usually ordered to kneel before his execution. Both young men thought they were about to be slain, and the fear caused them to stagger, heads spinning as they sought escape.

'Kneel down, goddamnit. I don't want to hurt you so don't give me reason to shoot y'all!'

Po's words gave them hope and overrode their flight instincts. First one, then the other went down on their knees and stayed there, peering up at Po. He moved around them, never lowering the rifle, until he was at the side door of the panel van. One-handed he clutched the handle and tugged. The door was not locked and it slid open on its guide rails. Warm air and the smell of humanity wafted out, despite it being hours since the van must have held several occupants. Po gave the interior of the van only a cursory glance before his attention snapped back to his prisoners. Nothing inside told him that Elspeth and Jacob had been in there, but he sensed they had.

'Whose van is this?' he asked.

The two men exchanged glances. One of them elected to speak, but he did so at a whisper, taking heed of Po's earlier warning. 'Everything here belongs to the community.'

'Is that so? But who's most likely to use it?'

'Whoever needs it most.'

'Who used it most recently?'

'I don't know.' The young man checked with his friend, who also shrugged an apology.

Po didn't want to put words in their mouths, but he was certain that Caleb Moorcock, or at least somebody acting on his behalf, had driven the van to Portland and back.

'When was it last used?' Po asked.

'I don't know.'

The second man shook his head.

Po actually believed them. Judging by their appearance and their lack of animosity towards him, Po doubted the youngsters were party to the inner workings of the Moorcock compound. He regretted having to do what was on his mind.

'Get up, one at a time, and get in the back of the van.'

'Please, mister, don't hurt us.' It was the second youth who'd spoken. His mouth trembled as he blinked up at Po through tears.

Po snapped out his hand. 'Give me that flashlight.'

The young man held it up, and Po saw how hard he was trembling. He took the flashlight and stuffed it in his belt. 'Go on. In the van.'

The young man scrambled to obey. He sat up towards the front of the van on a bench seat fitted to the wall. Po shook his head, nodding down at the floor. The young man went to his hands and knees to obey.

'OK, now you,' Po told the elected speaker.

As the young man stood, he glimpsed into the van's interior and perhaps he imagined it as his tomb. Something snapped inside him. With a shriek of desperation he lunged and tried to grapple the rifle from Po. Po easily avoided the swiping hands, and instead he turned the rifle in his grasp and gave the youth a sharp jab of the butt in the chest. The man staggered back, his knees colliding with the step up into the van and he sat down hard. Po gave him another sharp jab with the rifle butt, this time to the chin, and the young man splayed backwards, unconscious. The other man had watched open-mouthed, silenced by dismay.

'I hoped I wouldn't have to do that,' Po growled, 'but your buddy gave me no choice. What about you, son? You goin' to try to be a hero?'

Showing his open palms, the young man whimpered, 'I won't give you any trouble, mister.'

'Good. Here's what you're going to do. Grab your friend and drag him inside. Make sure he can breathe and isn't goin' to choke on his own tongue. I'm going to lock you both inside, and then I'm going to walk away. But here's the thing, son, if I hear one peep outta either of you, I'll come back and shut you both up for good. D'you hear me?'

'Y . . . yeah, I hear you, mister. I understand. I won't make a noise.'

'Good idea.' Po waited while the youth manhandled his sleeping pal inside the back of the van, then he gave the youth one final reminder, by placing his finger to his lips. The youth nodded and clamped his lips tight. Po closed the door on them, and stood a moment, listening. Inside, the conscious youth didn't even move, for fear the door would be yanked open once more and they were blasted to death.

Po backed away, and then he turned and jogged for the open door. He took a quick scan around before fully emerging from the bunker, and once outside, he closed the door and fitted the padlock in the latch and snapped it shut. He'd cowed the youth into silence, but he couldn't rely on it lasting. Once the youth realized he was no longer in imminent danger, he'd escape the confines of the van. He would likely try to get out through this door and finding it locked would kick up a ruckus. Po intended being well away from the bunker by then. He began a rapid walk away, taking the same path he'd originally followed to reach the bunker along the warped concrete road.

He cursed his ill luck. Not only had he failed to find Elspeth or Jacob, he'd advertised his presence in the commune by coming into conflict with three of its residents. None of them knew who he was, but once they raised the alarm it wouldn't matter. Po would be hunted. That in itself wasn't his major concern because if the caliber of enemy could be judged by those he'd already met, he fancied his chances; however, returning to the compound to continue his search had just become a task ten times more difficult than before.

He'd wanted so much to demand answers from the two youths. He could have forced them into telling him where Elspeth and

Jacob were likely being held, but doing so would have given Caleb and the other Moorcocks a heads-up for when he would return. He had no wish to forewarn them that he was coming back. For now, they might suspect that his reason for being inside their community was to steal from them, not to liberate their prisoners. The youths might have no idea where Elspeth or her son was, but had he mentioned them then the game would be up. For now he must bite his tongue, hold in his frustration and get the hell outta there before everything blew up in his face.

From behind him came distant pounding, then the thin strains of a voice. The youth had found his way out of the van, but the outer door was locked. Po wasn't worried that the sounds would travel across the defunct parade ground to the houses, but there might be somebody closer. He picked up his pace and approached the hut where he'd left the older man trussed and gagged. For now, the man was silent. Po felt a momentary pang of concern that perhaps he'd hit the guy too hard and he'd never wake again. His concern was fleeting; back inside the bunker, the youth showed he was more resourceful than Po had at first given him credit for. He repeatedly hit the horn on one of the vehicles, and the sound carried further than any dull thuds or muffled hollers. The racket was certain to draw curiosity, soon replaced by a hostile response once Po's presence was discovered. He relinquished the rifle, tossing it aside, while feeling for the flashlight in his belt with his other hand. There was no possible way he could safely return to the river by the same route he'd followed in: he'd be captured in minutes if his pursuers chased him in vehicles. He must negotiate the labyrinth of crags and deadfalls, and in there the flashlight would be a handier tool than a firearm. By the same measure, so would the knife currently nestled in his boot.

TWENTY-FOUR

'Time's up,' said Tess as the countdown on her cell phone hit zero. She shifted in the darkness but didn't move far. 'So let's go get him, us.'

'We should wait a bit longer,' Tess cautioned. Her words went against her grain, but they must be sensible about this. The two hours timescale she'd agreed with Po was specific, but not chiseled in stone. He could be mere minutes from returning, and they might spoil his chances of getting out undetected if they immediately stormed the bridge.

Pinky leaned close and peered at her with one eye almost pinched shut.

'We'll give him another ten minutes,' she said.

'A lot of harm could be done to a man in ten minutes,' he said.

'I know, but like you said earlier, Nicolas has skills. We have to trust that he hasn't been spotted and is on his way back to us.'

'The guards are still relaxed,' Pinky pointed out, and edged back into the shadows. 'They haven't been alerted to watch for him, them. Maybe all will be well, but don't you think I should go back to the car and be ready.'

By the time they had returned from collecting the pistols from their hotel room the police cruiser had disappeared. Pinky had driven the GMC to a wholly different hiding spot and they had disembarked, and walked back to the ravine between the crags, where Po should return shortly. Their vehicle was only a minute up the road, concealed further back in the woods so it wouldn't attract the attention of the patrolling cops again. They could fetch it if they decided there was no other play than to storm the commune, or – a move they were both in agreement with – they could approach on foot, subdue the guards and liberate their pickup truck for the task.

'Just another ten minutes,' Tess repeated.

Earlier, Pinky hadn't exhibited much concern for Po. But as the seconds had ticked down and his best friend had failed to return,

Tess had noted him licking his lips frequently, and also touching the butt of the pistol he'd pushed into his waistband. He was almost as anxious as she was, despite his admiration of Po's skills. He stepped forward to check downriver towards the bridge again. He looked back at her. 'Still not reacting.'

Tess nodded silently. She peered over to where the river rumbled through the boulder-strewn terrain, watching for any flicker of movement that might indicate Po was on his way back. For now the forest lay still. Not even a bird was startled from its roost. She was tempted to go up to where Po had jumped the river, ready to grab and haul him to safety on his return leap.

She checked her cell phone. The last message from Po was the one saying he was in, and where she'd exhorted him to be careful. She tapped out another message now: *WHERE ARE YOU?*

She waited. Beside her, Pinky loomed, staring at the cell phone as if he could hurry a reply by force of will alone.

No message was forthcoming.

The tracker app failed to work.

'Don't let it worry you: it's like I said, the signal here is very weak,' said Tess, with a lack of faith in her own explanation.

'We shouldn't've let him go in there alone, us,' Pinky moaned. 'One of us should've backed him up.'

By 'one of us' Pinky meant him.

'He'll be back any minute,' Tess said.

'How much longer do we wait till we accept we made a huge mistake, us?'

'You're right. Go fetch the car, Pinky. I'll wait here in case he does come, and you can pick me up. If we have to take those guards hostage, I will, and I'll force them to take us to Po.'

'Sounds like a plan,' said Pinky. The trouble was that it was anything but a plan: it was more a foolish kneejerk response to a previous failed plan, but she was as anxious as Pinky was, more so probably, and only wanted to have her man safely back with her. She wasn't kidding about forcing the guards at gunpoint to do her bidding.

Pinky slipped away into the night. It was a minute's walk to the car, and probably as long for him to get it started and drive it back here. By then Tess's revised timescale would have come to an end. She'd given Po as much time as she ever would.

Way off in the woods dogs bayed.

A rifle fired . . . the sharp crack echoed among the treetops.

Tess stepped forward, as if getting an extra yard closer would help her to hear better.

Further up the road Pinky must also have heard the gunshot, because he exclaimed, and then the slap of his running feet told her he'd thrown caution to the wind. Tess drew her pistol and went across the road, heading for the boulders where she'd last seen Po. He was nowhere in sight. She turned following the baying of hounds: it sounded like a pack of them was on a fresh scent trail. Maybe the dogs and the gunfire signified a normal night hunt on the Moorcock property, and that some kind of wild game was the prey, but she wasn't hopeful. She couldn't see the bridge from her new vantage point, but the reaction of the guards might clarify events for her. She began jogging towards the bend in the road, to get a look at their response. Behind her, hidden among the trees, the GMC's engine coughed to life. Tess kept going and gained the corner. The guards were beside their vehicle. No, one of them was actually leaning inside, and the second stood close to the open door listening. He was paying no attention to the dogs, but to something being relayed to him by his pal; Tess assumed they were in radio contact with somebody deep within the encampment.

She was torn between continuing towards the bridge and waiting for Pinky to catch up. He'd initially go to where he'd left her last, and finding her gone, he'd come after her. Tess kept moving towards the bridge, picking up pace with each step. The dogs bayed and howled, getting more excitable every second. More gunshots rang out. Shouts and orders rang from several quarters of the woods. It didn't bode well for Po.

The GMC roared up alongside Tess, and without missing a step, she hauled open the passenger door and jumped inside. Pinky hit the gas and the door slammed shut.

'It sounds as if Po's got half the community chasing him,' she said.

'So let's go help even the odds, us!'

TWENTY-FIVE

U nder normal circumstances the fence erected decades ago would not cause much of an impediment to Po. With its outward facing security measures, he could easily climb the fence and then negotiate the barbed wire for a safe drop to the ground outside. However, being pursued by dogs and armed men he was pushed for time; a lack of time necessitated hurry; and hurry caused inattention. Trying to scale the fence under those terms would see him ripped to shreds and easy game afterwards. He couldn't allow it. Instead of climbing the fence he followed its march through the trees, seeking someplace where the wire had been cut or beaten down by previous trespassers onto the land, through which he could escape without damaging his body. The problem being, the more he followed the fence, the deeper into the tangled woods he went, and the further he'd be from his extraction point he'd agreed with Tess. He had no time to check, but assumed that by now his two hours' window had firmly closed on him. He hoped that Tess and Pinky didn't do something rash like try to come to his rescue.

Pursuit had followed swiftly on his heels. The youths he'd shut in the bunker must have raised enough of a ruckus to bring help running, and the instant they had warned of an interloper then the dogs had been put on his scent. He wondered if the dogs were kept for the sole purpose of hunting unwelcome visitors to the community's land, and how many people before him had been ran down by them. In his mind's eye he'd pictured the scene, a man torn to pieces by a slavering pack of hounds, and it had sent a qualm through him when the man in his imagination was him. The nightmarish vision had made him fleeter than normal as he'd ran through the Moorcocks' land to where the fence reared up to halt him. On this side the forest had been tamed, beyond the fence it was a tangle of ancient woodland, thickets and crags. The old wood gave him more potential places to go to ground, to put his back against something impenetrable so he could face the pack one at a time as they came at him, where, armed with his knife, he would make the dogs pay for every strip of flesh they tore from his hide. For now the old wood was out of reach, but at least he had the benefit of maneuverability while moving between the spaced-apart trees.

There was no break in the fence. He'd spotted places where the wire had been patched and was now as sturdy as before; it enforced the message how badly the Moorcocks demanded that trespassers stayed out. He saw signs fixed to the exterior, spaced regularly at about a hundred paces. He had hoped to find that further inland from the entrance gate the fence would be less maintained, but his hopes had been dashed.

A rifle fired.

The bullet came nowhere near to Po, but the gun's retort caused him to flinch in anticipation all the same. Whoever had fired, they did so at the crashing of his progress through the woods; they did not have their eyes on him yet. The dogs were a different story entirely: they were on his scent and coming fast. Somewhere ahead and to his left he heard voices raised in question: how the hell had his pursuers anticipated his movements and gotten ahead of him already?

He ran, swerving around the boles of trees that reared out of the gloom, with the fence no further than a couple of body lengths' distance to his right. The baying of the dogs grew louder. He slowed, only enough to cup his hand over the flashlight and inspect a new portion of the fence he'd come across. It appeared to have been clipped apart, a long zipper of severed links that would open wide enough to permit entry to a human. Sadly on close inspection the clipped fence had since been mended, with newer, stronger wires entwined through the cut links: Po wasn't escaping by that route. His pause had cost him seconds, and the dogs were gaining. He shoved the flashlight in his pocket and dipped down to his boot and drew his blade. Hurting an innocent animal severely went against his grain, but not at the expense of allowing a pack of mutts to eat him alive. He gripped the knife's hilt in his right hand, the flat of the blade angled against his forearm. With his knife gripped in this position it was less likely to be knocked from his grasp if it collided with a tree as he ran. He set off again.

Another rifle barked, and again the round was spent somewhere in the woods, but a second shot followed and this time Po heard it strike a tree that was too close for comfort. He ducked – too late – and kept running as bits of exploded bark rained to the forest floor behind him.

More voices echoed through the woods. Some were behind, but again some originated from his front left. Those in front sounded as if they were controlling the hunting party dogging Po's heels, as if they were purposefully corralling him to a point where a trap could be sprung. It was time to change tack. Instead of weaknesses in the fence, Po began to look to his surroundings and within another ten paces spotted something he could use to his advantage. There was a tree standing perhaps ten feet away from the fence. It was tall and as thick as a telegraph pole, but it was also devoid of foliage. The tree was old and at some point its tip had been broken off about fifteen feet up. Scraggly boughs stuck out the trunk: a perfect ladder.

Immediately on seeing it, and recognizing it as a worthy way to waste more precious seconds, he lunged towards it and threw his shoulder into the tree. It swayed dramatically, and another three or four feet of rotting wood broke off at the top and plummeted to the earth, barely missing him. The perils of widow-makers were well known to woodsmen, and Po was no exception in knowing how dangerous an old tree like this could be. In his haste he'd almost brought about his ruination. However, now that the uppermost portion of the trunk had collapsed, he threw his entire weight at the tree trunk, pushing with both legs as he drove it towards the fence. Under his heels he felt the sward ripping and a network of old roots began tearing out of the shallow earth. The tree suddenly gave up any resistance to him and began to topple. Po stood clear, praying that there was not another weakened section of the trunk six or seven feet along the trunk where it might snap in half. The falling tree collapsed onto the uppermost wires of the fence, almost matching the same angle at which the stanchions supporting the razor wire protruded outward.

Po had not relinquished his knife while toppling the tree. He considered doing so, because he'd need both hands to help him scale the trunk. He decided no, but it was because the decision was snatched from him. Two dogs flew from the gloom at him, and unlike the dogs tracking him, these had a different purpose so came almost without warning: attack dogs rarely voiced their intention to rip their target apart. They were large German shepherds, swift, silent and potentially lethal. The leading dog came at him like a missile, its jaws extended to clamp on his arm, to negate his weapon, and to use the leverage to yank and spin him to the floor.

Po danced to one side, bobbing and weaving like a pugilist. The dog's teeth snapped on air, and it twisted mid-flight, its claws raking at him for purchase instead. Then it was beyond him and its momentum had taken it to the forest floor. The dog scrambled to regain its feet, to renew its attack.

Po was already engaged with the second dog. It had been stalled a moment by the first shepherd's attack, so hadn't sprang at Po. It ran in instead to grab at his leg. He kicked out but it was as fluid as oil, and faster than him. It swerved and span and clamped down on his heel. The dog powered backwards, digging its feet into the earth for leverage. Po cursed, hopping backwards after it. If he fell, his fight would be over. He was tempted to stab the dog, but only as a last resort. He twisted, grabbed the bole of the toppled tree and kicked savagely with his trapped leg. The crushing force of the dog's jaws was terrible, but Po's saving grace was that the dog had crunched down on his boot and it resisted the sharp teeth. The dog shook its head, yanking him side to side.

The other dog was upon him. It grabbed at his left arm, where it was wrapped about the tree trunk. His leather jacket wasn't strong enough to fully thwart its teeth. He felt the bones in his forearm grinding together. Uncharacteristically, Po roared in torment. But he didn't give up. He wrenched around, dragging the dog on his arm with him, and he pounded it in the ribs with the hilt of his knife several times. The dog was driven by a killer instinct, though, and didn't let go. Po slammed it around the head and muzzle, and this time it released him and cowered away, its tail tucked under it as it regarded him with rolling brown eyes. Po swore savagely at it, and then turned his rage on the second dog. It had not given up trying to upend him the entire time it had held his heel. Po booted it away, then sent another kick at its rump. The dog span about, snapping and snarling at him. Po took another kick at it and the dog leaped sideways to avoid him and it rebounded off the fence: it was the reaction Po was hoping for.

Before it could gather itself to attack again, Po ran up the toppled tree. Its angle was too sharp to carry him to the top, but he got his boots four or five feet off the ground before he had to grab at the ends of broken branches to help haul him up. The dogs renewed their attack, the cowed one more tentatively, both leaping and snapping at his heels. The braver dog attempted to scramble up the trunk after him, but it didn't have the benefit of thumbs. It fell off the tree, and then Po was clear of its teeth.

The uppermost portion of the tree trunk had squished down the rolls of razor wire, but the barbs were still a potential threat unless Po took his time to negotiate them. He didn't, he scaled to the pinnacle of the trunk, then leaped for all his worth.

The drop took him by surprise. Not only had he to jump from the height of the fence, he'd added to it by leaping up and outwards from the top. He sailed out and into the lower boughs of the forest on the other side, crashing through them as he plummeted to earth. Something raked his side from his hip to his armpit, and another knotty branch dug a painful furrow up his left thigh. As he landed, both heels close together, they sank deep into the loam, and his forward momentum carried him over both ankles so that he almost somersaulted. It was a graceless landing, and the force of it stunned him, so he'd no conception of windmilling between tree trunks and checking up against a fallen trunk.

The temptation to stay exactly where he'd landed was strong. He was numb for the moment, and his brain full of cotton wool. A curse wheezed between his teeth.

The baying of hounds and shouting of men was growing closer.

There was no staying put if he intended evading pursuit.

For the moment he'd foiled the attack dogs, but in no time his human pursuers would arrive and any of them with a gun could halt his escape. He pushed up from where he'd fallen, feeling every muscle, ligament and bone shifting and rearranging it seemed, until he had his legs under him. His left thigh was on fire, his knee twisted and his heel also felt unstable. He lurched as he attempted his first step, and he bit down on a curse. His right foot felt sore too, but it held him. He checked towards the fence and the two shepherds slavered and growled at him between the chain links. Po grimaced at them, but couldn't raise any genuine ire; the mutts were only doing their jobs. He felt for his flashlight, it was gone. Miraculously though, he had held onto his knife. He dipped down, sheathing the blade in its boot sheath for safety, then turned towards the twisted old wood, and limped into the darkness.

TWENTY-SIX

'Drive past the bridge, Pinky,' Tess instructed urgently.

'Say what? I thought we were gonna—'

'Yeah, but it looks as if the truck's going to come out and save us some trouble.'

While they were still on the approach to the bridge, Tess had watched the guards. One of them had left his pal in the truck, so that he could raise the barrier at the far end of the bridge. The pickup was already rolling forward.

'What are they up to, them?'

'My guess is they've been told to watch out for Po, and the guy in the truck's coming out to patrol this side of the river. Keep driving, Pinky, and don't look at them. Once we're out of sight we'll turn and come back. Then we'll only have the one guy at the bridge to deal with, and I don't think he has access to a radio to call for help.'

It was an assumption, but a fair one.

Pinky had his own version of a plan. 'I could ram that mother off the road, and then go and smack the one at the bridge around. But you're right, it's probably best your way.'

He kept driving, and they both kept their faces forward as they passed the bridge. The pickup was most of the way across, slowing down, so that the man on foot could run ahead and move the sawhorses. He glanced at the GMC but gave it no further attention as he began dragging the barriers aside. Pinky didn't slow, he sent the GMC around two curves before finding a passing place at the shoulder, where he quickly performed a turn, and aimed the car at the bridge once more. He began crawling the GMC forward, and as an afterthought knocked off the headlights so their approach was not announced. At the final curve he stopped and they peered out towards the span of the bridge. There was no sign of the man on foot.

'They must've both got in the truck after we passed them,' Tess surmised.

'They've both gone to cut off Nicolas's escape route,' Pinky said, 'which probably means he isn't coming back this way.'

'Forget about crossing the bridge then,' Tess said. 'It's more important we stay this side of the river and stop them from catching Po. If they have guns and they spot him trying to jump the water . . .'

Pinky put his foot down. Driving without lights was risky on the twisting road, but he'd got the measure of the road beyond the bridge having traveled it back and forth a few times now, so he kept the lights turned off. It was the pickup's taillights that gave up the guards' position in the road ahead; ironically they had parked in the same ravine between the boulders that Tess and Pinky had used earlier. Unobserved by the guards, Pinky slowed the GMC and pulled in as tight to the shoulder as possible. He and Tess slipped out of the car, their guns ready, and they moved to intercept the would-be interceptors.

The pickup wasn't tucked in tight the way they'd tried to hide the GMC earlier; there was no reason for the guards to conceal it. The truck was parked across the entrance to the ravine, on the hardpack where the police cruiser had earlier halted. Tess wondered if the cops had mentioned coming across a romantic couple hiding back there to the guards, and now that the alarm had been raised about a trespasser on their land, they had reason to be more suspicious and decided to investigate. It was fortunate the guards hadn't arrived a few minutes ago, or it would have seen them trapped on foot in the ravine. As it were, they were back on foot, but this time they held the advantage, if marginally.

One of the guards was still in the truck, speaking into a CB-style handset. The other man was out on the hardpack, staring across the river. He had a rifle canted across his middle. The roaring of water between the rocks camouflaged any noises that Tess or Pinky made. Also, they were behind the glow of the pickup's high beams, and invisible to the man on the road.

'You get him,' Tess whispered, indicating the man on foot, 'I'll handle the other one.'

'Should I kill him, me?'

Tess clucked her tongue. 'We can only use reasonable force, Pinky.'

'Good job I checked, eh?' He squeezed her a smile.

She shook her head in dismay, anticipating Pinky's next muttered words as he moved for the man: 'Now I just have to figure out what constitutes reasonable force when dealing with a sumbitch intent on murdering my best friend.'

As Pinky strode directly past the pickup, his pistol extended, she mirrored him. The driver was a hawk-faced man sporting a straggly beard and mustache. He was dressed in casual work clothing and boots. There was a gold band on his third finger. Tess should not forget that he was just an ordinary man, probably with a family at home, doing as he'd been commanded to hurt Po whether he liked it or not. But neither should she forget that he shouldn't be taken lightly; he was armed, though right then, his gun was on the pickup's dashboard.

He was listening to his radio as Tess moved alongside him, partially distracted. But he was also on edge, his adrenalin up after being brought in on the hunt to capture Po. He knew without looking directly at her that she was a stranger, and therefore a potential foe. Also, his gaze was fixed on Pinky as he lunged into the beams of light, and spotting Pinky's gun, the driver dropped the handset and snatched at his revolver. Tess jammed the muzzle of her pistol under his ear with enough force to shove him sideways in the seat, and his fingers fell short of grasping the revolver's handle. Tess reached with her left hand and swept his gun to her. She picked it up and held it behind her, out of his reach as she allowed him to return to a more upright position. 'Don't try anything stupid,' she hissed through the open door, 'if you don't believe I'll shoot you you're sorely mistaken.'

Before she'd even got out the words, Pinky had dealt similarly with the other guard. Tess was only vaguely aware of a brief swirl of action that ended with the guard sitting in the dust, holding his head, while Pinky slung the appropriated rifle over the rocks and into the river beyond. Pinky bent, clutched the man by the back of his collar and yanked him onto his knees. He pressed his pistol to the nape of the man's neck. Tess couldn't hear the dire warning her friend gave. She concentrated on her own prisoner. 'Put both your hands on the steering wheel.'

The driver complied. He darted sideways glances at her, licked his lips. 'What's going on? Who are you people?'

'I'll ask the questions,' she snapped.

The man's fingers worked on the steering wheel, squirming like eels. His eyes darted towards her again. She withdrew the gun a few inches so he could clearly see the business end close to his head.

'Don't try me.' Tess could read the signs that he was fighting an internal war of indecision: the movements of his fingers indicated he was torn between obeying her and launching at her throat. 'Keep your hands on the wheel, your eyes forward and answer my questions, and you'll get to go home to your family. Try anything stupid though . . .'

He got her message. His fingers tightened around the steering wheel, and he stared ahead. His Adam's apple rose and fell with a dry gulp. He had a good view as Pinky made his friend stand, and then nudged him between the shoulder blades with his pistol to start him walking towards the pickup. His friend looked inconsolable.

Voices babbled through the radio; the accents were too thick for Tess to distinguish more than one in five words. But she got the sense of the flurry of messages: Po was still on the loose and eluding his pursuers. She smiled, but otherwise her face was expressionless. For a moment she was unsure how to play out this situation. For now, nobody inside the commune knew who they were, how many of them there was or why they were there. Po's incursion had been to try locating Elspeth and Jacob, in order that a rescue mission could be launched later. If Tess asked about either of them now, it would give the game away. Getting the man to elicit information without specifically asking about the prisoners was the best way to proceed.

'There's somebody in those woods across the river,' she said. 'Why are they being chased?'

'You know why.'

'I don't. Tell me.' Tess tapped the gun muzzle on the man's ear.

In the meanwhile, Pinky forced his prisoner down next to one of the pickup's rear wheels; he checked Tess was OK.

To the driver Tess said, 'Well?'

'Your friend is trespassing.'

'Did I say the person is my friend?'

'You don't have to.'

'It's a bit extreme, isn't it, to have a hunting party chasing a trespasser? They must have done something more than walk where they aren't welcome.'

'He hurt some of our folks.'

Tess kept her features emotionless. 'For what reason?'

'Who can say?'

'You can.'

The driver shook his head.

Pinky interjected. 'How's about I bust your pal up some more, you going to *say* then, you?'

'Who are you? Are you cops? FBI?' the man responded.

Tess sneered. 'If you're wondering if we're constrained by a set of rules, think again. My friend will beat your pal to an inch of his life and not even blink. Then guess what . . . you'll be next.'

'You don't frighten me.'

'I frighten your buddy,' Pinky replied. He wafted a hand under his nose. 'I think he's already soiled his pants.'

Tess diverted the conversation from the dead end it was heading to. 'My guess is this trespasser saw something he shouldn't have. Is that a fair assumption?'

The driver rocked his head.

'What has Eldon Moorcock got going that he doesn't want outsiders to see?'

'Who says he's got anything going on?'

'Back to *that* question again? You say or—' Pinky aimed a swift kick at his prisoner. The cowed guard cried out in alarm. The driver had no way of seeing that Pinky's foot hit the tire, and not the man.

'Whoa! Take it easy, man,' cried the driver.

'Next time I won't miss,' Pinky snarled.

'Get talking,' Tess urged the driver, 'before somebody does get hurt.'

'I don't know what Eldon's up to. He has this bunker—'

'What does he keep in it? Don't lie again. You know exactly what he keeps there. You're out guarding that bridge all night to ensure nobody looks inside it. You're out here now chasing a trespasser 'cause he might have gotten a glimpse at what Eldon's hiding.'

'I swear to you, I don't. Look at us, ma'am. We're the schmucks who get to freeze our butts off all night guarding a bridge. Do you really think Eldon shares his secrets with us? He treats the likes of us as if we are worthless.'

'It's a poor life for either of you, then,' said Tess. 'So why do Eldon's bidding? You've come here, armed, to do what? To murder somebody you know nothing about, or why he's actually here, on behalf of a man that treats you like dirt?'

'We only came here to help capture him, not murder him.'

'Only to then hand him over to somebody intent on murdering him all the same?' Tess stepped back from the pickup's open door. She frowned down at the man that Pinky had disarmed. What to do with their prisoners was a quandary unique from what was in store for him should Po be captured. 'Is that what Eldon will do: kill him? Or is there someplace where he keeps people while he punishes them first?'

'Ha!' said the man, proving he was no simpleton. 'That's what this is all about, right? You're not here because of what's in the bunker, you're looking for somebody.'

Tess's head ticked to one side.

The driver said, 'If you're here because of Orson Burdon, you're looking in the wrong place. The cops already asked about him, and are satisfied there's no evidence he ever set foot on our land.'

'That's what the cops were doing here earlier, asking about Burdon?' Tess had no idea who the guard was referring to, but she could use it to her advantage. 'The police didn't ask to search your land?'

'They'd need a warrant.'

'All they'd need is Eldon Moorcock's permission. Eldon wouldn't give it?'

'Why should he? I told you, there's no evidence Burdon ever set foot here.'

'And that's what's in store for this other trespasser, eh? He gets captured, he disappears, and there's no evidence to ever indicate he was here?'

The guard refused to answer; it was obvious he was being maneuvered into a trap.

His silence didn't matter to Tess. What he refused to say was more important than the lies and half-truths he spoke. Apparently Orson Burdon had gone missing, and the guard believed it was

Burdon that Tess was interested in locating. She'd allow him think
that to hide the truth.

Another flurry of conversation broke out over the radio. From
the annoyance in some voices and the misery in others, it sounded
as if the search for Po was not going the way the hunters had
intended. The baying of dogs sounded distantly, and closer by
there was a faint crackle of movement through brush, but they
were the only indicators of the search. Tess commanded the driver
to get out the truck.

'What are you going to do?' he asked.

'Unlace your boots,' she told him.

'Wh-why?'

'Out the truck and do as I damn well say,' she snarled. She
wagged the gun at him and he rushed to obey. He sat in the dust
to pull out his laces, offering no form of visible threat. He had
claimed to be unafraid of them, but he was a liar: he had been
frightened before that he was going to be shot, and now she'd
offered a lifeline he was eager to comply.

Already, Pinky had picked up on her intention, and had
instructed the other guard to take off his belt. Pinky looped the
belt through the pickup's rear fender, then instructed his prisoner
to present his hands. He cinched the belt around the man's wrists,
then pulled the belt so tight it creaked with the strain. The restraint
wouldn't hold the man for long, but they didn't need it to.

Pinky watched his prisoner, but moved closer to Tess, to act as
a threat while she first tied his wrists together behind his back,
then used the second bootlace to secure him to the front fender.
Again, the lace could probably be rubbed through within minutes,
but she only required a small window of time to leave.

'Can I trust you to stay quiet until we've left?' Tess asked.

'Who is going to hear us?' the driver replied and squeezed out
a grimace.

Without warning, Pinky stooped down and clubbed a right hook
against the driver's jaw. Knocking the man out was the lesser of
two evils, but the suddenness of the blow caused Tess to flinch.

'Jeez, Pinky, did you have to do that?'

'Guy proved he couldn't be trusted to keep his yap shut. What
else was I supposed to do, me, shoot him?'

Tess looked down at the man secured to the rear fender. He had his teeth clamped shut. His eyes were as shiny as silver dollars. Pinky aimed a finger at him. 'Now *him* I trust to stay quiet.'

They retreated from the pickup, keeping an eye on the seated man. He ensured he kept his face averted and his chin squashed tight to his sternum. Once they were past the boulders at the edge of the ravine he would no longer be able to see or hear them, but Tess still indicated to Pinky that they should hurry quietly with a wiggle of two fingers, and then touching one to her lips.

They got in the GMC, Pinky again driving, and immediately Tess leaned between the seats, peering into the back.

'Are you OK, Po?' she asked.

She had heard the faint crackle of his progress through the woods at the riverside. He had crossed the river and snuck into the GMC while she and Pinky kept their prisoners distracted. He was alive, but disappointed.

'I couldn't locate them,' Po growled. 'We have to go back.'

'Not yet we don't,' said Tess. 'For now we have to press the pause button. Pinky, let's get out of here.'

TWENTY-SEVEN

Elspeth knew Caleb as a man who rose quick to anger, and who reacted to even perceived slights by growing hot under the collar and launching into irrational outbursts. After hauling her from the cellar, where he'd made those dire threats about getting the truth from her, and abandoning Jacob in the darkness, his rage had been palpable. Soon, though, the situation had become more terrifying because he'd lapsed into silence and he'd seethed coldly as he dragged her away. He had cast glances that both threatened dire retribution and then in the next second pleaded with her. Jacob's shocking denouement about his parentage had thrown Caleb off-kilter worse than any words Elspeth could have hurled at him. Caleb, being a bully, thrived on control, but here he had none. He could beat the truth out of Elspeth, but Elspeth could lie, or tell him whatever he wanted to hear, and then what? He would still remain unsure of the truth. With this understanding he was slightly lost.

He had dragged her to another chamber deep within the hive of subterranean rooms and tunnels and thrown her inside. There was power feeding the lights there, and Caleb had flicked them on. Slamming the door behind him, he had stared down at her while she gathered her feet. She had risen up and faced him. He turned his face aside and wouldn't meet her gaze; he looked ashamed, and tears tracked from his bloodshot eyes. Despite herself she pitied her abuser. There was once a time when she had loved Caleb Moorcock, and for a moment he had reminded her of the man that had stolen her heart. That was before she had been subjected to his relentless cruelty, though. Any love she had ever felt for him had since dried up and formed a walnut-sized lump where her heart should be.

'It can't be true,' he croaked, and still couldn't look at her.

'It isn't. Jacob misheard and—'

'You've fed that boy lies for years, Elspeth, but this is the worst of them.'

'I didn't lie to him. I didn't tell him anything, he misheard me and—'

'Now he thinks Po'boy Villere is his father!'

'He has somehow gotten that into his head. But I didn't—'

'He isn't stupid. And he isn't a child. He's old enough to know exactly what he heard.' Caleb finally looked at her, and the only shame he exhibited now was what he believed himself subjected to. 'You must have put the idea in him.'

'No. I didn't. You have to believe me.'

'I don't believe you. I *can't* believe you. You ran away from me, Elspeth, and you stole my child from me. I got you both back, but you've poisoned Jacob against me. How can I ever trust you or anything you say again?'

'Caleb, *please*. Look at how you treat us, how you hurt us. I had to try to take Jacob somewhere safe. You've got to understand that?'

Caleb sprang at her and grabbed her by the front of her shirt. He swung her around, jamming her against the wall of the small room. 'I warned you what I'd do if ever you tried to leave me.'

'I don't care what you do to me anymore. I only care about Jacob. If you cared for him you wouldn't put him through this torture.'

'I'm making a man of him, the way my parents made a man out of me.'

'Your parents abused you, Caleb! What you are doing to Jacob, there is no other name for it: it's *abuse*!'

'Do you think any other man could make a better father? Oh, that's right! You think Villere would be a better dad, a better role model for Jacob.' Caleb thought for a few seconds and concluded a fiction that fitted with his narrative. He stared at her with eyes now as hard as marbles. 'It's why you ran off to Maine, isn't it, searching for your old boyfriend. That was your intention, wasn't it, Elspeth? You thought you could convince Jacob that Villere is his father, by feeding him your stinking, poisonous lies, and you'd all live happily ever after. Jacob heard what he was supposed to hear, but Villere wasn't having any of it, right? He's got another woman now, and they want nothing to do with you or your brat; they kicked you both out on your asses, that's what happened? That's how you ended up back on the street and how I recaptured you?'

'I was only trying to protect my son . . .'

'Your son? He's my son too! He isn't Villere's, he's *mine*!'

Caleb could never control his fists for long.

He struck Elspeth then, a backhanded slap that sent her to one knee. She covered her face with her hands; he would punch her body instead, and she could withstand it longer than she could being beaten around the head. He loomed over her, bunching his fists and Elspeth steeled herself against what might prove to be her worst beating ever.

A distant car horn had been bleating for some minutes, ignored by them while they had been entrenched in their own drama. But now the horn had fallen silent, and voices had risen up in its place. Footsteps clattered down the hall outside and a hand pounded on the door. 'Caleb,' a voice hollered, 'you'd better come quick. Eldon wants you right now!'

Caleb still stood over Elspeth. Through her fingers she watched his features contort through several conflicting emotions. The hand beat upon the door and his name was called again. Caleb bent to her, hissing in her ear, 'We aren't finished here, Elspeth. I'll be back soon and we'll take up where we left off.'

He had left the room then, and she was aware of urgent conversation, and then the slap of boots on concrete as Caleb and the other man ran off to obey Eldon's summons. Why there was an urgent need for him to leave she couldn't tell, but the interruption had saved her from who knew how badly a beating, perhaps this was the one she had been destined not to survive. Maybe there was a benevolent god watching out for her, and he had taken pity on her and sent some divine intervention. She doubted it; any explanation would be far more mundane, and yet she sent up a prayer of thanks all the same.

In the past Elspeth had taken her beatings and afterwards was usually incapable of doing much more than the simplest of tasks. This time was different: she'd been spared his fists. Her hair felt as if it had been yanked out in bunches, and her knees and palms were sore from being dragged along the floor, but otherwise she could move without discomfort. She pushed up to her feet, one hand braced to a wall for support and she gave her limbs a mental going over. Caleb had struck her a couple of times, no less when he'd thrown her about in front of Jacob, but she was unhurt. She felt stronger than she had in, well, in forever, and much of that was in strength of mind. On the previous occasions she'd been assaulted she had been fearful of what might follow, so had acted meekly around her abuser. Victims of abuse often questioned their own shame and perceived it as guilt, and convinced themselves that somehow they were to blame for everything they got. That was the superpower of the abuser. This time, though, she felt as if he had lost some measure of dominance over her, and she was prepared to push the boundary more. She went to the door without pause.

Normally Caleb would have set a guard to watch her, or he would at least have locked her within the room until his return. From what she'd heard though, he had run off with the man that had come to find him, and also, in their haste, they'd forgotten to throw the outer door bolts. Despite her new resolve she paused at the door, her fingers hovering over the handle as she contemplated her next move. Doubt assailed her for a moment. Had her husband concocted a nasty trick, where he would coax her into a false sense of security? Was he hiding outside, ready to pounce on her from the darkness of the tunnel, to drag her back here again for a worse punishment than the one previously in store? She couldn't allow fear to control her, not after she had resolved that this was the last she'd ever allow Caleb to lay his hands on her.

She nudged the door open an inch at a time, listening keenly. Voices echoed down the tunnel, but the source sounded distant. Dogs yapped and bayed. She heard the revving of an engine. Whatever had gotten the community excited it had their full attention. Elspeth crept out into the tunnel. The tunnels had originally been hewn from the hills and bedrock, but they had been fortified with concrete. The ceiling and walls were uniform grey, along which electrical conduit had been strung, some of it now brittle with age. At regular intervals bulkhead lights offered luminance, but as many were out of commission as those that worked. The tunnel led arrow straight in both directions, pockets of light and dark reaching out into the hillside. Elspeth had no idea where she was in relation to her son, but only had one choice of direction if she planned on avoiding recapture. To her left the distant clamor arose, so she immediately turned and ran to the right.

The further she progressed the less the electric system had been maintained. She came to a junction in the tunnel and peered into an adjoining corridor. In there it was total darkness. She cast around, seeking a switch and found only a cable that had long ago been chopped clean through. None of the lights worked from there forward. When she concentrated, she thought she could make out a graying of the darkness somewhere in the distance and thought it was where another corridor met this one. She began pacing forward, one hand against the wall to steady her. She passed open doors and others that were locked tight. None of those held her son, so she kept moving. Occasionally cobwebs caught in her hair, and one time they got in her mouth and she spat and wiped at them in revulsion. With each step the grayness ahead grew brighter. Finally she reached the intersection of the tunnel and one she found to be much larger than the two she'd just traversed. The ceiling was higher, the walls further apart. The ground was scuffed by the passage of feet and different pieces of equipment. She recognized this tunnel, though she had never been this deep inside the hillside before. To return to the cellar she must go left towards the loading bay in the bunker, then negotiate another couple of passages. Caleb had been determined to take her somewhere out of the way while beating the truth of Jacob's parentage out of her. She supposed though, had she gone back the way he'd dragged her, her journey would have been shorter.

She began trotting down the wider tunnel. There the lights were maintained, and she could see a good distance ahead. She could also hear voices again, but the previous clamor had lessened; there weren't as many people and dogs near the entrance to the bunker anymore. She must still be careful; it would take only one person loyal to the Moorcocks to spot her and her latest escape attempt would end. Sadly for her, the majority of people in the community were loyal to the family, and the rest were plain terrified of the consequences if they weren't.

She dressed in flowing garments to conceal her shameful scars. Right then she silently cursed the way that they ruffled and flared around her. Though she ran as silently as possible her clothing swished and flapped, as if a bird was trapped within the tunnel. Ideally she should rid herself of the bulky garments for something more practical, but these were all she had access to. She paused

to writhe out of her blouse – she'd already lost her shawl and
scarves somewhere between Maine and here and was now down
to her undershirt – and to reach down and pull the rear hem of
her dress between her knees. She pulled up on the material, knotted
it and shoved it into her waistband at the front, forming a pair of
baggy pantaloons out of the fabric. When she moved on it was
quieter and more to her satisfaction.

Long before she reached the loading area at the front of the
bunker, she discovered a side passage she'd never been in before.
But its general orientation took her away from the voices and
nearer her son. She went down the corridor, again surrounded by
darkness, heading for a pinpoint of light some distance ahead. In
the narrow confines her breath was a constant rasp she thought
might carry to the ears of those in the loading bay. She progressed
with her lips tight, trying to breathe shallowly through her nostrils.

The passage exited into a square chamber. It was approximately thirty by thirty feet, and the ceiling was much higher than
the tunnel's, beyond the reach of her fingertips even should she
jump. A large airlock-style door dominated one wall. The floor
was buffed shiny because of years of footfall in and out of the
vault. This vault, she knew, was out of bounds to all but Eldon
Moorcock's sons and a few of his most trusted supporters. Elspeth
ignored the huge door and instead turned to peer down the main
tunnel that led into the room. It too led towards the loading dock,
although a turn in the passage a hundred yards or so distant
obscured her view of it. There was no movement between her and
the turn. She began moving, picking up pace with each step, glad
to find that the volume of her breathing was no longer an issue.
She reached the turn and paused. She bobbed a quick glance around
the corner. The tunnel twisted once again, turning at a right angle
towards the loading dock. The voices were louder now, but that
was to be expected. There came a whine followed by a deep-
throated rumble. Without seeing, Elspeth recognized the sounds
as the huge bunker doors opening. Engines coughed to life. Some
of the community's vehicles were being mobilized. She briefly
wondered what was going on outside: was the community under
some sort of attack? She hoped that an FBI task force was raiding
it, and she could throw her and Jacob at their mercy. She must
rescue him from the cellar first.

She slipped around the bend and paused again at the next, her back flat to the wall as she snuck a peek around the corner. There were two figures no more than twenty feet away from her. They were too intent on delving inside another room than to notice her. She knew both young men, they were brothers, whom she'd watched grow from children to adulthood and could have called them by their first names, but to do so would damn her. She ducked out of sight as the brothers emerged again from the room carrying rifles. They hurried back to the loading bay, to join, she understood now, a hunting party.

She sent out a silent prayer of gratitude to her unidentified benefactor. For a second she entertained the notion that whoever it was had come to help her save her son, but who would do that and why? Nobody could know that they had been snatched and brought back here. Nobody except . . . no, she couldn't hold out any hope that either Nicolas Villere or his partner Tess had figured out that they were in trouble and had traveled across country to try to save them. Elspeth had walked out on them when they'd offered to help, and for all they knew she had jumped on a bus and taken Jacob as far away from here as possible. That's if they even gave her and her son as much as a second thought after they'd left; she supposed that Nicolas and Tess might feel that they had dodged a bullet when she'd refused to divulge who her son's biological father was. Even if they suspected they had been grabbed, would they purposefully avoid seeking their whereabouts, and allow the issue of Jacob's parentage to be brushed under the carpet?

None of that mattered!

She shoved aside any thoughts of a rescue party or otherwise. Saving her son was down to her alone. She rushed towards the room the brothers had recently vacated and peered inside. It was shelved on three sides and all the shelves were stacked with enough weapons and armament to launch an invasion of a small country. There were hunting rifles, assault rifles and even a couple of those boxy Uzi machine pistols made popular in the movies. Elspeth had no clue about shooting any of the larger weapons: she went instead to a shelf holding several different makes and models of handguns. There were pistols, but Elspeth found them too intimidating to handle, so instead she reached for a standard revolver. She had fired a six-gun years ago, and the revolver reminded her of its simplicity. She checked and found the chamber loaded with bullets. She shoved the gun into her waistband and concealed it under the material she'd bunched there. Using the gun would be a last resort.

She checked outside before leaving the armory. There was still sound and movement in the loading bay, but most of the vehicles had already left, and now by the sound of things the last few stragglers were boarding a truck to join the chase. Some of them whooped and hollered as the pickup set off, high on excitement and without consideration of the consequences. The doors began rumbling shut again, meaning alas that somebody was still inside the bunker, manning the electronic controls. She padded down the tunnel aware that the least sound might now travel to the ears of who was still inside. There was a crossroads in the tunnel and she ducked to the right and hurried towards the holding room her son had dubbed 'The Cellar'.

Caleb didn't deem it necessary to have a guard on the door. But having dragged her out earlier, she recalled him throwing the bolts to bar Jacob inside. As she got closer her heartbeat tripled in speed: the bolts were undone and the door stood open an inch. What a fickle twist of fate it would be if Jacob had already escaped his cell and she was unable to find him. She lunged towards the door and was about to tug it open when voices filtered out to her. She halted, her hand creeping to the butt of the revolver stuffed down her skirt. She approached, by increments, listening for any clue who was inside the room with her son. She heard Jacob whimper something and that was all she needed to hear. She dragged open the door, even as she tugged out the gun and thumbed back the hammer.

Jacob stared at her a second, open-mouthed with surprise. Standing with their back to her, the person looming over him with a stick raised in threat, was slow in responding to her presence: there was no possible way that Elspeth should have been there.

'Get away from my son,' Elspeth croaked in warning.

Ellie-May Moorcock turned slowly to appraise her. The older woman's lined face was the color and texture of tanned leather under the feeble light invading the cell. She didn't lower her walking stick. She looked past Elspeth, obviously searching for her eldest son. It was a moment more before her gaze drifted to the gun in

Elspeth's hand. An emotion flickered over Ellie-May's features, but it was not fear. She had spent too many years terrorizing the younger woman to fear her abused daughter-in-law even when armed.

'And what do you think you're going to do with *that*?' Ellie-May smirked. 'What are you doing here, anyway, I thought Caleb—'

Elspeth ignored the old harridan, instead peering at her son. 'Was she about to hurt you?'

'Grandma said she was going to take her stick to me the way Caleb should've,' Jacob whimpered.

'Yes,' Ellie-May snapped at Elspeth, raising the stick up over her shoulder, 'and I'll take it to you too, you willful bitch.'

'No, Ellie-May, you won't.' Elspeth grabbed the stick and held it aloft. The older woman strained to yank it free, but Elspeth was resolute.

'Let go, you worthless whore.'

'That's the thing, Ellie-May, you call me worthless but that's fine. It means I'm nothing to you, and believe me, the feeling is mutual.'

Ellie-May surged forward, trying again to wrench free her stick. She was a couple of decades older than Elspeth, a tad bent over, but she was strong and robust and potentially dangerous if they got in a grapple.

Elspeth didn't shoot.

She clubbed the gun down on the old woman's head, and Ellie-May squawked once as she collapsed at her feet.

Jacob yowled in alarm. Despite what the old woman was about to do to him, it was still his grandmother he'd seen beaten down by his mom. He was confused, and he could even be forgiven for feeling some sympathy for his grandma. But Elspeth wasn't about to dwell on her. She threw aside the walking stick, reached and grabbed Jacob. 'Come on, let's go,' she said, and led him from the cell. She looked back. Ellie-May lay in a heap on the floor. For all she knew she could have hit her hard enough to crush her brittle old skull and Ellie-May was already dead, or she could be fading quickly. She couldn't let the old witch perish!

Actually, she could.

Elspeth pushed the door shut and threw the bolts.

TWENTY-EIGHT

'Are those bite marks in your jacket?'

After escaping pursuit, Pinky had returned them to the hotel in Muller Falls. Their friend had retired to his room, giving them some space for a few minutes. It was Tess's first opportunity to check Po over. He sat on the double bed, his fingers kneading his thighs. He glanced dispassionately at the holes in his sleeve.

'Couple of mutts almost took me down.' He raised his leg, showed Tess the ripped hem of his jeans and the teeth marks in his boot.

'Have they broken your skin? You might need—'

'I'm up to date on my tetanus shots.' Working occasionally in Charley's Autoshop, where cuts and abrasions were potential everyday injuries, Po protected himself from infections with inoculations.

'I'm more concerned about rabies,' she said.

'They were trained attack dogs, Tess, not raccoons.' He chuckled at the notion she'd put in his head.

'Still, you could get a nasty infection if—'

'Chill out, will ya, Tess? They didn't break my skin. I got a couple of nicks on my face and hands running through the woods, but otherwise I'm fine.'

'You're limping.'

'I'll walk it off.'

'Show me your leg.'

'What? Why?'

'Because from the way you're rubbing your thigh it must hurt like crazy.'

Po nodded. 'I had to jump a fence to escape the dogs. I near speared my leg on a branch.' He stood and shucked tentatively out of his jacket. Tess helped him pull out of the final sleeve. He grimaced, but hid his true discomfort from her. 'Another branch got me good up my side,' he admitted.

'Let me see.'

He raised his shirt, drew the material up almost to his ribs and hissed in pain. Tess took over, lifting the shirt up all the way to his armpit. She hissed too.

A raw scrape marked him from his hip to next to his pectoral muscle. Some of the skin had been scraped off entirely, and the wound was dotted with dried blood. Each rib must have taken a beating.

'There's nothing broken,' Po said to forestall her, 'but it stings like a son of a bitch. My leg's the same. Scraped up but, otherwise, I'll live.'

'I still want to check it out.'

'I told ya, Tess, I'll walk it off. One of those dogs got its teeth into my heel and tried to shake my leg out its socket. It messed up my knee and twisted my ankle makin' that jump, too: I'm sore, but nothing's broken. I'll be fine to go back out there.' He reached to retrieve his jacket.

'No deal.' Tess pressed him down on the bed once more. 'We aren't going anywhere until you're cleaned up and I'm happy that you're unhurt.'

'The longer we waste here, the longer Elspeth and Jacob are in danger.'

'We still don't know if they're even in the commune, Po. We are going to look like a bunch of idiots if it turns out they did get on a bus, and right now are sitting on a beach down in Florida.'

'You know they're there, Tess.'

'I suspect they are, but we still have no proof.'

'More's the reason I need to go back.'

'We will, but not until after the heat has died down. Right now you've got that place literally up in arms. If we go back now we'll be walking into a shooting gallery.'

'Now's the time we should go back. It's the last thing anyone would expect, right?'

She shrugged. He did have a valid point. 'I'm going to fetch some soap and water and clean your wounds first.'

Po reached for her wrist. 'Let's save it for later, Tess. I can't rest here thinking that boy's bein' abused again.'

'He might not be yours . . .'

'Does it make any difference? He's a child, and the man who's supposed to be his goddamn protector is the one stubbin' out cigarettes on his bare skin. Jacob doesn't have to be mine for me to want to save him, Tess.'

'Yeah, I know, I get that. I just don't want you getting up your hopes only to find out he's not your son.'

Po lay back on the bed, pushing his fingers through his hair as he exhaled. Tess sat on the mattress alongside him. She put her palm flat over his heart. It pounded like a trip hammer.

'I genuinely don't know how I feel about all this, Tess,' Po said. His eyes were shut, but he held his cupped hands over them. She thought perhaps he was ashamed she might see him weeping. 'You might not agree, but there's a part of me that wants Jacob to be my kid, another part knows things will be much easier for us all if he isn't.'

'We'll deal with it together, whatever the outcome,' she promised him.

He removed his hands and peered up at her. His turquoise eyes were clear and hard. 'We have to save him first.'

'We will.' Tess patted his chest. 'Don't get up. I'm fetching soap and warm water.'

Po got up regardless of her instruction. He tested his legs. His right ankle seemed to trouble him more than his other leg, despite the left being the one attacked by the dog. Still, he nodded and told himself again, 'I'll walk it off.'

Tess was happy to note he didn't reach for his jacket again. She was confident she could go in the bathroom for a minute and be reasonably assured he'd still be there when she returned. The hotel was old-fashioned and twee in its décor: a good thing. It meant it had items to hand Tess would never find in a modern chain hotel. She found a ceramic bowl tucked inside a cupboard built to incorporate the washbasin and pedestal. She sluiced it under the warm faucet, then half filled it. She dug out a face cloth and sponge from the toiletries she'd brought from home. When she returned to the bedroom, Po had moved to stand by the window. He looked out over the front of the grounds towards the main road through town.

'Those cops just went by in a hurry,' he said.

Tess set down the bowl of water.

She joined him at the window.

'D'you think they've been summoned by the Moorcocks?' he asked.

'I doubt it very much. The impression I got was they deal with their problems themselves and the cops are as unwelcome on their land as we are.'

On the drive back from the riverside, Tess and Pinky had regaled Po with what had happened concerning the guards from the bridge.

'You said something about those guards assuming you were looking for some missing fella?' Po prompted.

'That's right,' said Tess. 'Some guy called . . . wait a minute . . .' She racked her brain for the correct name. 'Orson Burdock. No, Burdon. They said Orson Burdon.'

'You said the cops spoke to the guards about him but they were brushed off.'

'Yeah,' said Tess, and she lowered her voice to do a reasonable impression of the guard she'd interrogated. '"I told you, there's no evidence Burdon ever set foot here".'

'Meaning any evidence had been cleaned up already?'

'That was the impression I got. The guard was kind of smug about it, as if Eldon had gotten away with murder . . . and I mean that literally.'

'It tells us somethin' about our friendly neighborhood law enforcement officers, right? If they're being kept in the dark about this missing guy, it's fair to assume they ain't dancing to Eldon Moorcock's fiddle like I first thought.'

'For the record, I never suspected the cops here were corrupt. That was all down to you and Pinky.'

'I still think we should keep them outta things till we know more. It's like you said, I've still no proof that Elspeth or Jacob are here, and I'd like another go at rescuing them before we involve the cops.'

Tess turned away from the window and collected the washbowl and cloths. 'Come over here and sit down. Let me get you cleaned up.'

Po took another lingering look out of the window, but by now the police cruiser was a distant memory. 'Didn't you say you tied those guys to their own truck?'

'Yeah. It was the best we could do under the circumstances.'

'That's maybe who the cops have gone out to. Perhaps somebody unconnected with the commune found them trussed up and called the police.'

'I hear you, Po. If those guards describe Pinky and me, the cops will know exactly where to come looking for us. I'm not concerned: I'll fully explain what we are doing here, and demand that they take action to confirm that Elspeth and Jacob are safe. If I have to, I'll have Emma Clancy get her boss to pull some strings with the local district attorney's office and have an entire task force mobilized.'

She was overstating her authority, but she'd at least try to galvanize positive action out of the police if they did get involved.

'Is that the entire police force that Muller Falls can muster?' Po wondered. 'Two guys?'

'It's a small town; they're probably fortunate to have any policing budget whatsoever. There's probably a county sheriff's office, and imagine that if anything major happens here they call in assistance from them or a larger neighboring PD, or probably from the state cops.'

'Or there are other cops here we are unaware of yet?' he proposed. 'Two guys can't be expected to cover three shifts, three hundred and sixty-five days of the year.'

Po left her with a damp cloth in her hand. He walked to the adjoining wall to Pinky's room and gave it a solid thump with the ball of his fist. 'Yo, Pinky!'

Earlier Pinky quipped to the police about the hotel walls being thin, and he hadn't been fully joking. 'Yo?'

'Want to come in here, bra?' Po said.

'Give me a moment, you.' Pinky's voice was barely muffled by the wall.

'What's wrong?' Tess asked.

Po ignored her momentarily while he went over and opened the door to the shared landing. As he returned he said, 'I think it's time we got outta here. If they're all the resource the town has access to, I just had a horrible thought why those cops might've been summonsed outta town . . .'

'Oh, God,' said Tess, also realizing that trouble was potentially heading directly at them. She set aside the damp cloth, and instead began pulling together her few belongings she'd unpacked and spread throughout the room.

Pinky stuck his head around the open door. 'Whassup?'

'It's time to get the hell outta Dodge,' Po told him, 'and hole up somewhere a posse can't find us.'

'Give me a second and I'll be good to go, me.' Without explanation, he spun about and ducked back inside his room. He had brought a small knapsack containing his overnight essentials in from the GMC; his spare clothing was in a suitcase still in the trunk. He need only grab the bag; it was highly likely his pistol was already secreted about his body. Tess had placed its twin in her tote bag.

'Leave some stuff lying around,' Po suggested to her. 'We shouldn't officially book out, just go out without saying a thing. If anyone checks our rooms let them think we're going to come back.'

How would they know where to look? Tess didn't voice her thought: Muller Falls wasn't overflowing with hotels, motels or B&Bs, so a search party sent to town by the Moorcocks wouldn't take long to check them all. Judging by the lack of tourists here, she'd bet that any local questioned about where 'the strangers' were staying could point directly at this hotel. Po had a point. If they were expected to return here, their hunters might waste time staking out the hotel rather than trying to pick up their trail. She tossed some non-essentials back on the bed and left the snacks they'd purchased earlier scattered on a counter top. The washbowl and cloths were a good addition, which she placed on the stand next to the double bed. Po had pulled back into his leather jacket by the time she was ready to leave. Her gaze went to the teeth marks in the sleeve, then tracked down to his left heel where his jeans were tattered and his boot scuffed: she couldn't believe he'd gotten away from the attack dogs without major injury. She was thankful he had though. He seemed to be walking stiffer than before.

They closed the doors to their rooms and went down the stairs. The hotel was a family run affair, by people who had lives beyond serving their guests. The pleasant couple that had checked them in on arrival, and later showed them to their rooms, was nowhere to be seen. A TV on low volume, and the accompanying laughter of a couple of teenage boys, hinted that the family had retired to their private rooms at the rear of the hotel, and were relaxing before retiring to bed. Po let them out through the exit door and pulled it shut behind him. They immediately got in the GMC, all taking their designated seats without question or complaint. Tess again had the back seat to herself, and Po was the elected driver. It made sense; he was the most skilled when it came to defensive driving tactics. Immediately he showed the most sensible tactic. He took a right turn out of the hotel, and drove towards the north end of town, the opposite direction from where an angry mob from the commune might approach.

TWENTY-NINE

T he skin at the back of Caleb Moorcock's neck prickled. Unconsciously he rubbed a calloused palm up and down the back of his head as he listened to the whining excuses of the bridge guards. Already they'd both stressed, several times, how it was not their fault that they had been outflanked and taken hostage at gunpoint.

'Forget about that. Describe the woman to me again,' Caleb said.

The guard who had been knocked out massaged his jaw. 'She was blond, nice looking, maybe yay high.' He held his hand level with his bruised chin, then immediately looked abashed that he'd allowed a small woman to take him captive. 'She took me by surprise and stuck a pistol under my ear.'

'And the dude was a big odd-looking black guy with thickset legs?'

'Yeah. He had a funny way of talking too.'

'Weird, like he was referring to everyone in the third person?'

The guard blinked at him, unsure what he meant. It didn't matter. Caleb had already concluded he knew who had captured the guards. The instant that he'd learned of the trespasser, his reaction to the description of a tall, rangy built man was to picture Po'boy Villere. It was no coincidence that the other two sounded like his partner, Teresa Grey, and his pal Pinky.

Caleb shivered as he peered out across the bridge. The barricade and sawhorses were still pushed aside, since the guards had only recently returned to their posts after freeing themselves. His neck prickled again, and he rubbed at it. Partly he was excited that he might yet get to take out his anger on Villere, but he was also partly anxious. His father had not been amused when he thought Caleb's actions might have attracted the attention of a private investigator: he didn't want any kind of law enforcement officer – private or otherwise – sniffing around his business. But here they were: Villere had trailed Elspeth back here, and his partner had followed. He was unsure how Eldon would take the news, but there being an investigator in the area wasn't something he could keep to himself.

The second guard, the one spared a punch in the jaw from Pinky, stood to one side, his eyebrows arching towards the top of his head. He rubbed at the raw wounds the belt had cut into his wrists before he'd been able to free them both. Caleb eyed him dispassionately. The guy expected punishment for his failure and by God it would come, but Caleb decided now was not the time; he'd allow both guards to stew in their own juices a while longer. Besides, he needed them on side for now.

There was a noisy group of around two dozen men behind him, as well as three trucks besides the one the guards had brought back across the river. Two German shepherd dogs strained at their leashes, as eager as Caleb was to pick up Villere's trail. The other hounds had been taken along the riverbank to where Villere had entered the Moorcock land with the smallest hope that he hadn't made it back to the river yet and was hunkered down in the woods. Caleb thought it was probably a wasted exercise, because by now Tess and Pinky had skedaddled, and most likely because Villere had returned to them. He turned to them with one hand raised in the air. The talking and speculating halted and all eyes focused on him.

'We can't stand by and allow outsiders to come and go on our land as they please,' he announced. 'Otherwise it will soon be a free-for-all, and before we know it we'll have strangers hiking all over the place, and getting in our way and treating it as their own. My father bought this land, but your families settled it: it's your home and you need to defend it *now*. Tonight a man stole onto our land and hurt some of our kin . . . old Royston Mitchel still hasn't shaken off the knock he took. And these guys here' – he indicated the guards – 'they were threatened and beaten by others. Are we going to allow that to happen without challenge?'

Zealous voices answered him, hooting, hollering and cursing, but not everyone living under the thrall of the Moorcock family were of the same psychotic nature: some of them shuffled their feet, stayed to the back of the mob and hoped they wouldn't be forced into whatever madness Caleb had in mind.

'I want some volunteers.' Caleb stared at several of the younger more easily coerced men in turn, giving them no option except to volunteer, then ranged his gaze wider. Several men stepped forward unbidden, mainly those that'd already answered his first summons to arms. The less eager he noted as they kept their heads down and tried to stay in the shadows. He wanted nothing from those cowards. He smiled and nodded at each of his volunteers, and within a short time had them loaded in or on the pickup trucks. He'd have liked to take the dogs with him, but they took up too much space. He put their handler to use though, assigning him to watch the bridge, seeing as the original guards had proven unfit for the job. He told the two demoted guards to squeeze in the cab of their own truck, while he took the driver's seat and led the small convoy of rowdies over the river.

Usually the inhabitants of the commune steered clear of Muller Falls. Very occasionally they visited to partake of the town's services but in general the commune was self-sufficient. Sometimes some of the youths from the commune would sneak into the town in search of alcohol or members of the opposite sex, and it had not been unknown for some of the older men to act similarly when the opportunity arose, but mostly the townspeople and those from the commune stayed apart. There was an unhealthy distrust between some of the older folks on both sides. There had been a previous time when a similar convoy as this one had struck out for town, but that was in the very early days of the community and had been led there by Eldon. It had followed an incident where some rowdy townsfolk had ambushed a couple from the commune and beaten them up. Eldon had responded to violence with violence, under the decree that they were obliged to protect their community from outside aggression. They had wrecked a bar, broken several shop front windows and also set fire to a community hall before retreating again behind the fences. The incident had shaken the town, and the woeful police department of the day was loath to respond, and instead of the justice being pursued, it had been allowed to slide. Things could have been worse, it had been reasoned: Eldon's posse could have found the men responsible for assaulting his people and hanged them like he'd first sworn to do. Rather than harbor Villere and his friends, the townsfolk would quickly give them up to avoid a repeat of the last time they tried to hide the offenders.

Initially Caleb would have preferred it if his brothers had

accompanied him to town. It was one thing having your buddies backing you up, quite another when it came to blood kin: brothers would die in defense of each other. He checked around and saw that his volunteers could barely be called his buddies; at best they were neighbors, at worst his thralls. He couldn't rely on any of these men the way he could with Darrell or Randy, but he shouldn't worry. He was all about proving his manhood, rather than guys who would fight back-to-back with him, he required an audience, *witnesses*. Besides, the way that Darrell had challenged his decisions about the way he'd grabbed Elspeth and Jacob over in Maine, he could do without listening to his brother's misgivings about what he planned now. Caleb was the eldest; he didn't need guidance from any kid brother, especially when it came to handling his business.

Before he had taken the truck a mile along the road towards Muller Falls the CB radio kicked to life. Caleb recognized Randy's voice despite it being raised several octaves and his words spilling out in his urgency.

Caleb grabbed the handset and keyed it. 'OK, calm down, Randy, and speak slower. I can't make out a damn word you're saying.'

'Pa wants you back here right this minute, Caleb,' Randy said in a rush.

'Tell Pa I've got something to do first.'

'Something more important than finding your wife and kid?' asked Randy. 'Something more important than finding the son of a bitch that just beat our mother unconscious?'

Caleb stood almost upright on the brake pedal and the truck fishtailed to a stop. The men on the back all crushed together, thrown in a heap of arms and legs against the cab. The pickup following close behind almost rear-ended the truck. Behind it the latter two trucks had time to stop, but the convoy was left parked at odd angles in the road. Some of the men jumped off the flatbeds, expecting imminent trouble.

'What do you mean, somebody has hurt Ma?'

'They knocked her out, Caleb, like she was nothing to them,' Randy's voice was almost manic, 'and when I get my hands on them, I'll rip out their guts and stamp on them. You hear me? I'm going to tear them apart. Pa wants you here so you can do the same, so you'd better get on back here.'

'Who hurt Ma?' Caleb demanded. He was trying to get things clear in his head: had the trespasser – Po'boy Villere, who else could it be? – given the dogs the slip and then returned to the commune to continue whatever deviltry he had in mind? If Villere was responsible for hurting his mother he'd . . . well, Randy had said it best. He'd gut the son of a bitch and stamp on his innards.

'We don't know, she hasn't fully come around yet. But it has to be the same one that hurt the others, right?'

'How'd he get at Ma, I'd have thought she was safe with Pa and you?'

'Ma wasn't home. After dinner she left to go check on how things were going between you and Elspeth. She was found unconscious in their cell and your wife and son are gone. At first Pa was concerned that you'd been hurt too, but Darrell checked and learned you'd headed to town with half our menfolk. You need to get back here with them now, Caleb, cause by all accounts we've still got somebody roaming around here, and most likely Elspeth and Jacob are with them.'

'How long has Ma been out?'

'How do I know?'

'How bad is she, Randy?'

'For Christ's sakes we're talking about our mother, Caleb! She's bad enough and somebody has to pay for hurting her.'

Caleb was uncertain what to do. He stared once beyond the windshield; he was certain that Villere had fled the scene and returned to his friends and they had holed up in the nearby town. But if Randy was right and Villere was still in the commune, and his wife and son accompanied him, then Caleb should . . . wait a minute!

'Elspeth wasn't in the cell with Jacob,' he stated. 'I took her to another room so's I could deal with her alone.'

'We know, Bertram told us.'

Alec Bertram was the one who'd initially hailed Caleb when the alarm about the trespasser was first raised. Bertram had run with him back to the loading dock where two of the younger men had been captured and locked in the van.

'Somebody needs to check on her,' Caleb said.

'We did. Weren't you listening just now? I told you, you need to get back here to help find them, your wife and son are both missing.'

'That goddamn bitch! Don't you get it, Randy? It wasn't the guy we're looking for that hurt Ma, it had to have been Elspeth! She got out of her cell and went to fetch Jacob and found Ma there instead.'

'If that's the case, you'd best forget any feelings you had for that whore,' Randy swore, '"cause I meant what I said. I'll kill her if I get my hands on her first. Otherwise, you should do it for what she did to Ma.'

'Don't you worry about that, bro. Nobody, and I mean nobody, hurts our mother and gets away with it. If you catch her, don't hurt Elspeth, bring her to me, and I'll see her punishment fits her crime.' Caleb slammed the handset down so hard that it bounced out of its holder and hung by the extendable cord between the knees of the older of the guards. Both men had kept silent while Caleb had spoken with Randy. Caleb snapped a glare on the older man.

'If you had done your damn jobs none of this would have happened. Now my mother has been hurt and you useless fuckers are responsible.'

'No, Caleb, that's unfair—'

Before the excuse had fully tumbled out of the inept guard, Caleb backhanded him across the nose. Every ounce of rage he felt towards Elspeth, and to Villere, was behind the blow. His knuckles smashed the cartilage, and the man slumped forward, groaning in dismay as blood flooded into his cupped palms. The younger guard looked ready to throw open the door and run for it, but Caleb didn't give him the chance. He slammed the truck into a series of tight maneuvers, until he had it facing the opposite direction on the narrow road. He drew up alongside the foremost of the other trucks. He wound down his window and called to those staring at him from the cab.

'You guys continue into town and locate the strangers. Keep an eye on them and if they make any move to leave, follow them and let me know immediately.'

He hit the gas and pulled away. The others in the convoy were left wondering what was going on, but without leadership they would decide to follow the others, or turn and go with him back behind their fences: either way suited him.

THIRTY

They didn't continue far before Po found a wide spot in the road. He spun the car around so it faced back towards town, then brought the GMC to a halt. Beyond the northern boundary of Muller Falls the road didn't progress many miles before it first went from being paved, to dirt, and then to nothing apart from a few overgrown hiking trails. As Jenny, the server at the café, had informed them there were few things out this way to attract tourists, everything worth seeing was out of bounds on the Moorcocks' land. Some might say they were on the proverbial road to nowhere but it had served their purpose for now. Without saying a word, Po switched off the lights and engine and stepped outside. He lit a Marlboro and cupped its ember behind his cupped fingers. After a moment Tess and Pinky left the vehicle and they all stood at the front of the hood.

'What are you thinking?' Tess asked Po.

'I'm thinking we might have overreacted, but it was still the right thing to do. We don't want to bring trouble to the folks of Muller Falls, and besides, what good will it do any of us holding off a bunch of crazy militia men with shit for brains?'

'Agreed. But I meant what are you thinking we should do next?'

'You know what I want to do. I want to go back and rescue Elspeth and her boy.'

'There's no way we can get in the way you did last time. Even if a posse wasn't sent after us, you can bet that they've got guards at all the weak spots they can think of. Sneaking in won't be as easy now.'

Po smoked a moment, then said, 'Can you bring up those maps for me again?'

'Sure I can.'

Tess collected her laptop from the car and set it on the hood.

'I'm most interested in the old map, the schematic version.'

Pinky peered over his shoulder as he watched Tess tapping keys. The map Po was interested in appeared on screen.

'Those dotted lines,' he said, indicating double rows of faint dashes, 'I know now they're subterranean service tunnels used by the National Guard when they were here. Look there . . .' He traced a route across what used to be the parade square to a road and hence forward to a structure built into a hillside. 'That's where I ended up inside,' he told them, and tapped the bunker, 'but look at these.'

Radiating out from the bunker were several underground spokes, some of which led deeper into the hillside, whereas others ran perpendicular with the bunker's interior, leading away to other buildings on the site and beyond. Po's gaze ranged over the map, tracking tunnels, and tracing them back to their sources. He stepped back with a grunt, almost mashing Pinky's toes under his heels. Pinky gave him space and Po used it to step out to take another few draws on his cigarette. Pinky took a closer look at the map and then checked with Tess for clarity.

But she had seen what Po had, and she mulled things over a moment. She pushed her hair back behind her ears, then set her fingers on the keyboard and began tapping. She brought up other maps, and Pinky understood where the night was leading. He swallowed uncomfortably.

Po flicked aside his cigarette and returned to stand beside Tess. He popped a mint in his mouth, and then leaned closer. He grunted again, but this time in approval. 'Was just about to ask if you could find anything about any cave systems around here.'

'We are going spelunking, us?' asked Pinky, sounding less than enthusiastic at the prospect.

'My name's Tess Grey,' Tess reassured him, 'not Lara Croft. I'm only looking for a route onto the property, not one that will take us miles underground.'

'Good.'

'Do tight spots bother you, Pinky?' asked Po with a tight smile.

'Been in plenty in my time, but none like being stuck head first in a hole in the ground.'

'There's no need for you to come if you don't want to. Neither of you need come. I can be in and out again like the last time.'

'The last time you were almost captured and eaten alive by those dogs,' Tess said. 'You need somebody there to watch your back.'

'Those caves, they're going to be dark and narrow and full of bats?' Pinky asked. 'They sound delightful, them, but unfortunately not for a guy of my generous proportions.'

'Like I said,' Po repeated, 'you don't have to come, Pinky.'

Pinky dropped his head, stared at his feet then shook his head morosely. 'What is it the Brits say: in for a penny in for a pound? We're in this together, Nicolas. I'm coming, me.'

'Me too,' said Tess. She returned her attention to the map on the computer screen and pointed out a cave system to their west. 'That looks like a possible way inside. Unfortunately it's on the wrong side of the river from here, and I don't recall any bridges marked on the aerial map.'

'So we get wet,' Po said, ever the pragmatist.

'Wet and cold and covered in guano, what more could we ask for, us?'

Po grinned at his friend. 'Well, you did move north dreaming of high adventure.'

'True, but why do all our adventures have to be so damn uncomfortable . . . and *wet*?'

'I warned you guys to bring gumboots,' said Tess, wishing she'd followed her own advice. 'Hey, look, the river's wider beyond this bend here, so it should be slower and easier to cross. Once we're across it looks like we've a short hike to the cave system, and if I'm right, this tunnel here emerges on the slope of the hills inside the boundary fence.'

'And if you're wrong it could lead all the way down to the bowels of hell,' Pinky muttered under his breath.

Tess said, 'Do you happen to have a flashlight in the car?'

'Actually I do. Let me get it.' Pinky went not to the trunk, but to the front passenger side, where he dug in the glove box. He came out with a small flashlight that he flicked on and off again, checking the strength of the beam on the palm of his hand. 'That should do for an emergency, but wait up, I've a better flashlight in the trunk.'

Po moved close to Tess, whispered, 'Can't think of a reasonable excuse to get Pinky to stay behind, but maybe those caves aren't the best environment for him.'

Tess shrugged the suggestion aside. Given a choice she would prefer not to go crawling around a cave system leading to who knew where, but when she had thrown in her lot with Po it was in its entirety. The same could be said for Pinky's loyalty to his friend too. 'We'll keep him safe,' was all she could offer.

'You still armed?'

'I am.' The pistol was in her tote bag though, and the bag too cumbersome to go with her. She lifted out the pistol and gave it a check over before shoving it into her belt.

'I have my knife, but I'll source something else if needs be.' As he briefly told her that there was an armory somewhere inside the bunker, Pinky returned, toting a lantern.

'Look at what I found. Didn't know it was there till I shifted the spare tire. It's one of those wind-up lamps. There are all kinds of bits and pieces in there for if the car breaks down. Couldn't think how we could put a reflective triangle to use though, so I left it alone, me.' He jiggled the lantern at them. 'Makes me feel more like a real caver now.'

'You said you had another flashlight?' Tess asked.

'Right here.' Pinky jutted out his hip. He had shoved a much larger torch than the first one in his trouser pocket.

'We should fetch some of that water with us,' Po said, meaning some of the bottled spring water they'd purchased for the trip.

Pinky groaned at the prospect of being underground long enough that they'd need to rehydrate. All such thoughts served to compound the onset of claustrophobia.

'It's not for us,' Po said, steering him away, Tess assumed, from visions of being entombed deep underground and dying of thirst, 'it's for Elspeth and Jacob if they need it. I imagine they're not being treated with kindness by her damn in-laws.'

'We should grab a couple of bottles each,' Tess suggested, and went to the car to follow her own instruction. She shoved her laptop in her tote and then had Pinky lock them in the trunk: she took her cell phone with her. Phones had proven mostly unreliable out here in the wilderness, but she'd rather have it than not when it came to signaling the cavalry.

Po and Pinky jammed bottles of water in their pockets, then all three of them stood again at the front of the car. They each looked at their closest friends, and further words were unnecessary. They were woefully unprepared for a rescue attempt, let alone a caving expedition, but they were as ready as they could reasonably hope to be.

'Let's do this then,' said Po, and they turned westward, cutting across the wooded side of a valley, following a tributary to the river.

THIRTY-ONE

H er son was on the cusp of adolescence, where he regarded
himself as a young man rather than a child, and he saw
it as his duty to protect his mom from danger. On the
other hand, to Elspeth he was her baby boy, to be coddled and
cherished above all other things. It caused slight confusion whenever a threat manifested, with one trying to get the other out of
harm's way to the other's frustration. In the end Elspeth had to
take Jacob by his shoulders, and with earnest determination she
instructed him to do as she asked. He acquiesced, because after
all he was only ten years old and not really a man at all.

She led them through the labyrinth of tunnels, one watchful eye
over her shoulder and her ears pricked for any hint of pursuit.
Twice now they had almost blundered into people in the tunnels,
but had the fortune of finding hiding places until it was safe to
move on.

She'd felt some instant satisfaction from knocking Ellie-May
cold, but soon she regretted harming the old witch, because she
had ignited the collective outrage of her community, and not
least the blood lust of the Moorcocks themselves. They thought
they were gods of their domain, so for somebody to strike the
matriarch was akin to the worst blasphemy ever. People were
now hunting her who once she might have expected pity from.
There were families here, and several individuals, who she might
once have turned to for help, and as terrified of the repercussions
they might be, they would have helped. Not now. Not after she
had hit Ellie-May, an indefensible crime in the eyes of their
overlords. There were other women here that suffered similarly
as she did at the hands of their husbands, and Jacob was not
the only child to be abused either, and Elspeth had hoped that
once she had gotten her boy free of Caleb's clutches she could
somehow help them too. If they spotted her now, she feared those
selfsame women and children would join the chase to hunt her
down. She could hope for help from nobody and could rely solely

on stealth to escape again. And where stealth failed, then there was always the threat of the revolver she took out and held by her side.

The tunnels were uniform in design, but only to a point. They occasionally met larger chambers that she could only guess at their uses, and some of them met and intersected with a network of natural caves that honeycombed the hillside. Usually the tunnels ended where the caves began, and had been barred off. Some of the barricades had collapsed over the decades, while some had been vandalized. Elspeth was tempted to take to the cave system, hoping to find a way through the mountains to freedom perhaps beyond the Canadian border; she was also terrified of stumbling from a tunnel into a cave without realizing where she'd gotten wrong-footed, because in reality she knew she'd soon be lost and they would perish long before they found an exit. The manmade tunnels, long and narrow as they were, all led somewhere in the site, to the bunker or to an adjoining structure; as long as they followed these then they'd find a way back to the fresh air.

Jacob progressed silently, tripping along at Elspeth's side. When the tunnels descended into darkness, he clutched at her clothing, fearful of being separated. His claustrophobia was held mostly in check while they kept moving, but on the occasions she'd made him duck for cover, she'd heard his breaths wheezing in his chest as he fought to control his growing panic. They had traversed an illuminated portion of tunnel but were again approaching an intersection where the tunnel at right angles with the first was a deep well of blackness. Elspeth preferred to take that route, where there was little possibility of stumbling into a search party whose lights would give forewarning, but she felt Jacob draw back, sucking in deeply. She looked around at him and found his eyes huge and reflecting the overhead lights.

'Come on,' Elspeth coaxed him, 'we just have to go a little bit further.'

'No, Mom, we mustn't. I've been here before. That tunnel . . . I think it leads to Booger Hole.'

'Booger Hole offers us a way out,' Elspeth reminded him.

'Not if he's home.'

'Jacob, there's no such thing as the booger.'

'There is, Mom. My pa . . . uh, Caleb warned me about going

near Booger Hole. He said that children who wandered too close are snatched and taken by the booger deep under the mountain where he skins them alive and eats their raw flesh.'

Elspeth clucked her tongue. Tales of the booger amounted to local fairy tales, or maybe to cautionary tales designed to keep disobedient children in check. Many backwoods communities told similar stories concerning wild men that roamed the wilderness, each with their particular takes on the boogeyman myth; here it was said that their local booger was a seven-feet-tall wild man – their version of Bigfoot, Elspeth supposed – notoriously violent and a rapist of women: he was the perfect metaphor for the type of beast represented by her husband.

Rather than try to convince her son the booger didn't exist, she chose to fight through his wall of trepidation with humor. She raised the revolver and wagged the barrel. 'Let's see the booger try stealing anyone after I put a couple of rounds in his hairy butt.'

'It's not funny, Mom. The booger is real. There was this time I heard him howling from deep inside his cave.'

'He won't touch you if you're with me,' Elspeth said, growing exasperated and again wagging the gun, 'not while I have *this*. Now come on, Jacob, before somebody catches up.'

'If they do catch up they probably won't follow,' said Jacob, his voice barely audible.

'Then that's a good thing.' Elspeth took him by his hand and urged him into the connecting tunnel, and almost immediately the darkness folded around them. He dragged his heels at first, but soon he tucked in tight to his mother's side and matched her steps.

THIRTY-TWO

Walking in wet footwear was horrible enough, coupled with jagged stones and sharp twigs digging into her ankles and calf muscles every few seconds it was almost intolerable, but Tess continued without complaint. She knew what she was letting herself in for when demanding she join Po on his second rescue attempt, so had resolved to keep any uneasiness to herself. Pinky was a little more vocal, but again, his curses and admonishments were aimed at self-motivation and avoiding turning back. The thought of entering the tight confines of the cave network filled their friend with dread, but Tess would bet her life on him entering it. This was Po's undertaking, so he absolutely kept quiet about his discomfort. Of the three of them, his high-topped boots would've given most protection against the shallow but chilly water they'd waded through, but nevertheless, he'd gone into the trek already carrying some minor injuries. Tess noted he limped on his left foot and avoided fully setting down his heel whenever possible. He carried on though, following the mental map he'd etched in his brain, leading them unerringly towards the cave system.

They almost missed the entrance in the dark. This was no gaping maw in the hillside, the opening was barely four feet high and six or seven feet wide. It was mostly obscured by a pile of boulders tumbled there in the distant past. Po crouched at the entrance, one hand supporting his weight as he leaned forward to peer inside. Behind him, Tess checked the beam of the small flashlight given to her by Pinky. The disc of light it emitted was meager at best: a shiver of revulsion rode up her spine as she contemplated entering the cave. She looked back at Pinky. It was late in the evening, thick clouds obscured the heavens so there wasn't the hint of star or moonlight, but Tess fancied that she could clearly see Pinky's features in the gloom. His skin was damp and shiny with sweat; it was as if he was partially luminescent.

'Po,' she cautioned, to save Pinky's embarrassment, 'maybe we should rethink this idea.'

Po grunted, and hunkered down a bit more. He aimed the beam of the larger flashlight into the black hole. Pinky wound the handle on his lantern furiously, causing the glimmer to brighten. He stood beside Po so the lamp's light joined that of the torch. They both glanced at each other doubtfully.

'I think you might be right, Tess,' Po conceded. 'From what I can tell it's a goddamn warren in there. There's no way of telling which is the right way to go, or even if it would lead us through the hill and beyond the fence.'

'I vote we try scaling the fence instead,' said Pinky.

'I second the motion,' said Tess.

'I genuinely hoped this would be an easier way inside. I should've known better.' Po stood. The opening didn't extend much higher than his sternum; it'd be torture for a man of his tall stature to try negotiating the cavern at a constant crouch, so God help Pinky's chances of getting through. 'I guess the fence it is.'

Pinky turned his face aside to hide his relief, but his corresponding whistle of victory gave him away. Po squeezed his friend's shoulder. 'The alternative's still gonna be a bitch.'

The hills loomed overhead, stretching away in both directions as a series of high crags and canyons tangled with thickets of trees. The boundary fence was on the far side of the hills – here the crags formed the southern rim of the river canyon. They would have been formidable barriers even without the inclusion of a fence.

'I can't see any way through from here,' Tess said.

'We'll have to go that way,' said Po, with a quick stab of his flashlight beam to their right, 'otherwise we'll end up being pushed back to the river canyon, and the going gets much tougher over those boulders.'

Tess frowned again at the crags. Her preferred way would be to return to Muller Falls, and recruit the local police department in the hostage rescue attempt. However, she understood the inherent problems they would face in getting the police on their side. There was still no evidence whatsoever that Elspeth or Jacob were inside the commune, or – if they were – that they were being held against their will, let alone being harmed. As far as Elspeth's testimony about abuse and criminality went, it was hearsay at best, and downright lies at the worst. To all intents and purposes, this was still an information gathering exercise that might very well end up with them leaving the commune with empty hands and their tails between their legs. But it was important to Po that they make the attempt, and she would support him.

'Lead on,' she said.

'You two should go back to the car,' he responded. 'There's no need for all of us to risk our hides.'

'No. We're coming with you or, so help me, we'll drag you back to the car by your ears,' she warned him.

Po shook his head at the ridiculous threat, but he didn't argue. He turned and loped away, the discomfort in his leg forgotten for the moment. He used the flashlight to pick out fissures and crevices in the rocks. Tess and Pinky walked abreast, in the circle cast by his lantern, but soon the path narrowed and she was forced to move ahead of him. They worked their way up a dry riverbed, prone still to flash floods judging by the weathering in the rock face. To their south the crags appeared insurmountable. At that rate they might have to walk all the way to the foothills of the mountains before they found a path back towards the old military installation.

The dry river followed a steep incline to its source. Po went up some rocks with the agility of a mountain goat, but paused at the top, with his left heel raised to take his weight off it. He used his flashlight beam to dig between the taller crag, and he nodded. 'We might lose a layer or two of skin but it looks as if there could be a pass here.'

Tess scrambled up to join him, while Pinky peered up at them from below. 'Show me,' Tess asked.

Po pointed with the flashlight beam, and she saw where the rock was deeply fissured. Higher up the forest trees hadn't taken root, although the gap in the boulders was still choked with under-brush. It looked negotiable though.

'Looks do-able,' she admitted.

Po gestured for Pinky, but their friend had turned his back to them, and he peered down the dry riverbed they'd scaled.

'What is it?' Po asked.

'Thought I heard something,' Pinky replied, his voice a whisper.

On the boulder, Po and Tess crouched, so they weren't presenting their silhouettes. They switched off their flashlights.

'What did you hear?' Po whispered. 'Movement?'

'Voices,' Pinky corrected. 'Distant but distinct. Listen, you.'

All that Tess could discern was the sound of the river, a good ways off now but still a constant rumble at the edges of her hearing. Po's face grew pinched in concentration, and she heard him huff out a breath. 'I hear them,' he said.

Tess strained to hear what he had, but couldn't.

Below them, Pinky switched off his lantern, and he moved to conceal his shape among the boulders.

'I don't hear anyone,' Tess whispered, prompting Po to reach out and gently tap her wrist in signal. He used the same finger to point to the north. In that direction the terrain was forested and met the river. They had abandoned their GMC out there beyond the river.

'Sounds as if they've discovered our ride,' he said.

'It could be anyone,' Tess reasoned. 'Hunters, kids from town . . .'

'Unlikely. Why would a random hunter get all bent outta shape 'cause he came across a SUV in the dark?'

She conceded the point, except she still couldn't hear whom he was referring to, let alone anyone getting excitable over their discovery.

'We should get moving, and quick.'

'They're miles away, right?' Tess felt as if they'd been hiking miles, but thinking things through, they had zigzagged in their course: as it stood Pinky's GMC was probably less than quarter a mile away as the crow flew. 'Besides, even if they're closer, they'll have no idea where we've gone. Even if they guess we tried finding the caves then . . . oh.' She halted. It didn't matter whether their hunters knew where they were, they would assume that they were attempting a second incursion of the commune and the alert level would be raised. Sneaking over the fence undetected might become impossible.

Tess took out her cell phone. Not to make a call, but to check her ability to do so. She had no service. It probably meant their pursuers had no way of alerting their kin inside the fences, not unless they had another form of communication device available: she recalled the CB radio in the bridge guards' truck and decided they were probably *de rigueur* around here.

Pinky clambered up the rocks, sprightlier than expected in wet shoes. Tess offered a hand to help pull him up despite him outweighing her by at least twice. He gained the perch they stood astride, and then Po gave ground, hopping forward onto the next in a series of stepping stones they could use to reach the fissure. Tiny pebbles and a few bigger stones clattered down the larger rocks. 'Watch how you go here, the footing's unstable,' Po cautioned.

Tess flicked on her flashlight. The beam was as dim as ever, but still better than nothing. She picked out her path over the rocks, preparing to follow Po. As she did she heard a shout. The voice was thin, distant, but there was no denying it was the sound of triumph: she'd just bet that their pursuers had discovered where they'd forded the river at its shallowest point hereabout and had celebrated how hot on their trail they must be. What kind of idiots were these people: had they no idea what might be the consequences of finding their prey? Did they not understand that men the likes of Po Villere and Pinky Leclerc were not weak quarry, but apex predators who could turn on them? And though she'd rarely boast, it was true that she was no slouch in a fight either. If it was in their favor, they could wait here, launch an ambush and wipe out their hunters with little effort. Of course, it was not in their favor, and besides, they might have to kill and Tess couldn't countenance the idea of becoming a murderer, even if those chasing them didn't know that. She practically danced over the rocks after Po.

It was a squeeze negotiating the tight fissure. It was bad enough for Tess to fit through the narrowest parts, and there were times when Pinky had to climb higher to find egress or risk sacrificing his skin to the jagged rocks. He made it through though, puffing and panting, cursing under his breath, but largely whole. Tess took the skin off her knuckles, and also got some gorse caught around her leg, and it scratched her ankles raw before she'd managed to drag her foot loose. For his part, Po's leather jacket got scuffed and torn but these were simply fresh scars on his already chewed jacket. They paused at the edge of the crag to peer out over the Moorcock lands.

Below them Tess spotted a fence.

It was formed here of a few strands of wire strung between the trees. Periodically signage was affixed to the fence to deter trespassers. It was not an insurmountable barrier, as she'd feared. 'I'm

glad we didn't waste our time crawling through those caves now,'
she said.

Po squinted down at the fence. 'That's just the outer fence;
once we get nearer the military compound there's a more formidable one. The caves – far as I could tell from your maps – go all
the way under the second fence and intersect with some of the
tunnels on the base.'

'Oh, right. I thought for a minute there we were going to get
a break.'

'Nope. One small consolation is, once we scale the second fence
the going gets easier underfoot. Before then we have to contend
with that.'

He indicated the tangled forest below them.

'Hopefully there's some kind of game trail we can follow,' said
Pinky.

Tess studied the old woodland. It was reminiscent of a fairytale
landscape dreamed up by the Brothers Grimm. She could imagine
it to be the home to ogres, demons and evil witches. 'I bet you
packed your machetes alongside your gumboots,' she quipped.

Po craned around, listening to the sound of distant voices. 'It
sounds as if those guys who found our car have decided to follow.
We should get moving.'

They found an easy enough route down off the crag, following
a water-worn ditch to the forest floor. The fence didn't slow them
more than a few seconds, but the instant they entered the woods
it was apparent how carefully they must move. There was little
ground on which there weren't fallen trees and limbs, and in some
places the thickets were so dense that they had to backtrack to
find another way around. 'Now you might understand why I took
my time gettin' back to you the last time,' Po said as he helped
Tess scramble over a fallen tree.

'I'm surprised you made it out, period.'

'Like I said, it gets easier once we're beyond the next fence.'

Pinky rolled his eyes at the thorny branches as he dabbed blood
from his cheek with the back of his hand. 'There's a part of me
that's looking forward to climbing the razor wire instead of this
hellish stuff.'

They were all collecting nicks and scratches as they progressed,
but the cut on Pinky's cheek was the most visible. Tess found a

tissue she'd pushed in her pocket earlier in the day and handed it over.

Their flashlights and lantern helped, but as they closed in on the compound itself, Po urged them to turn them off. They picked their way through the last few hundred or so yards of wild wood-land with more trepidation than before. Tess got a smack in the face off a springy branch and was fortunate not to lose an eye when she walked on to one much stiffer. Pinky got a matching cut on his opposite cheek, and this time there was no tissue to help mop up his blood. He used the sleeve of his jacket instead. Po made it through without any fresh injuries, but his sore leg was troubling him worse than when they'd set off.

They stood facing the fence erected by the military, but maintained since then by those living behind it. It was eight feet tall, the upper-most part of it angled outward and strung with razor wire.

Tess exchanged a look with Po.

'Was easier coming from the other side,' Po admitted.

'If you boost me up between you, I could perhaps throw a jacket over the wires. Then we could maybe climb over . . .'

'Or we could use this,' said Pinky and fished a set of formidable looking pliers out of his trouser pocket. 'They were among the tools in the trunk when I found my lantern. Thought they might come in useful, me.'

'Pinky, I could kiss you,' said Tess.

'Again? Well don't let that ugly brute stop you,' he said with a mock frown at Po's expense.

'Gimme those,' said Po, and took the pliers from his friend.

These were not bolt cutters. The tool was designed for grip-ping and twisting, not cutting wire as sturdy as the type forming the fence, but it came with a function for stripping wires of their plastic coating, and with enough leverage could cut through thinner wire. Po didn't test them against the fence itself, as it would take an age to cut a hole large enough for them to slip through. He used the pliers instead to untwist the wire fixings that held the fence to the nearest upright post. Once he'd removed the securing wires to a height above his head, he reached down and grasped the fence at ground level. It was buried in the earth and had been for decades. 'Could do with a hand here, guys,' he said.

Tess stood to one side of him, Pinky to the other, and they each grabbed the lowest edge of the wires. 'On three,' Po instructed, and began to count down. 'Heave!'

The wire tore from the ground trailing tough grass and clods of earth, but it was loose enough from the post that they were able to yank the lower edge clear of the floor. 'Tess, you go under first,' said Po.

She immediately went down to her knees and scrambled under. She popped up at the other side, and then lent her strength to help hold the buckled wire up.

Pinky followed her. He had to roll onto his back and kick his way under the fence. Together they strained to hold up the fence as Po squirmed under and climbed to his feet. They let the fence drop to its original position; unless a close check of the ground was made, it'd be unlikely anyone would spot that it had been the place of an incursion.

They were inside, or, as Tess chose to see it, behind enemy lines.

THIRTY-THREE

B y the time he returned to his parents' family house, his mother had been transported there and laid on a bed. When Caleb looked down at her, Ellie-May's face was barely recognizable as that of the Moorcock matriarch. In an almost catatonic state her features were lax, ironing out most of the deep furrows and wrinkles that normally characterized her, and her weathered skin was so pale now it verged on translucent. For the first few seconds he studied her he feared she had perished before he'd made it to her side. A closer look showed a pulse throbbing in the side of her neck, and every now and again her eyes rolled behind their lids. Randolph's wife, Patricia, sat at Ellie-May's shoulder, acting as her nurse: the most the dull-minded woman could do was offer moral support, plump up a pillow, and perhaps hold a glass of water to his mother's lips – she knew nothing more about nursing or medicine.

'Mom needs a doctor.' Darrell prowled around the bedroom chewing his lips.

'I've sent Randy for Bob Richardson,' said Eldon, who stood at Ellie-May's opposite shoulder, staring down at his wife. His tone might not exhibit his anxiety, but Caleb could tell his father was worried from the way he occasionally sucked in the end of his mustache and chewed down on it.

'A *real* doctor,' Darrell responded. 'Bob Richardson's a damn quack!'

'Bob was a medic over in Nam,' Eldon snapped. 'He knows more about medicine than any man I know.'

'Mom needs to be in a hospital, Pa, and seen by a real doctor.'

'We look after our own here,' Eldon growled, 'always have and always will do. Your mom's taken a bump to her head, but that's nothing to her. You wait and see, when she wakes she'll tell you it weren't nothing. She's tough as old boots, is Ellie-May.'

Darrell looked to Caleb, hoping for some kind of solidarity. Caleb ignored his brother and instead directed his words at their father. 'Who d'you think did this to her, Pa?'

Eldon craned towards him, the tendons in his neck standing out like plucked guitar strings. 'That was what I wanted to learn from you, Caleb.' He thumbed at the prone woman. 'Has this got something to do with you fetching Elspeth and Jacob out of Maine? I warned you, I didn't want any private investigator pushing their nose into my business and look at what came of that warning.'

'We can't say this has anything to do with me bringing them home, except maybe that—'

'Don't give me any of your lies, Caleb. I know you were on your way to Muller Falls for a goddamn showdown, I know you sent some of our folks up there despite me ordering you back here. Am I supposed to believe that these strangers showing up here is unconnected to you stealing your kin home?'

'I can't think of anybody else they could be,' Caleb admitted. 'I made a mistake in assuming that they wouldn't follow us back here. I should've ensured they couldn't follow us back before I left Maine. Events kind of overtook me though, Pa, and I already explained how and why I acted the way I did. But here's the thing, the timeline's all wrong for it to have been Po'boy Villere who hurt Mom.'

'You'd better explain, boy.'

'I was with Elspeth when the alert was raised that a stranger had been inside the bunker. The guys he took hostage and locked in that van, they already said he left before they raised that ruckus with the car horn. We know that to be true because he was chased and almost brought down by Terry Fisher's dogs before he managed to escape over the fence and disappear. Whoever it was struck Mom, they did so after I joined those hunting down the sumbitch.'

'Stands to reason who it was,' said Darrell.

Eldon was no idiot. He too already had a strong inkling who was responsible for knocking his wife unconscious.

'So what are you going to do about Elspeth?' he demanded. 'It's one thing having a wife run away, another for you to bring her back only for her to raise her hands to your ma. Whatever way you're handling her, it isn't working, Caleb.'

'Why'd Mom go to see Jacob?' Caleb countered. 'Didn't she trust I had it in me to chastise him the way I saw fit?'

'Don't you go second-guessing her when she isn't awake to defend herself.'

'I'm only trying to imagine why Elspeth would hurt her, and I'm guessing she caught Mom in the act of hurting Jacob.'

'You're making excuses for the bitch now? You're trying to validate her reason for hurting your mother?'

'That's not what I'm doing. I'm only trying to figure out what went wrong for Mom to end up getting hurt like this.'

'I'll tell you what went wrong,' Eldon spat, 'you let that wife of yours get off too lightly all these years. D'you see what became of you being too lenient with her? Bitch thinks she can hit your mother and get away with it.'

'She can't, and she won't.'

Eldon reached across the bed and grabbed Patricia roughly. He shook her, all the while aware that his message would have been more pertinent if it was aimed at a different son. 'What do you think should be done to anyone capable of hurting Ellie-May?'

Patricia kept her gaze averted. Through her teeth she mumbled, 'They should be punished.'

'That's right, they should be punished,' Eldon said. He grasped Patricia harder, almost dragging her across his unconscious wife. 'How would you punish them, Patty? What would Randy do to you if you were disobedient?'

'He'd punish me bad, Eldon,' Patricia muttered.

'That's right. And what if you hurt his mother?'

'Then he'd probably kill me.'

'He sure would. Randy knows how to treat his woman, right, and I damn well believe if Darrell had himself a wife, she'd know who was boss too. Caleb, you've been far too soft with that woman of yours, and now look at where that's gotten us.' Eldon released Patricia, who cowered away and returned to helping Ellie-May, doing her best to avoid Eldon's attention again. The patriarch stomped towards his eldest son. His mustache bristled, and droplets of saliva rained on Caleb's face. 'When you get your hands on Elspeth, I expect her to be stripped naked and whipped from one end of the town square to the other.'

'After the hateful shit she's put in Jacob's mind, and for what she did to my mother, trust me, Pa, she'll suffer much worse than that.'

'What's this hateful shit you're talking about?'

Caleb gritted his teeth. He looked from his father to Darrell, and lastly to Ellie-May. These were his folk, his real family, while Elspeth meant nothing to him now. Before now he'd shown her some leniency as the mother of his child, but if what Jacob said was true, then he owed her nothing. He gave his father a fierce grimace. 'Let's say there was once a time when wives were put to death for less.'

Eldon returned the fierce grin. 'Now you're talking my kind of language, son.'

THIRTY-FOUR

Po dropped to his haunches, raising one fist skyward. None of the three had served in the military, but through its usage in movies and TV shows the signal had become recognizable. In equal measures to Tess it meant 'stop' and 'be quiet'. She did both. Behind her Pinky also came to a halt, and he went one act further by dousing his lantern. Tess took her prompt from Po, also sinking down so that she presented a smaller silhouette in among the tree roots. Pinky pressed up against the bole of a tree. Here the forest was cultivated, and the trees grew in regulated lines, making finding concealment more difficult.

It was unnecessary asking what had alarmed Po. Tess could hear. Some distance ahead a vehicle drove at speed through the forest, probably carrying a bunch of armed rednecks intent on cutting off their route. To their east she could hear the yapping of dogs. Those that had found their GMC and followed them across the river must have discovered that they had entered the private land by now and were somehow coordinating a welcoming committee with their neighbors. This was not the time to waste crouching in the woods; every second should be spent penetrating further into the commune if ever they were going to find Elspeth and Jacob.

'What's wrong?' she whispered.

Po's posture was one of a stalking cat. He lowered his fist, and without turning to her said, 'I hear somebody up ahead.'

She couldn't hear anything beyond the sound of the far-off engine, and the more distant pack of hounds. Actually, her senses had grown more attuned with her surroundings, so as she concentrated, that was not the entire truth. She could define the breeze in the treetops, and the creaking of branches, the cry of a night flying bird. Also she could hear the whistle of Pinky's exhalations behind her. Po once told her that if she centered herself, opened her mouth in an oval and closed her eyes, she would hear better: it was true, as she had tried his woodsman's technique on previous

occasions and found it worked, but she daren't close her eyes just
then. She leant forward, peering between the regimented trunks
into the dimness and she caught a hint of movement. It was a
shadow against shadows, but it was there. The more she watched,
the more moving figures she spotted: they appeared to be spilling
upward out of the very earth.

'They got ahead of us,' Po whispered. 'I should've seen that
comin' goddamnit.'

It stood to reason that people that had grown up on this land
would be intimately familiar with it, and would know all its short-
cuts, including the route through the cave system. After discovering
where they had crossed the river, the hunting party must have
followed them to the crag, but instead of going up and over as
they had, they'd taken the shortcut through the hill, under the
perimeter fence and gotten ahead of them. From what Tess could
tell, they were climbing out of the bowels of the earth by way of
a ladder. A couple of them had flashlights that they flicked off
now that they had broken ground, but others flashed the beams
around seeking their quarry. They could have no idea where their
prey had gotten to yet; for all they knew Po and his friends were
stuck back at the fence trying to find a safe way over. The hunters
conversed briefly, before they split up, with three of them heading
back north towards the fence. The others went towards the repurposed military encampment, forming a scrimmage line as they
moved through the woods. Tess could tell from their outlines that
they carried rifles.

The three men sent to check nearer the perimeter fence took an
oblique angle to where Tess crouched. She tensed, with her finger
on the trigger guard of her pistol: she was unaware of the exact
point at which she'd swapped her flashlight for her gun. Po made
a calming gesture with the flat of his hand, watching intently as
the trio crept past. Tess tracked their route through the trees with
her gun, conscious that Pinky did likewise with his. The trio
continued and was soon lost in the darkness. By the time they had
disappeared, so had the others who had emerged from the tunnel.
Po stood. He worked his ankle, gingerly testing his weight on it
before he waved Tess and Pinky to follow.

He took them to the tunnel entrance. If they'd missed the hunting
party coming out of it, Tess doubted they would have discovered

the tunnel. At ground level a circular concrete base stood barely nine inches above the forest floor, and at its center a hinged trap-door allowed access. Undergrowth had taken root around the tunnel's entrance, adding to the trapdoor's camouflage. They could have passed within feet of it and been unaware of the hatch. They stood around the trapdoor, waiting for somebody to speak. Po said, 'We can continue through the woods, and risk running into that group again, or go back to my first plan and sneak inside the camp via these tunnels.'

'I'm still not keen on going down there, me,' Pinky admitted.

Po opened the trapdoor. A concrete chimney descended into the earth. An iron ladder gave access to the tunnel floor below, as Tess had suspected. She figured that the network of tunnels had been constructed with several ingress points such as this one, as well as with various ventilation shafts. Possibly the military had inte-grated the natural cave system into their design to assist with the airflow through the tunnels. Pinky gave the ladder a shake of his head: it was narrow and some of the visible rungs were corroded.

'Nu-uhhh, definitely not keen,' he stressed.

'I'll use the tunnels,' Po suggested, 'to complete the search I started earlier. Once I've found Elspeth and Jacob we can then work together on getting them safely out.'

'You're assuming that they're being held underground,' Tess reminded him.

'I am making an assumption, but only partly. If you were Caleb and had snatched them off the street, where would you hide them? Me, I'd keep them underground where I obviously hide my other secrets.'

There was still the issue of whatever criminal enterprise Eldon Moorcock had going, and Po was correct in that evidence of it was probably hidden underground too. Po had mentioned seeing some kind of bank-style vault during his earlier incursion of Eldon's bunker . . .

Tess shoved her pistol in her waistband and took out her cell phone. 'I've enough of a signal to text with; how's your phone, Pinky?'

He checked. 'Yeah, I've enough juice for a text.'

'I'm going with Po,' she said. 'Do you think you can make it to the commune without being seen?'

'I can go invisible, like a ninja, me,' he smiled. 'I'm just not too skilled at fitting through tight spaces.'

'We might need some form of transportation once we find Elspeth and the boy, how's about you go about securing us a ride?' asked Po.

'Sounds like a plan.' Pinky looked down into the tunnels again, and then gave Tess a sorrowful shake of his head. 'I should be going with you guys, but one look at that rusty ladder reminds me of my limitations. Rest assured, though, I'll be up here, me, waiting for when you come out.'

'Keep your cell phone close by, and we'll coordinate with you,' Tess said as she tucked hers in her breast pocket.

Pinky stared off into the darkness.

Po aimed a finger in the general direction that the scrimmage line had moved off in. 'The compound's thataway.'

'So are those rednecks,' replied Pinky. 'Unless you want me to shoot some of them dead, I should maybe take a more circuitous route, eh?'

Po clapped his friend on the shoulder. 'Just don't get yourself shot.'

'Go on,' Pinky said, and ushered Po back to the trapdoor, 'I'll keep an eye out until you're safely underground. Tess, you'd be better taking this than that little old thing.'

She accepted the wind-up lantern from him. Down in the tunnels it would prove far more helpful than the tiny flashlight she'd used until now. She hooked it over her left elbow, waiting anxiously while Po descended the ladder. If his injured leg gave way, it would tumble him into the depths. She held her breath until he safely reached the tunnel. 'Be careful,' she advised Pinky.

'I'm not the one climbing down into the bowels of Hades,' he reminded her, then flickered what was supposed to be a reassuring smile.

Tess puffed out her cheeks, leaned close to Pinky and admitted, 'I wish now I wasn't so freaking adamant about accompanying Nicolas.'

She was only partially kidding. Before she lost her nerve, she held onto Pinky's offered hand, and rested a heel on the uppermost rung. It held her weight; the same might not be said for those below. Pinky supported her until her head was at ground level, and she was able to take the rungs in her hands. She clambered down, and felt Po assist her with his hands at her hips for the last few feet. Back on firm ground she peered up the chimney. Pinky craned over the opening above, a deeper silhouette against the night sky. It was probably no more than twenty feet but he looked a mile away. Pinky raised a thumb. Before Tess could answer his gesture, he lowered the trapdoor and they were enveloped in darkness so thick it felt cloying. Tess hurried to juggle on the lantern.

The glow from the lantern danced off the uniform walls.

'How will we know which way to go?' Tess asked.

'The commune's that way,' said Po, indicating the tunnel directly ahead. Behind them there was dankness emanating from the tunnel, hinting at the warren of natural caverns it intersected with a little distance behind them.

Tess was aware of their immediate direction of travel; she was more concerned with how they'd orientate themselves once they reached the crisscrossed tunnels he'd described being in earlier. Po aimed his chin at the nearest wall, and she made out a faded number stenciled on the rough concrete.

'I'd guess those coded numbers give direction and purpose,' he said. 'We'll see once we make more progress, huh? By the time we reach the commune, I hope to have it figured out.'

'I have the lantern, do you want me to lead the way?'

'More importantly you have the gun,' Po said. 'Take it out, Tess, we don't know who we might meet down here.'

She drew the pistol and held it by her side. With her left hand she extended the lantern before them and set off walking. Po stayed directly behind, occasionally turning to tread backwards as he checked for signs of pursuit. Down there everything echoed, even the slightest scuff of a shoe or brush of an elbow against a wall was amplified. The glow from the lamp dimmed and she swiftly cranked the handle bringing it back to life: she couldn't imagine completing the journey if they lost the light she had.

'How far to the commune?' she whispered.

'Further than I'd like,' he said. 'It's roughly a half mile through the woods from here, but I'd bet down in these tunnels it feels ten times that far.'

'Pinky was upfront about his claustrophobia,' Tess said. 'I wish

I'd known before now that I have an intense dislike of subterranean tunnels.'

'You didn't have any inkling?'

'There was that time I got trapped down a well, but it was different then. I put my mind to escaping, so I didn't dwell too long on being trapped. Here, well, I'm finding breathing difficult.'

'You're not the only one. I think it has more to do with the stifling atmosphere than with fear. Try taking shallow breaths and we'll soon reach a place where there's more oxygen.'

Tess took his advice. Within another twenty paces her face was slick with sweat, and her clothing clung to her. It felt as if she was trying to draw air through damp cotton. Even the walls dripped. The humidity was horrendous.

'Po,' she said, 'I'm not handling this too well.'

He placed a hand on her hip, moving closer to her. 'Just a little further and things will get better, I promise.'

'I can barely breathe,' she said.

'Drink some water,' he suggested. 'It might help.'

She set down the lantern and accepted one of the bottles he'd shoved in his pocket. She chugged down most of the bottle before handing it back.

'Better?' he asked, after he'd emptied the bottle.

'Nope.'

He didn't reply, choosing instead to keep her moving with gentle pressure on her hip. Tess's feet were rubbed raw by her wet shoes; she thought it strangely ironic that the first time she'd seen Po with Elspeth and Jacob she'd suffered similarly sore feet, perhaps this was a sign that she'd soon see them together again.

After several turns in direction they came to a junction. A tunnel intersected the first, narrower, and in complete darkness. The tunnel they traversed was a main artery, the other a feeder vein: Tess knew that arteries led direct from the heart. Without checking with Po she continued on the same path. Ahead there was a change in the darkness. The uniformity of the blackness was broken by a faint slash of silver. She glanced back at Po. His features were lit by the glow of her lantern, his eyes sparkling, but the lines and angles of his features were deeply grooved by shadow. He grinned at her, indicating he too had spotted the glow ahead, and he reminded her of a jack-o'-lantern.

The presence of light meant they were approaching an area used by the commune's residents. Having studied the same maps as Po had, Tess felt she should be able to pinpoint their location, but she was clueless. She had some residual sense of direction and thought they were traversing a west to east artery now, but she could be totally wrong. She should feel some relief that they were nearing their destination, but she couldn't muster any. At least breathing was a bit easier.

Po halted.

Tess checked with him and found him peering intently into the darkness behind them. She didn't speak – in there her voice would travel. Besides, she didn't require clarification. The padding of footsteps had alerted him.

From what she could tell, several people pursued them through the tunnels. A single person, armed with a gun could mow them down while they were trapped between the concrete walls. She quickly doused her lantern so they didn't present a target. She tugged on Po's sleeve and he moved with her, aiming for where the darkness lightened ahead. It was probable that their figures were distinguishable against the lighter background, but less so than when limned by the lantern's glow.

To their right there was an alcove.

Tess pulled Po in after her.

She touched a finger to his lips, unnecessarily as he understood the need for silence. She urged him to lean closer.

'We can't outpace them,' she whispered, 'and will be easily spotted the further we go. We must wait here and ambush them. Are you ready for that?'

'Need you ask?'

She held up the pistol and felt him draw his knife from his boot sheath. 'I won't shoot unless absolutely necessary. Please don't kill any of them, Po.'

'Only if I must,' he said.

His reply might have given her more confidence if his menacing tone didn't promise a foregone conclusion.

THIRTY-FIVE

The stench of death repelled her. Elspeth threw her elbow across her face, retching as she turned. With bile in her mouth she ushered Jacob back in the direction they'd just come from.

'I warned you, Mom.' Jacob's eyes shone like silver coins against the gloom.

He was referring to the Booger Hole being home to a cannibalistic monster. It certainly smelled as if the cave was the repository of corpses, whether or not they had been gnawed on by some giant hairy hominid.

'We can't go that way,' Elspeth told him.

Jacob shrugged. He had suspected what they might find. Elspeth bent to the side and cleared her throat. A string of hot saliva dribbled from between her lips.

'Or can we?' She peered down the tunnel they had followed this far into the natural cavern. Did going back promise a worse fate than having to endure the stench of decomposition? Yes, the consequences of returning to the bunker outweighed enduring the bad smell tenfold. 'We have to,' she decided. 'Hold your breath until we are past, uh, until we're past . . .'

'Mom, I know it's a dead person. I'm not a little kid, so you don't have to hide the truth from me anymore.'

Elspeth squinted at him. His words were loaded.

'He's not a good man, but Caleb's still your daddy, Jacob.'

He shrugged again, a sharper gesture this time.

She again held him close as they moved ahead, cradling him against her hip while she kept the revolver aimed ahead. The stink intensified with each step. Elspeth's eyes streamed: whatever – no, whoever – had died here it had been recent judging by the intensity of the rot.

'He's there, Mom.' Jacob halted and pointed at the corpse unbidden. Their eyes had adjusted to the blackness of the cavern and were able to pick out some shape and hue against the deeper gloom.

'Don't look.'

'It's OK. He just looks asleep,' said Jacob.

Despite trying to avoid it, she glanced at the dead man. He lay against the side of the cavern, his chin tucked into his chest, one arm and one knee drawn up. Jacob was right; he looked as if he had fallen asleep and rolled to a comfortable position. In the dimness she couldn't see his wounds, but she could smell them – he stank similarly to the deer Caleb hunted and took delight in disemboweling.

'We should search him,' said Jacob.

'For what?'

'Anything useful.'

Elspeth shook her head. There was no possible way she'd lay hands on the corpse.

'I'll do it.'

'No. Leave him be, Jacob. Come on, if he was dragged down here there must be a way back outside again.'

Jacob moved and dropped to his haunches alongside the corpse.

'Jacob—'

'I'm looking for a cell phone or a weapon, or . . .' He danced his hands over the body, his fingers arched to avoid putting too much pressure on it, and then worked down the bent leg. He emitted a little exclamation, and then dug in the pocket he'd discovered. He pulled something out and held it up to show his mother. When she didn't immediately respond, he rolled his thumb, and the cigarette lighter sparked to life. The tiny flame was intensely bright to eyes that had grown accustomed to pitch black. Elspeth hissed and shied away, but in the next instant she grabbed at Jacob and hauled him away when he exclaimed in revulsion. She peered over his shoulder. Her son had been fortunate not to kneel in the pile of entrails that had oozed from the dead man's slit open abdomen. Another almost bloodless hole sat between the man's shoulder blades.

She had entertained the notion that the corpse was simply that of somebody that had gotten lost in Booger Hole and had perished, succumbing to thirst or exposure, but all along she knew what the body truly signified: murder. She had no way of knowing whose handiwork this was, but she had good reason to be suspicious of the Moorcocks. If her husband was not responsible for killing this man, then another of his demented family probably was. For years there had been rumors around the commune that Eldon and his sons had made other people disappear, and she now had a firm idea where they'd all gone.

'Hold up that flame,' she said.

Jacob sparked the lighter to life again.

The flame guttered, the tip bending towards the boy's hand.

Elspeth looked beyond the flame to where the source of a draft must originate.

There was no suggestion of an immediate exit from the cavern, but it had struck her that after the man had been killed, her lazy brothers-in-law would have spared as little energy as possible in disposing of his body. There must be an exit somewhere close by, and the presence of a draught told her where to seek it.

She encouraged Jacob to lead the way, holding the lighter aloft. Soon though, the metal fixings on the plastic tube grew too hot to hold. He hissed in pain, and let the flame go out. 'Here, give it to me,' she said.

She wrapped some cloth torn from her undershirt around the metal, then spun the wheel against the flint. The flame guttered and then held. Again she watched the tip of the flame tilt away from the cave's exit. It lit the deeper recesses of nooks in the cave walls.

'Look, Mom,' said Jacob in a hushed voice.

What she saw she might never be able to erase from her memory. There were more bodies, some of them in a much worse state of decomposition than the first they'd discovered. They were practically skeletal, robed in fragments of rotting clothes. Some of these corpses had to be decades old, dating from shortly after Eldon Moorcock purchased the land. Apparently her in-laws had been murdering their rivals as equally long as they'd been dominating their subjects. One thing she was certain of, they had no qualms about killing those who opposed them, and Elspeth was firmly in that camp now.

'Is that Mikey? Mom, I . . .' Jacob's question faltered.

Elspeth pulled him to her side, unable to give a comforting hand while holding her revolver and the lighter, but still able to offer her closeness. She held the lighter aloft to light up the alcove

Jacob stared at. 'I'm sorry, Jacob,' she said, 'but I think you're right.'

'But Mikey left to go and live in California with his uncle,' Jacob croaked.

Mikey, or Michael Stewart, was an older friend of Jacob who had grown outwardly rebellious as he hit his mid-teenage years. Months ago he had gone missing, and Caleb had announced that the youth had been granted permission to leave the commune. Supposedly Mikey had an uncle who had lined up employment and a place for the youth to live: it was lies concocted to explain the truth behind his disappearance. The boy had been killed, and dumped here in Booger Hole, and the true horror Elspeth shrank away from was if his own parents were complicit in the cover up.

'This is *soooo* wrong,' Jacob cried.

'It's awful,' Elspeth agreed, 'but we can't let it stop us now. We have to get away, so that we can tell somebody what really happened to Mikey and to these other people.'

She had to drag Jacob away. The boy sobbed, and each deep exhalation accelerated to a point where she feared rage would overtake him. He clenched and unclenched his fists, and several times he changed direction, but she drew him after her before frustration made him charge back to Mikey's side. 'Come on, Jacob,' she coaxed, 'if you want justice for your friend we have to get out of here and tell the cops.'

'No, no, no,' a voice said from the darkness ahead, 'I can't let you do that, Elspeth.'

She yelped, and jerked back, bumping Jacob. The boy swore, using coarse words his mother had never heard from his lips before. Under the circumstances she forgave him, because she too used expletives unbecoming of a lady. She backed away, grabbing for Jacob, and in the process losing the flame on the lighter. Her other hand swung back and forth as she aimed the revolver at the darkness ahead. A flashlight beam flashed on, striking her fully in the face. She cried out and cringed at the invasion of light.

'Drop the gun,' the voice commanded. 'I've a rifle pointed at your brat's head and will shoot him if you try anything.'

When first she'd heard the voice she had thought Caleb had found them; this was more horrifying though, as this man would have no qualms about shooting his nephew. Randy was insane.

The revolver went off in her hand.

The noise was incredible, almost deafening in the confines of the cave. The muzzle flash would have blinded her too had she not already had her eyelids squeezed tightly. The bullet struck the wall of the cave and ricocheted away. Randolph Moorcock swore in surprise, but proved in the next instant he wasn't bluffing about being armed. His rifle barked and Elspeth screamed in terror as she felt Jacob collapse to the ground.

She fired the revolver, deliberately this time.

Randolph laughed at how close the bullet came and fired back.

He was deliberate too, ensuring he missed her, but forcing her to hunker down as chips of rock rained from the ceiling.

'Much more of this shooting and we'll probably bring the mountain down on top of us,' Randolph called, sounding excited at the prospect of a devastating cave-in.

Elspeth had lost the lighter. She didn't require it: she could feel Jacob under her fingers. Thankfully the boy was moving. He felt furnace hot under her touch. 'Jacob?' she croaked.

'I'm . . . I'm OK, Mom.'

He must have dropped to the floor in reflex. She grabbed him and began scuttling to who knew where. She waved the gun behind them, using it as a threat to hold Randolph at bay. Her brother-in-law kept her in the flashlight's dancing beam, laughing at her pathetic antics.

She took cover behind a boulder, concealing Jacob as best she could from the gunfire. Randolph moved towards her, the flashlight bobbing with each step. Elspeth aimed at the light, but failed to shoot.

'Get her,' he said, and it struck her that Randolph wasn't the only person lurking in the cavern.

A figure lunged at her from the darkness.

Elspeth squealed, and the revolver discharged. A man cursed savagely, and she had no idea if she'd wounded him or not. It didn't matter because other figures rushed her, and a hand grabbed her wrist forcing it towards the ceiling. The revolver discharged again, the bullet thwacking the rock mere feet above. More dust and fragments of stone stuck in her thick red hair. A fist was driven into her midriff. She coughed in pain, but forgot about her discomfort in the next second when Jacob was torn from her grasp. Her son screamed and fought, but he was a skinny boy struggling against grown men. Two more men forced her arms down by her sides, and a third plucked the revolver out of her grasp.

'It's pointless fighting,' Randolph cooed from a few feet away from her. 'I've got you, and it always was going to be inevitable. There are only a few ways out of the bunker, and this is the one of them I guessed you'd try for.'

'Randy, please, you have to let me go.'

'Nope. That's the last thing I ought to do.' He darted the flashlight beam towards the freshest of the corpses. He waggled the beam so that the corpse shimmered. 'Can't have what happened to good ol' Orson Burdon coming to light, can I?'

'You did that?'

'That would be telling. Now hush. You've given running away a good go, twice now, and both times you've failed. Third time won't be the charm, Elspeth.' Randolph moved in closer, and she could clearly see him in the backwash from his flashlight. He had slung his rifle on its strap over his shoulder. In his hand he held a walkie-talkie radio. He pointed it at her. 'What do you think's going to happen to you now, Elspeth?'

She shook her head. She knew exactly what was coming for her, but wouldn't give him the satisfaction of gloating.

'Y'know, before I came looking for you, I had to go and fetch Bob Richardson to see to my mother's injuries. That was you who hurt her, right? Bad move, Elspeth. I promised not to kill you, but what do you suppose my pa's gonna do once I drag your skinny ass back to him? For sure, Caleb isn't gonna stand in his way.'

'I don't care what he does to me, just let Jacob go.'

'Jacob's coming with us. It's important he bears witness to what happens next.' Randolph grinned maliciously and again shone the flashlight beam over Orson Burdon's corpse.

She couldn't avoid looking again at the bodies scattered around that horrible place and shuddered in the knowledge that the Booger Hole could possibly end up as her crypt too.

THIRTY-SIX

P o snapped the point of his elbow into one man's face and used the recoil to power his fist into another's. The first man croaked in agony and buried his mashed nose in his cupped palms. The second man was knocked clean out and collapsed to the tunnel floor. Po ignored the latter and grabbed the former. He swung the injured man around in a tight arc and slammed him against the wall. Blood droplets showered Po's face as the man expelled a sharp yelp of pain. Po swung another elbow, a sweeping cross this time, and the hard tip clashed with the man's jaw with concussive force. The man's knees gave out and he slid to his butt, sleeping as soundly as his friend did.

Tess was only vaguely aware of her partner's swift work with the duo, she was too engaged in a fight of her own to pay attention. She must silence only one antagonist, but he was proving more resilient than those Po had taken care of with a few short, sharp jabs of his elbows. She had punched her opponent several times unanswered, but already she could tell that he was rallying and her chance of winning the fight growing precarious. The man's teeth were clenched in a florid face, his features backlit by a head torch her first punch had knocked awry. Her attack had come as a surprise, throwing him into momentary confusion, but now he had centered his gaze on her and it was filled with derision. Tess hit him again, using her palm to jab at his chin. He knocked her hand aside and grasped her throat in both hands. He drove her backwards into the alcove she'd launched from.

He throttled her.

During Po's incarceration, he'd had plenty of opportunity to employ the close-quarter combat skills he'd learned and gone on to perfect behind bars. Known jokingly as Jailhouse Rock, it was a martial art unique to convicts. He had mastery of the swift and vicious moves designed for battle so up close and personal it could be employed in a telephone booth, a tiny cage or even a shower stall. Tess's unarmed combat skills were designed for restraint rather than destruction, but from Po she'd learned a thing or two beyond the law enforcement manual that once dictated her responses to violence. She kicked the man between the legs, and when he folded towards her, she clamped her teeth on his ear and gnawed down. Her savagery released his choke-hold, causing him to push against her in a frantic attempt at escape. As he wrenched backwards she feared that she'd be left with a mouthful of bloody gristle: the thought was repulsive. Tess let go, but she followed his direction, and hooked a heel behind his knee. She shoved with both hands. Her opponent lost balance, but the tunnel was too narrow for him to fall cleanly. He caromed off the wall, and Tess grabbed his jacket and tugged him sideways. His feet tangled with those of his friends already lying on the ground. He stumbled, fell and went down on a knee in front of Po. Po glimpsed briefly at Tess, registered her difficulty beating her opponent, and hammered him with a blow that felled him.

'Thanks,' she wheezed, 'but I had everything under control.'

'It isn't a competition, Tess. You did your bit, I did mine.' He looked over the three unconscious men – one of them was stirring, his hands reflexively reaching for his broken nose – but Po wasn't heartless and wouldn't hurt the man any further than necessary. To her relief, he had been the one to change his mind and urge Tess to put away her weapon and try taking out this small hunting party less lethally. He bent down to the latest man he'd knocked out, pulled off the head torch, switched off the light and launched it down the tunnel. Po searched them all swiftly. None of the others had flashlights.

Tess collected Pinky's lantern and switched it back on.

'Lead the way,' Po said.

It was unlikely any of the trio would be in a fit state to trouble them in the next few minutes, but he set himself to protect her back. His old-fashioned manners could be deemed chauvinistic and be mildly abrasive at times, but Tess had no complaint when he was simply following his nature. His was the same protective impulse that had brought them across the country to help Elspeth and Jacob.

'You recognized those guys, didn't you?' asked Po.

'Yeah, they're the three who went to check for us at the fence.

They must've returned quickly and followed us down into the tunnels.'

'I just checked them over; none of them was carrying a radio or phone. I think we're still good to go.'

In other words, their hunters had been unable to report their findings at the fence and had made the decision to return to the commune via the tunnels. They had not expected to stumble across their quarry down in the dark, hence how easily they'd been dispatched. For now Tess and Po's presence down there was safe, but it would change as soon as the trio awoke and made their way to a populated area of the tunnels. Tess thought of Pinky: hopefully their friend was still safe and had avoided discovery too.

Ahead, the silvering of the light continued. From a hundred yards away Tess could make out the shape of an intersecting tunnel. This one was artificially lighted, suggesting they were approaching the rooms and tunnels regularly used by the Moorcocks. Without comment Po slipped past and approached the intersection. He still limped, but otherwise he looked fit and well: the brief fight in the tunnel had raised his heart rate, and the flood of endorphins had helped anaesthetize his pain. He put his back to the wall and took a quick peek around the corner. He waved at Tess to join him.

She turned off the lantern as she neared and set it aside now it was no longer needed. She leaned close to Po's side.

'This tunnel goes all the way to the bunker I told you about. See those symbols on the walls, I've been counting them down.' The nearest symbol daubed on the wall contained a number nine juxtaposed with an arrow. 'I recall seeing a figure nine painted on the wall near that armory I told you about. If I'm not mistaken the same number was painted next to that vault door too.'

'The vault was close to where you said you locked those young guys in the van?' Tess clarified.

'They're each very close to the other. Once we're back in the loadin' dock we'll find a way outside.' Po reassessed his words. 'Though I won't be leavin' till I'm certain Jacob isn't down here.'

'We'd best get looking for him,' Tess suggested. 'Those guys back there aren't going to stay asleep for much longer. If they wake and raise the alarm . . .'

Po nodded at her wisdom. He slipped out into the lit tunnel and began a quick trot towards the loading dock. Tess followed, holding the pistol down by her thigh.

The tunnel met a room. It was a featureless place and seemed to serve only to connect this with another part of the tunnel. Tess noted the figure '9' symbol was again painted on the wall. The same number featured on the adjoining tunnel wall, and again a directional arrow accompanied it. Po darted down the tunnel, now moving as if with abandon. Tess decided that speed probably trumped stealth now; she jogged to catch up. They approached a bend in the tunnel. Po halted, stepped backwards and Tess ran up against him. He quickly turned and held a finger to her lips. He stared into her eyes to convey the importance of silence. Moving through the next part of the tunnel was what sounded like a group of people. Tess nodded to show she was fully aware, and then raised the pistol to show she was also ready to back him up wherever the next few minutes took them. They moved together towards the corner, and this time Tess ducked under his armpit so that she too could scout their next move. There was nobody in the tunnel, but people were very close by: the sound of their passage was filtering down a short connecting tunnel. Judging by the scuffing of feet and murmur of voices there was a decent crowd amassed just out of sight. Po followed as Tess crept forward.

They found the entrance to the next tunnel, again signposted by the stenciled figure nine and watched people trooping past its far end in what amounted to a procession of sorts. Po's breath caught as Elspeth was led past, her arms gripped by two burly jailers. Tess pressed her left hand against his chest, calming him, halting any spur-of-the-moment reaction. Seconds later Jacob shuffled past, guarded by a bearded, thickset man with a large belly protruding over his belt. The boy's guard carried a hunting rifle slung over his shoulder. Po's breath remained caught in his chest. Tess glanced up at him, and would have urged caution, but he was calculating his next move. More figures followed in line, and unless Tess was mistaken they amounted to ten men altogether. Too many to attempt taking on without employing the lethal option: even then, the odds were against them, and besides, they couldn't risk Elspeth and Jacob getting caught in the crossfire.

The procession continued, and Tess guessed they'd entered a larger space as their footsteps and voices echoed. Po bent to her

ear and whispered, 'They're in the loading dock. Did you see they
had Elspeth and the boy? I wonder where they're takin' them?'

'We should follow,' Tess suggested. 'Maybe we'll get an opportunity to free them without having a pitched battle.'

From somewhere behind them a holler echoed through the
tunnels.

Po tensed. He drew his knife.

'We might have to contend with those stragglers before we
think about following anyone,' he warned.

Tess tasted bile. Was it too much to ask hoping to have found
a way out before the men they'd knocked unconscious wakened?
She held up the pistol. Using the pistol she could probably threaten
silence from them, but she didn't want to get parted from Po. Not
even for a second in those horrible tunnels.

There had been no reaction from the group now walking
through the loading bay, for now those in the tunnel had gone
unheard. 'Let's just follow. Hopefully our chance will come
sooner rather than later. Oh, hold it, Po.'

'Whassup?'

She took her cell phone from her breast pocket. It vibrated
almost silently in her grasp. 'It's Pinky,' she said needlessly.

Po craned to check her phone screen while she brought up the
message.

I pray you're still alive, Pinky had texted. *Something weird is
going on. They planning on building a pyramid?*

Tess and Po exchanged puzzled glances.

'Now isn't the time for enigmatic riddles,' Po growled.

What do you mean? Tess replied.

They're stockpiling aggregate up here.

'What the hell?' Po again frowned in puzzlement. But his
confusion lasted mere seconds. The rumble of the opening metal
shutter made a palpable din in the tunnels.

Tess followed him as Po used the racket to cover their approach
to the loading bay. They bypassed what looked like a bank vault
door, and then the open doors to antechambers and spilled out
into the dock. There was a small fleet of vehicles in the sunken
loading bay area, and a group of people stood around waiting for
the huge roller shutters to open enough for them to pass beneath.
There was enough space under the shutter to show that some other

vehicles had arrived outside, and a welcoming party had gathered
to meet the procession and their prisoners. As the door rose higher,
concertinaing on itself with a shriek of tortured metal and the
groan of pneumatics, Tess spotted a figure stood astride the bed
of a white pickup truck. It was a man as tall as Po, and perhaps
wider across his shoulders. He had oily black hair, brushed straight
back from his forehead. His features were long and lean, and he
had an aquiline nose and deep-set eyes. If she didn't know otherwise, she'd say this could be Po's long-lost brother. No, she decided,
as he grinned maliciously when Elspeth was pushed to her knees
in front of him, this was not Po's brother, but perhaps an evil
doppelgänger. This was Caleb Moorcock, and it was evident to
her now, that he was Jacob's genetic father.

Po was silent.

He must have been thinking the same thoughts and coming to
the same conclusion about Jacob's heritage.

Elspeth was grabbed again by some of the onlookers and lifted
bodily onto the bed of the pickup. Caleb Moorcock sneered down
at her, and then stabbed a finger at Jacob. Men as equally complicit
in his abuse as his father led the struggling boy towards Caleb.
The boy was picked up and passed into his father's hands. Caleb
held him at eye level for a few seconds, then scornfully cast him
down by his mother. The big-bellied guard clambered up to join
Caleb, and Tess formed the opinion this was another of Eldon
Moorcock's despicable brood. The redneck slapped his hand repeatedly on the roof of the cab, and the pickup started a slow turn,
the crowd dispersing around it. As the truck found its path clear
it began pulling away, joined by the other cars and trucks, and
those on foot scrambled to join the now engorged procession.

Tess clutched Po's forearm, and could feel how tense he was.

'I don't believe that Jacob is yours,' she said gently.

'I see that now,' he agreed, 'but it doesn't change a damn thing.'

'I never expected it to.'

'They're a mother and child in danger.'

'Then let's go rescue them, shall we?' she said.

'*Laissez les bon temps rouler*,' he said and flashed a humorless
smile.

THIRTY-SEVEN

T he procession halted at the end of the parade ground closest
to the Moorcock family homes. There the stained concrete
gave way to tilled earth, flower gardens, and to the west
an established orchard grove. Taken as a snapshot image, the
gardens and houses would not look out of place several miles away
in the town of Muller Falls, or in any other small American town
for that matter. The one thing that hinted at a sinister undertone
to the community was in a deep trench that ran cater-corner to the
parade ground. This trench was once part of the subterranean
tunnel network but evidently it had collapsed years ago, and subse-
quently only partially excavated. A pile of soil and broken concrete
stood at the lip of the trench, its volume added to in the past
minutes by a group of women and boys drafted in to assist with
the manual unloading of a lorry. They shoveled stones the size of
grapefruits off the truck and onto the growing pile. This Tess
assumed must be the pyramid that Pinky referenced in his text.

There was a sense of carnival about the inhabitants of the
commune. Other residents had spilled from their homes to join
the crowd gathering on the parade ground to watch. Some laughed,
others talked excitedly, and there was plenty of friendly pushing
and jostling among the onlookers as the pickup carrying Elspeth and
Jacob drew to a halt. Other people kept their heads down and their
opinion about the proceedings to themselves: not everyone here
was a crazed and murderous minion of their self-proclaimed king.
Throughout the commune other residents headed to join the throng
at the edge of the trench, probably summoned to bear witness.
Tess even spotted an old man being pushed towards the crowd in
a wheelchair. The hunt for Po was still underway: she could hear
the baying of hounds emanating from the woods, and also the
distant rumble of vehicles over the ill-maintained roads. She
wondered if the scouting party that had followed them to the caves
had since joined the throng here or if they were still seeking their
quarry. The trio knocked unconscious in the tunnels would surely

have recovered by now and be on their way to report the confrontation. Strangely, Tess and Po were given some leeway to sneak closer because of the excitement factor and the movement of so many people all heading in the same direction: at a distance they'd be mistaken for other members of the commune.

As they neared the procession, Po wavered slightly and Tess came to halt.

'We should split up,' he whispered.

'How many times have I to say it? There's no way we're splitting up.'

'If one of us is captured, at least the other has a chance at—'

'We are not splitting up, Po. We do this together or not at all.'

She knew exactly why he wanted to split up. It was so he could send her to some relatively safe place while he risked his backside to save Elspeth and Jacob. His old-fashioned chivalrous manners could be endearing at times, but infuriating at others. How many times must she prove to him that she was no shrinking violet?

'Besides,' she added, 'Pinky is out there someplace. He's our backup if we are captured.'

'I know. I only—'

'You only want to protect me. I know. I get that, Po. But I don't need to be wrapped in cotton wool when I can look after myself.' She raised the pistol. '*And* I have *this*.'

A number of people in the crowd carried hunting rifles, and had knives on their belts, but the majority was unarmed. It was primarily the henchmen surrounding Caleb and his big-bellied brother that carried assault rifles and pistols. Maybe they should have sought that armory room Po had earlier discovered and picked up some extra firepower. Armed only with his knife, there was little possibility he could convince Elspeth and Jacob's captors to release them; at least the presence of her pistol was more persuasive.

'It just feels wrong risking your life for the sake of Elspeth's when . . . well, you know, she used to be my girl. Tess, you mean more to me than a hundred of her.'

'We're here mostly for the boy,' she reminded him. 'But the boy needs his mom, too, and I fully intend getting them both out of this mess.'

'What d'you suppose is going on?'

'Caleb wants to make an exhibition out of punishing Elspeth. The Moorcocks want to send a clear message to all of their subjects. Witness what becomes of *anyone* who dares disobey *our* rules!'

'Look.'

The front door to the largest of the houses had opened. A huge, older man with a drooping yellow mustache paused at the threshold a moment, his head thrown back and his hands on his hips. He surveyed the scene before him. Then he nodded grandiosely and stepped outside, to follow a path through the garden towards the edge of the trench. Another man followed him, not as tall as Caleb, nor as fat as the other man on the pickup truck, but enough alike them both to be the third brother. He walked, eyes downcast, muttering something inaudible to his father.

Eldon Moorcock moved through the crowd, his subjects parting for him. He nodded at them, pompous and regal.

'What a sanctimonious piece of shit he looks,' Po decided. 'D'you think Eldon intends presiding over things? Who does he think he is: judge, jury and executioner?'

'I doubt he'll be the latter. Does he look the type to get his hands dirty when he has others to do it for him?'

'Maybe I shouldn't have used that word . . . executioner.' Po chewed down on his bottom lip. 'Surely they won't go as far as murdering Elspeth?'

'Elspeth believed it was a possibility,' Tess said, recalling their conversation back at Po's ranch when she'd begged Tess not to involve the police.

'You don't think she was being overly dramatic?'

Tess visualized the cigarette burns on Elspeth's thighs, and imagined the agony of those inflicted on her breasts; a man capable of perpetrating that kind of torture was capable of anything. 'If anything, she downplayed the suffering she endured before. If Caleb wants to put on a show, perhaps there's no line he won't cross. What was it you said in French a minute ago, Po: let the good times roll? Well, I prefer "*finissons cette merde*". That's right: Let's end this shit.'

THIRTY-EIGHT

It was almost an out of body experience for Elspeth as she observed her husband's performance. Caleb stood on the back of the pickup, his jaw set and his nose in the air, as if he was a Roman Emperor astride a war chariot. He even clenched his fists at his hips, striking the most imperious stance he could. Even as his father approached, he didn't relax his pose, drinking in the atmosphere as the residents of their community clamored for a closer look at his captives. He appeared mighty pleased with how quickly he'd brought his wayward wife to heel, despite the fact he owed Randolph for her recapture. But Randy looked content for Caleb to take the accolades, knowing well his eldest brother owed him big time.

Caleb looked to their father as Eldon strode up to the pickup. He didn't defer to Eldon's authority.

The older man peered over the side of the flatbed, staring into Elspeth's face. He sneered, and then spat a wad of phlegm at her. It hung in her hair. She made no attempt at brushing it aside; she wouldn't give him the satisfaction of seeing her disgust. In fact she barely responded to anything any of her abusers did or said anymore, because nothing would help except to make her more pathetic in their eyes. She only cared about Jacob and ensuring her son survived unharmed. Already Caleb had tried demeaning her, calling her the most horrible names, and casting aspersions on her alleged sexual proclivities with all and sundry. He had twisted and pinched her flesh and yanked on her hair so tight there were still long strands of it caught between his fingers. She took the abuse, and when she could, she reached out a comforting hand to touch Jacob. Her son sat with his back pressed into the corner of the bed, against the pickup's cab, his head down. He had no wish to witness his mother's further debasement.

The throng was noisy, but fell silent as Caleb threw his arms aloft. Some people had carried flashlights or lanterns from home, but the headlights of the vehicles in the procession amply lit up that end of the parade square. From her prone position on the truck's bed, Elspeth watched the enlarged shadows of people being cast upward against the trees and on her husband. Caleb's features were momentarily obscured, except for his eyes: reflecting an errant beam they gleamed in the darkness like embers. Elspeth shuddered at the depth of evil within them.

'All of you here know Elspeth. You know her as a neighbor, a friend, the mother of Jacob, mostly you know her as my wife.' Caleb jutted out his chin and curled back his top lip at the final description of her. 'What you might not know is how willful and obstructive a wife she is. Look at her—'

Without warning Elspeth was grabbed and hauled to her feet by Caleb and Randolph. Randy held her up, while Caleb stabbed a finger at her in emphasis. 'Look at the way she wears her clothes.' Her skirt was still pulled up between her knees and tucked into her waistband. 'Who does Elspeth think she is?' Caleb posed the question to the crowd. 'I'll tell you. She doesn't believe in obeying her husband's wishes any more, just look, she thinks she now wears the pants in our relationship.'

Some of her neighbors snickered in laughter at Caleb's summation. Others bent their necks, avoiding meeting her eyes.

'She doesn't,' Caleb asserted.

He reached and grasped her skirt, yanked the bunched material loose and snapped down his arm. Elspeth staggered but Randy grabbed her hair and craned her head backwards. Her fists trembled at her sides. Elspeth bit down on her bottom lip and endured.

'Our community was established on a set of rules,' Caleb reminded the crowd, 'and we all agreed to abide by them. One of those rules was that a wife must serve her husband without question.' Caleb searched the crowd, his gaze going from one woman to the next. 'Is there a wife among you who does not serve their master? You Georgia, do you do as Peter asks, or do you resist him? Mary, when Henry says "jump", do you ask "how high"? I bet you do. Oh, how I wish my wife was as obedient as y'all are. Elspeth has betrayed me!' Caleb shook his head in mock regret. 'She ran away and took my son with her. *My son.* And she tried to poison him with lies and took him to a man she pretended was his father. She tried turning Jacob against me. Is this crime against *me* forgivable?'

'Don't forget that the whore struck down Ellie-May,' Eldon suddenly barked. 'She should be struck down the way she struck down your mother.'

A murmur went through the crowd. Ellie-May commanded respect, but it was entirely through fear. Elspeth doubted there was a woman in that crowd who wouldn't like to have struck the harridan herself, yet – for appearances sake – they all oohed and aahed and took pity on the vicious old bitch. Elspeth wondered why she'd ever cared for her friends and neighbors when each and every one of them would sell her out to protect their own hides. Hot tears, heavy and tremulous, burned tracks down her cheeks.

'Mom was only protecting me.' Jacob's voice was barely audible.

Caleb lurched, grasped the boy by his shoulders and dragged him to his feet. He shook Jacob, emphasizing his point. 'Your mother beat your poor defenseless grandma. What kind of monster does that?'

'Grandma was beating me and Mom stopped her.'

Caleb shook his head in denial. Besides, it didn't matter. His mother wasn't the one on trial here, only his wife. He kicked out without warning, digging his boot sharply into Elspeth's thigh. If Randy hadn't held her up she would've collapsed. She resisted, but couldn't halt emitting a moan; the pain was deep within her muscle and grew each second.

Eldon reached for her over the edge of the pickup. Had he gotten a hold he might have dragged her to the ground and stamped her into the dust. Randolph kept her standing just out of reach of Eldon's grasping fingertips. Caleb bent at his waist, shoving Jacob aside to regard his father. 'Let me punish her as I see fit,' he said, and his words held no suggestion of request.

Eldon glanced at the trench, and then nodded sharply. He threw up his hands, commanding an audience.

'Elspeth has wronged us all,' he announced, 'and therefore all here should be allowed to punish her. But Caleb is right. She has wronged him more than any other; he should be the one to pronounce her punishment.'

'Darrell,' Caleb called down to his middle brother, 'help Randy with Elspeth. I'll bring Jacob.'

Darrell returned Caleb's gaze for no longer than a heartbeat, before he turned aside and walked among the crowd, as if he hadn't heard. Of the three brothers, Elspeth had discovered that Darrell was the least insane, but she couldn't hope for him to intervene on her behalf, as his loyalties still lay with his family. However, she might be able to play on him to help Jacob.

'Darrell,' she called after him. 'Please take Jacob away. He shouldn't be made to watch this.'

Darrell turned to regard her over his shoulder, but he held her gaze barely a second longer than he'd paid attention to Caleb. He walked away, lost in the crowd.

Caleb laughed nastily at the way Darrell had slighted her request, forgetting he did exactly the same to him seconds ago. Randy seemed oblivious. He walked Elspeth to the edge of the pickup, and then pushed her over the tailgate into the arms of the waiting throng. Men and women Elspeth had known for a decade treated her like a side of spoiled beef: turning up their noses they shoved her, guiding her remorselessly while Randy jumped down with a grunt and took control of her once more. Caleb followed, pulling Jacob after him by his wrist. Eldon joined his sons as they jostled their captives towards the trench. The crowd parted like moisture retreating from spilled oil.

Elspeth stared at the trench and understood her fate. For a while she'd existed in a state of distraction, dazed by the shock and disappointment of recapture. Now terror bloomed in her chest. She searched for any friendly face, anyone she could beseech for help. 'They killed Mikey Stewart!' she blurted. 'They murdered that boy and now they are going to murder me! Are you just going to stand by and allow these monsters to kill me? They killed Mikey, a child. Not only Mikey. There are others down in Booger Hole. They gutted a man, somebody called Burdon, and dumped him down there in the dark. If you let them do this to me, how can you be certain that you won't be the next to die?'

Her claim was met by some tittering, even some outright laughter, but several of her neighbors were taken aback, and she knew by the draining of their color that they suspected she was right. But taking her side would only court their own demises; not one person stood up for her.

'Toss her down there,' Eldon commanded sharply and he took hold of her shoulder to help cast her into the trench.

Elspeth squirmed out of Randolph's grasp, leaving behind

another hank of her hair, but Eldon only tightened his grasp and pushed her down to a crouch. Randolph butted her with his knees, then forced his expansive belly over her, crushing her down more; she also felt his genitals bump suggestively off her a few times, the repulsive toad!

'You there,' Caleb shouted, 'block that end of the trench so's there's nowhere she can run.'

Two burly young men answered his instruction, jumping down into the trench about fifteen feet away from the near end. They formed a human wall, spreading their arms as if prepared to tackle her.

'Now throw her down there like Pa said,' Caleb instructed Randolph.

Randolph grunted in effort as he forced her to the edge of the trench, then he pushed and nudged with his knees and belly until Elspeth had nowhere left to go but down. She tumbled off the edge of the ditch, skidding on the sharp decline and taking a small avalanche of dirt with her into its depths. The trench was approximately ten feet deep. At the bottom the earth had been cleared displaying some of the original tunnel floor, but mostly it was ankle-deep in earth and broken rubble. Elspeth tore the skin on her ankles against rebar-enforced concrete. She glanced up and watched as her neighbors flocked in to watch the show. Many of them had moved to the north side of the ditch, standing at the base of the recently added-to hillock. She spotted Caleb again, but she ignored his hateful sneer, seeking instead her son. Jacob's wrist was still grasped by Caleb, and her husband now used it to stop the boy from plummeting down and joining her in the trench.

Eldon reared up behind his eldest son and assisted to control his grandson by twisting Jacob's ear savagely. Jacob yowled.

'Leave him be, you bastards!' Elspeth bent at the waist, hands fisted by her sides as she screamed.

'Yeah,' said Caleb to Eldon, 'leave him be, Pa. It isn't too late for Jacob to prove he's worthy of the Moorcock name. Say, Pa, why don't you pass him one of those rocks?'

Eldon grinned at the suggestion. He released Jacob in order to seek among the stones piled next to the trench. Eldon stood, bouncing a smooth round stone the size of a baseball on his palm. 'Here you go, boy.'

'Take the rock,' Caleb ordered Jacob.

'I won't.'

'You will. Take it, or I'll have Uncle Randolph unsling that rifle and put a bullet through your mom's knee. Don't think he'll do it?'

Whether Caleb was bluffing or not, Elspeth believed. She cried out to Jacob. 'Son, it's OK. Just take the stone like your daddy tells you.'

'But he's going to make me—'

'We both know what he's going to do, Jacob, but it's OK, baby. I'd rather it was you first.' She peered up at Jacob, no longer afraid for herself. Knowing what Caleb was about to force Jacob to do, she withered inside because she couldn't take the guilt away that the boy would suffer forever more.

Caleb stretched out the boy's arm and turned it palm up. Eldon slapped the rock in Jacob's palm.

Caleb looked around at the others gathered closest to them. 'I invite you all to pick up a stone of your choice.'

Some people balked, comprehending fully where events were leading. Others, though, were caught up by the bloodthirsty pack mentality prevalent in groups like theirs and scrambled excitedly to find a missile to their liking. Caleb watched them, while holding onto his son. Nearby a woman slipped and went down into the ditch followed by an avalanche of dirt. She shrieked and clawed at the walls of the trench, fearing she might be next for her community to turn on. Some of her friends laughed at her plight, before guiding her to run to where the youths blocked her passage like a couple of linebackers. She ran to them, head ducked, anticipating being struck down. The youths parted for her and she ran whimpering in relief to a place she could climb out. Elspeth had watched her every move, had even contemplated trying to follow the girl out through the guards. They wouldn't have given way for her though.

She again looked up at her accuser.

Caleb said, 'Want to tell these good folks the truth, Elspeth?'

'What version of the truth? Yours or the *actual* truth?'

'Tell them how you lied to Jacob, how you tried convincing him he was another man's child.'

'You know I didn't do that, Caleb.'

'Tell them Jacob's mine. That there is no doubt and that you only lied to him about Villere.'

'He is your son,' she said, 'but after what you're about to make him do, I doubt he'll ever look at you as his father again.'

'I'm trying to save you, Elspeth. Admit to your lies, admit them, otherwise how am I to believe you didn't betray me and sleep with another man?'

'I won't admit to lying because I didn't lie. You're only playing word games, Caleb, so you can accuse me of adultery, when you know it's untrue. You have no grounds to punish me like this, no grounds to force these folk into joining you in a terrible miscarriage of justice.'

A rock struck her in the midriff. It had been thrown with force, but thankfully she was unhurt, the rock too small to cause major injury. She blinked in surprise at who'd thrown the rock. Eldon snarled down at her. 'For hurting Ellie-May I'll see you buried.'

'Damn it, Pa,' Caleb croaked, 'I wanted Jacob to be first to cast.'

'Too goddamn late,' snapped Eldon. 'Now quit your games and let's just do this, so's I can go check on your mom.'

Jacob, as it happened, had dropped the stone they'd forced into his hand.

'Pick it up,' Caleb commanded.

'I won't. You can't make me.'

Caleb swore under his breath, then turned to the crowd. 'You heard my father. Let's do this.'

He shoved Jacob down at Randolph's feet, so that he could dip down and select a grapefruit-sized stone. He weighed it in his palm.

Elspeth turned to present her back, even as the first rocks began raining down. Some were tossed lacking enthusiasm, and they missed her, but others were thrown sure and with force. One of them – she'd bet aimed by Caleb – glanced off the side of her head, almost taking her ear with it. She croaked, sinking to her knees, and was pummeled remorselessly.

THIRTY-NINE

T ess pulled the trigger three times in rapid succession. The retorts were loud, the muzzle flashes stark. And yet they almost went unnoticed by those nearest the trench. In a murderous fervor they scrambled for fresh missiles to join those already hurled into the pit. The punishment levied on Elspeth was inhuman, it was horrible, and Tess was almost overcome by revulsion at its barbarity. When her gunfire failed to halt the madness, she ran forward, again pulling the trigger and screaming at the top of her voice. 'Stop this! In the name of Christ, stop what you are doing!'

Shocked, some of them afraid, the crowd parted before her. Some people it seemed snapped out of the momentary madness that had overtaken them, and they turned their faces away in self-disgust. Others wept. But those closest to the Moorcocks responded differently. Some raised weapons, and others attempted to halt Tess's forward rush. With her teeth clenched in fury, Tess smashed one man down with the butt of her pistol to the side of his neck; another she forced away by ramming the gun's barrel under his chin and pushing him over backwards. She realigned her aim, this time with her barrel pointed directly at Caleb Moorcock's chest.

'You animal,' Tess screamed at him. 'Stop this now or so help me I'll—'

Caleb grabbed Jacob and dragged the boy in front of him, using him as a human shield. 'Oh, yeah?' he crowed. 'What will you do now?'

Tess's aim faltered.

Eldon Moorcock sheltered behind Caleb's pickup, watching over the hood as Tess approached another few steps. Tess ignored the older man, believing the one in control of the crowd to be his eldest son, and therefore the one to stop first. Members of his community sought direction from Eldon, but he ignored them. Most of them simply dropped the rocks they'd gathered from the pile while others scattered into the darkness beyond the lights. Tess snapped orders at some of those nearest, commanding them to get back: they obeyed. She reached the rim of the trench and took a quick check on Elspeth. The woman had retreated under her bloody arms, and she had pulled her knees up to her chest. Several smaller rocks were caught in her dusty clothing; many more were heaped around her. Tess had no idea how many of the missiles had struck her, or to what extent her injuries were. She tasted bile as she returned her aim to Caleb. The bastard sneered at her. Jacob squirmed in his grasp, desperate to aid his mother.

'It's over with,' Tess told him. 'Let the boy go.'

'Fuck you. Who do you think you are walking in here as if you own the place and ordering *me* around?'

Tess took careful aim. Caleb was much bigger than his son, it was unlikely she'd make a poor shot and hit the boy.

'Are you fucking kidding me?' Caleb hauled Jacob aloft, holding his son between them as he retreated backwards.

'You're a dirty coward,' Tess called after him.

'Yeah, and you're dead bitch!'

Tess dropped to one knee, unbeknown saving her own life.

She had no way of telling that Randolph had ducked at the first sounds of gunfire, and he'd scuttled away with other members of the community as she approached. He'd taken cover behind one of the other trucks in the procession. Unslinging his rifle he'd taken aim, keeping Tess in his sights as she reached the edge of the trench and threatened his brother. On the tail of Caleb's proclamation he fired, but Tess's head was no longer a target. The bullet whistled over her and buried itself in the trunk of a distant tree. She heard the retort, caught the muzzle flash, and in reflex she returned fire. Her bullets drilled the truck Randolph hid behind, causing him to jerk and flinch with each impact. He worked the rifle, clearing the breach and inserting a fresh cartridge. By the time he bobbed up and settled his rifle on the truck's hood, seeking her, Tess had disappeared.

She rolled over the edge of the trench, continued rolling amid an avalanche of dirt to the bottom, where she scrambled up and ran to Elspeth. She placed her left hand flat on the woman's back, while swinging her gun to cover them both. Thankfully Elspeth trembled beneath her.

'Elspeth, it's Tess. I've got you.' She shook the woman gently. 'Can you move?'

Elspeth didn't move. She cowered.

Tess tried again. 'Elspeth, I've got you covered. But you must move.'

There was no telling how many of the stones had struck her. Her arms were scraped and bloody. She'd managed to protect her head from most of the missiles, but the cumulative effect of dozens of stones striking her could have caused untold internal damage. Tess plucked away the smaller stones buried in her hair. 'Elspeth, answer me, can you move? We have to get you out of here.'

Elspeth emitted a whimper.

'You must be in agony, but we can't stay here or else—'

Elspeth unfolded, and craned her neck to see Tess. Her eyes were dazed, out of focus. 'I . . . I can move. Where's my son?'

'Come on, Elspeth. Help me to help you.'

'Where's Jacob?'

Tess pushed her hand under Elspeth's armpit, assisting her to stand. 'Let's get you to safety first.'

Elspeth pushed up, shedding more stones and pebbles. 'No, I have to get Jacob away.'

'It's OK. Nicolas and Pinky are going to rescue Jacob. You don't have to worry about him.'

Tess chewed her lip. She had no possible way of guaranteeing her friends would be successful, but she must convince Elspeth that Jacob was in safe hands, otherwise they might end up trapped down there and at the mercy of the Moorcocks; a stoning to death could be on both their cards. 'Let's go this way.'

The burly youths were still in the trench. However, they were no longer big or brave now that they'd no reason to impress anyone. They cowered, terrified of Tess's pistol. She snapped the barrel at them and commanded them to get the hell out of her way. They complied, scrambling up the steep walls of the ditch. For each two feet they climbed, they slid back down one of them. Tess propelled Elspeth before her, aiming towards where the collapsed tunnel was yet to be excavated. There the earth sloped to ground level, offering an easier climb out than the youths faced. Tess craned to look back, to try to get a sense of what was going on at the other end. It had been formulated in as many seconds as it took to count off one hand, but hopefully her plan had worked, and her distraction had allowed Po to get his hands on Jacob. There was noise and flashes and several voices hollering in competition, but she could not be clear about anything. Once she had Elspeth out of the trench, and somewhere safer, then hopefully she could reunite her with her child.

FORTY

All her misgivings concerning splitting up had disappeared the instant Tess realized there was no way to save Elspeth *and* Jacob if they stuck together. She had grabbed Po fervently, instructing him to 'go and get the boy' while she strode forward into the baying mob sending bullets flying skyward.

Po didn't require telling twice.

He raced away from Tess so that none of those nearest her would tell she was accompanied, and seconds later he lost himself among those rushing to escape the scene. He was not running blindly, he had his gaze fixed laser sharp on a target, having just watched him turn aside from his family. His sprained ankle no longer troubled him, but his knee felt as swollen as a basketball. Despite his injury he ran smoothly and almost silently where others stumbled and thrashed in the darkness beyond the circle of lights. At no time did he lose sight of his target, who, after first denying his brother, was now circling back. Po hadn't heard Caleb name him, but he suspected this was his brother Darrell, while the fat-bellied punk assisting Caleb had to be Randolph. Before going missing Elspeth had briefly described Caleb's brothers to them; Po hadn't given the brothers much thought at the time but he must have subconsciously absorbed their descriptions.

Darrell Moorcock was not as tall as Caleb, nor as heavy as Randolph, but he was no weakling either. He was of above average height, with a manual laborer's build, and was probably ten years Po's junior: he was a potentially dangerous opponent. Po wasn't slowed a beat. He launched at Darrell in a flying dive and tackled him to the earth. They rolled together, Darrell stunned by the impact at first, and then Po began to scramble, to gain a superior position. They both came to their knees. Darrell wrenched around to face him, setting his teeth in a tight grimace. 'Nicolas Villere?'

'You know me then?'

'We've been hunting you!'

'Well, here I am.'

Po hammered Darrell's collarbone with his left fist.

Darrell clutched at his broken shoulder with one hand, but the suddenness of the blow didn't totally halt him. He swung a clubbing right at Po and skimmed his chin.

Po launched in, forehead cracking Darrell in the cheekbone, forcing him to turn aside. Po swarmed him, looping his arm around Darrell's throat, grabbing the hand that sought to protect his broken clavicle. Po rammed his chest against him, and they again performed a sideways roll, ending with Po astride Darrell's back and his arm encircling his neck. Po's blade had almost magically reappeared and he inserted its tip between the man's teeth. Darrell could clamp down on the steel, but would be unable to halt the blade sliding in through his soft palate and into his brain. 'Keep fighting,' Po told him, 'and gimme an excuse to kill you.'

Resistance fled Darrell.

'Good. Now get up.' Po retained his hold, despite how awkward it proved for them to stand. They got there though, with only a little blood coming from Darrell's sliced lips. Po scrutinized what was going on at the head of the trench. He spotted Eldon, and Caleb, who had wrapped his arms around Jacob and held him against his chest like a swaddled baby. Tess had disappeared from view. Randolph crouched behind a truck, pointing a rifle at empty space. Panic surged through Po after spotting the latter but it was a momentary blip, because from the looks of frustration and concern on the Moorcocks' faces they were the ones they deemed in immediate peril. Tess must've jumped into the trench to help Elspeth. He hoped so. He switched his concern from Tess to the boy.

'Walk,' he snarled in Darrell's ear.

Darrell was arched at his lower spine, his head contorted on his neck. It made walking difficult. Po unhooked his forearm, but gripped Darrell's collar. He slid the knife out from between his teeth, reinserted its tip in the hollow beneath his ear. It was no less a threat but the man could move easier. Po directed him towards his kin.

'Hey! Dough Boy!' Po ensured that the youngest brother easily saw Darrell's plight. 'Drop that rifle or say goodbye to your bro.'

Threats always came with the caveat that you must be prepared to follow them otherwise they lost their potency. When Randolph was slow to comply Po exerted pressure on the knife. Darrell yowled in pain and added his exhortations for Randolph to drop his weapon.

Randolph hadn't the sharpest of minds, that or he couldn't care less about his brother's plight. He took cover on the far side of the truck, realigning his rifle so that he could get Po in his sights. Po twisted his captive to take any bullets first. At this range Darrell's torso would slow but not stop a high-powered round. 'I suggest you tell your little brother to behave,' he told Darrell.

'Randy for fuck's sake!' Darrell croaked hoarsely.

'Put up your goddamn rifle!' Eldon hollered at his youngest son.

Randolph's mouth worked, but only so he could draw spit. He hawked out phlegm on the hood of the truck without taking his aim off Po. 'If he hurts our Darrell, I'll make him pay.'

'We can make an exchange,' Po called. 'Darrell for Jacob.'

Caleb cocked his head over his son's shoulder. 'Are you for real?'

'You want your brother to live, let Jacob go.'

'Fuck you.'

'Let him go,' Po repeated. 'Let him go to his mother.'

'And if I do?' Caleb sneered at the notion. 'Y'all just walk away and forget about us?'

'No, Caleb, you know that isn't going to happen. But at least then us men can fight it out without putting a kid's life in danger.'

'You're some hot shit, Villere, huh? You think you're man enough to take us all on?'

'You're less of a man who needs your father and brothers to help you in a fight, then?'

'I ain't afraid to fight you alone.'

'So let Jacob go and face me.'

'I said I am not afraid but why would I? I don't have to do shit you tell me to.'

'Then say goodbye to Darrell.'

'Stick him again,' shouted Randolph, 'and I won't have nothing stopping me from pulling this trigger.'

'Yeah, well let's see just what happens when I do *this*—'

Po stabbed Darrell through the neck.

That, at least, must've been how it looked to his brothers and

father. In reality, Po, had struck his knee into the pressure point
at the rear of Darrell's knee, forcing him to collapse sideways with
a squawk. In the same moment he'd turned the blade towards
himself, but so he could ram his knuckles into the side of Darrell's
neck. The combined pain dumped Darrell on the ground, stunned
and wondering if he was still alive. Po hurtled towards Caleb,
leaving Randolph to his own fate.

Randolph saw his brother fall, and as dull as his brain was, his
mind exploded in a flash of fury and grief combined, and it took
him another second or two to return his eye to his rifle sights and
to try to track Po. He fired, but missed. He sighted again. His brain
fully engaged, he was unaware of the roaring of an engine or his
impending doom until it was almost too late. In the final second
he stood and twisted around, opening his mouth in challenge.

Pinky rammed an appropriated truck into Po's would-be slayer,
squishing the fat man's thighs against the pickup he'd taken cover
behind. The big truck that Pinky commandeered was larger and
heavier than the one it pinned Randolph to like a bug. The smaller
pickup was shoved into Caleb's truck, and in turn all three juddered
towards the edge of the trench.

Po saw Eldon fall down behind the trucks, albeit unharmed for
now. He left the father alone, concentrating instead on reaching
Caleb and Jacob. He had no view of Pinky, but trusted his friend
to look after himself, and the fallen brothers.

'Caleb!' Po hollered.

The man plunged over the rim of the trench, trying to run from
Po now he was alone. As he scrambled down the embankment, he
lost his grip of Jacob and they spilled apart. Each landed in heaps
at the bottom of the trench. Jacob had a bloody nose, but had
otherwise survived the drop unhurt. Po stood with his feet braced
at the top, glaring down at Caleb.

Caleb scrambled to grab Jacob again, except the boy was too
spry. Jacob bounced on the balls of his feet while he avoided his
father's grasping hands. Po charged down the incline and set
himself between them. He still held his knife. He deliberately
sheathed it in his boot, never taking his gaze off Caleb.

'You should have stayed in Maine,' Caleb growled.

'Wrong. You should have stayed behind your goddamn fences.'

Jacob moved and crouched by Po's side.

Caleb seethed. 'He'll never be yours. He was and always will be my son.'

'You don't deserve to be called a dad,' Po said.

'You don't deserve to live.' Caleb drew a pistol from his belt and aimed it at Po's gut. 'What, you expected me to chase after you unarmed?'

'You are the lowest form of coward there is.'

'Shoot him, son, and let's get this over with.' Eldon Moorcock peered down into the trench. His mustache bristled as he goaded his son to murder. 'You saw what he did to your brothers. He stabbed Darrell; he crushed poor Randolph's legs. Kill him. Kill him good.'

'I did neither of those things,' said Po.

'Kill him all the same,' Eldon barked.

'Sure, Pa, just watch.'

Caleb brought the pistol up a few inches so it aimed directly at Po's heart.

A scream of denial split the air.

It was Jacob, in a mad rage. He screeched an elongated 'Nooooo,' even as he unfurled and sent a surprising missile hurtling at Caleb. It was one of the full water bottles that had slipped from Po's pocket. It was small payback for what his father had put his mother through, but it was the best he could do.

Caleb ducked the bottle, but it still struck his shoulder, exploding and knocking aside his gun arm so that the bullet intended for Po drilled the embankment behind him. Po didn't wait; he sprang at Caleb, one hand snapping down on his wrist, one sinking fingers into his throat. He churned through the dirt as he drove Caleb backwards. Caleb repeatedly pulled the trigger, and bullets shot for the sky. Po's fingers remorselessly closed around his trachea, squeezing the curses out of him.

Locked in battle, Po had no idea of what was going on at the rim of the ditch, but two desperate dramas were played out there too . . .

Darrell, recovered from the blow to his neck, had regained composure. He stumbled to the edge of the trench, intent on helping his brother, but behind him Pinky loomed, having alighted the stolen vehicle. Pinky could have shot him dead, but he didn't.

Instead he wrapped Darrell in a bear hug and hauled him off his feet. Darrell struggled, trying to batter Pinky with his elbows, and kicking backwards to bark his shins. 'I'll kill you, you goddamn nigger,' he swore savagely.

'Seriously? That's all you can come up with, you? Are you freaking kidding me?' Pinky tossed Darrell from him in disgust. Darrell cartwheeled, spinning through vacant space until he landed in a graceless heap at the bottom of the trench. Dust clouded around him, but he didn't stir . . .

On the opposite side of the trench, Eldon clutched his hands in futility as he watched Darrell get hurled like trash into the ditch. His gaze darted to the pile of stones heaped at the edge of the trench. He scrambled towards them, intending using the missiles to pelt Po into submission and allow Caleb to gain the upper hand. He went to his knees in the dirt, grasped for a chunk of ragged concrete, and felt Tess's pistol touch him at the nape of his neck. 'If you know what's good for you, you'll put that down,' she warned.

'No *woman* tells *me* what to do,' Eldon snarled and tried to slap away her gun.

'Yeah. Keep on telling yourself that, you misogynistic pig!' Tess brought down the butt of the gun on the nape of his neck. Eldon collapsed face down in the pile of rubble.

Beside Tess Elspeth stood. She didn't spare Eldon's downfall more than a second's notice. She barely gave Caleb much more attention, only noting how Po had crushed her husband against the embankment. His gun had fallen from his weakened fingers while Po continued squeezing the life out of him. The only thing important to her just then was Jacob. He scrambled up the embankment, crying out to her in the voice of a child five years or younger than his actual age . . .

In that instant Po's mind was a void in which a single light flared; the light was the embodiment of his existence, he had one reason only to live, to avenge Caleb's victims. He'd shaken the gun out of Caleb's grasp, and had practically crushed the bastard's windpipe, but he continued squeezing. The bones in Caleb's wrist resisted him marginally more than his neck did. Caleb flopped now, with no resistance left in him. He could no longer make a discernible word; he was seconds from death. Po's senses returned to the moment, the magnitude of what was about to happen avalanching through his brain. He snapped open his fists, allowing Caleb to sink back against the embankment, and stood over him, breathing raggedly. He had killed before and had come close to slaying again. He shuddered the entire length of his body.

It was probable that Caleb had been unconscious, and for the past fifteen seconds or more had no concept of his battle with Po To him he was still engaged in the life or death tussle. He emitted a strangled shriek, and with neither forethought nor clear intention he kicked out and found Po's swollen knee. In its weakened state, Po's knee collapsed and he fell against Caleb and the fight was on again: round two. They grappled for dominance. Caleb was bigger and heavier muscled, but Po had drained most of the vitality out of him. Sapped of strength, he had no appetite for a prolonged fight. He broke free and scrambled for where Darrell lay unmoving in the dirt. He shook and slapped Darrell, trying to rouse him, and was rewarded by a pained moan: Darrell was in no shape to help him.

'You're done.' Po rubbed at his sore knee as he limped after Caleb. 'Have some dignity and accept defeat.'

'I'm a better man than you!' Caleb's face was lit with insanity. 'I'll show you, you piece of crap.'

'I'm not a child or a woman half your size for you to bully. Trust me, Caleb, I'll beat your head like a drum if you keep this up.'

'No, I'll take your hide and make a fucking drum skin out of it!'

Caleb twisted towards Po, snapping aloft a knife he'd taken off Darrell's belt. Unbeknown to either, it was the same knife Darrell had disembowelled Orson Burdon with. He lunged at Po's midriff, and as unsteady as he was, Po had little chance of evading the blade.

A chunk of concrete struck Caleb. It whacked into his exposed ribs and in reflex his elbow recoiled. The knife missed Po by inches. Caleb yowled – the concrete had cracked a rib – and he blinked up at the rim of the trench. Over him stood Elspeth, Jacob, Tess and Pinky. Each had armed themselves with more stones. It would've been sweet revenge for Elspeth to toss another rock, to punish Caleb in the manner he'd planned killing her, but Po took away the opportunity. He lurched forward on his wobbly knee and kicked Caleb's head with such singular ferocity it was a miracle his neck didn't snap.

Po clambered up the embankment. Elspeth hugged Jacob, but the boy pulled loose and stood before him. The kid's nose was bloody and he was covered in dust. 'Sorry you had to watch me do that to your daddy,' Po said.

'It was nothing to what he has done to my mom. He deserves to be hurt worse.'

'He's still your father, Jacob.'

'I know. But I stopped him from shooting you.'

'You sure did. I'm indebted to you, son. That trick with the water bottle probably saved my life. You ever need anything, and I'll be there for you. D'you understand what I'm saying? You need only ask, y'hear?'

Jacob nodded, and accepted a bump from Po's knuckles on his.

Tess took hold of Po's hand and squeezed it. They turned to the sounds of movement. There were people all around them. Some held weapons, some of them military grade assault rifles. Nobody used them. Eldon Moorcock was stirring and Tess went to stand over him, keeping him under guard with her pistol. He awoke slowly, his vision foggy at first. Suddenly, it was as if Tess was thrown into stark clarity, and Eldon gasped, expecting another bash around the head with her gun. His gaze darted, seeking allies, and he spotted a man nearby. 'Decker,' he croaked, 'you have to help me. Shoot this bitch!'

Tess checked out the man facing her. Was this the same Decker who'd accompanied Caleb to Portland, and who had assisted in the kidnapping? She thought it was the same man. He looked cowed, in the knowledge that he was in serious trouble. The rifle hung forgotten in his hand.

'What are you waiting for?' Eldon bellowed. 'Help me, Jer. I swear to you, if you don't do as I say—'

Decker dropped the rifle in the dirt and walked away.

Other members of his community turned their backs and walked away too. The tyrannical reign of Eldon Moorcock and his sons had ended.

AFTER

The sound of water rushing over the falls had become so familiar that Tess rarely noticed it any more. She fully believed though that – should the Presumpscot River ever dry up – the silence would be so sudden it would be deafening. She noticed the river now, as well as the breeze rattling the leaves in the treetops. She noted the grumble of Po's Ford Mustang, where he'd left it running with its hood up. After leaving it standing in the elements for several days he'd driven it back from Pinky's place and immediately set to the car's maintenance routine that'd been put off. Having worked on the car, Po had retreated from the car to rest a while. He was seated on the porch swing, kneading his aching knee. After their return from out of state Po had visited a clinic: the prognosis on his knee was not ideal, but better than the alternative. He had hurt his anterior cruciate ligament, torn his cartilage, and there was localized inflammation, but with rest and treatment he should heal without surgery. For the last few days Tess had encouraged him to alternate hot and cold therapies on the swollen joint, until Po had grumbled he didn't have time for all that Voodoo mumbo-jumbo. Now he only massaged it when it was sore, but the caveat being he didn't complain about the pain in earshot of her. When he saw her, he stopped rubbing and sat back in the swing.

'How are you feeling?'

'Fine,' he lied.

'Take some more painkillers.'

'Don't need them.'

She sat beside him and settled her hand on his injured leg. 'To think I was worried you'd broken your ankle,' she said, and gently massaged his knee.

'My ankle was only twisted, and maybe a little gnawed on by that mutt, but otherwise it's fine.'

'Things could've turned out much worse than they did.'

'You can say that again.'

Elspeth had been mere seconds away from death. A single stone, striking her in just the right spot, could have ended her life in an instant. They were fortunate to have arrived in time to intervene. Tess still winced at what she'd borne witness to: lapidation, or the stoning of a person was horrifying to see, an ancient form of punishment that should not exist outside the pages of the Old Testament. Sadly the stoning of alleged adulterers still happened in what should be a more civilized, more enlightened world. Elspeth had been pummeled but her injuries were superficial, scrapes and bruises mostly, and nothing she hadn't contended with for more than a decade since falling under Caleb's thrall.

They sat in companionable silence for a while.

'My knee isn't as sore as Randolph Moorcock's must be,' Po said with a chuckle.

'Pinky sure did a number on him with that truck,' Tess said, and also laughed at the memory. She felt no guilt at her dark pleasure, because she'd later learned that Randolph was a murderous piece of crap who'd shot dead Orson Keeler Burdon with his own bow and arrow. Had he gotten his way and Pinky failed to stop him, he'd have shot Po dead too.

There was a part of her that still shied away from vigilantism, but having been partnered with Po for the last few years, she didn't view it with the same jaundiced eye as she had when she had been a cop. Randolph Moorcock deserved every minute of agony he'd endure before his shattered legs were fixed, and she only wished that his brothers and father had suffered similar levels of agony. When Pinky tossed Darrell head over heels into the trench, the impact had knocked him unconscious, but he'd gotten away with his crimes with a few bumps and bruises, and the snapped clavicle courtesy of Po. Eldon had a sore head from where Tess struck him, and Tess had learned that another member of the family, the abusive matriarch Ellie-May, had never quite regained her faculties after Elspeth knocked her down for beating Jacob. As for Caleb, Po's final kick had broken his jaw, and it was the least payback he deserved for the pain he'd put his victims through. True vigilantism might have found all the family slain and dumped in Booger Hole alongside the vengeful ghosts of their victims, and there was part of Tess that would be satisfied with their fate, but then, they all faced life imprisonment so she wouldn't complain.

It turned out those two cops that Po and Pinky had first been suspicious of had turned out to be the best of their kind. As soon as Tess had an opportunity, she had dialed 911 and the duo had responded. It had been Officers Wilson and Rossiter who had taken the Moorcocks into custody, rather than a deputy from the county sheriff's department – Tess had since learned that some of the deputies were allegedly corrupt, accepting bribes from Eldon Moorcock. State police detectives had taken over the investigation, and the FBI had also gotten involved when discovering how Caleb and his brothers had crossed state lines in pursuit of, and in the commission of kidnapping, Elspeth and Jacob. Several other members of the community had been arrested for conspiring with the Moorcocks, and more would answer justice once the extent of their crimes became known. Supposedly narcotics had been discovered behind that vault door in the bunker, with Eldon and his sons complicit with a cartel using the commune as a stepping stone for their produce this side of the Canadian border. For now Tess was unsure where the criminal allegations would end. Elspeth and Jacob were currently hidden in a witness protection program, safe from harm but also out of her and Po's reach. There still remained a burning truth to be uncovered. One she'd resolved to discover after helping clean Jacob up and dabbing some blood from his nostrils with a handkerchief. She had taken care to protect the bloody cloth.

'Do you want to hear the results?' she asked.

Po sucked in his bottom lip and frowned.

Tess took out a folded sheet of paper. It was a copy of an email she'd printed off only minutes ago.

'Elspeth swore that Jacob isn't mine, Caleb said he isn't, and there's a piece of me here' – Po tapped the side of his head – 'that tells me he isn't.' He moved his hand and it hovered over his heart. 'But then I have this feelin' that I can't shake right here.'

'That's only because you're a good man, and you feel protective of an abused child.'

'You've read the results then?'

'I couldn't avoid reading them.'

'So the blood tests were negative?'

'I'm sorry, Po, your DNA wasn't a match.'

'I'm not sure how I feel about that,' he admitted.

'You wanted Jacob to be your son, but he isn't.' She faced him, touched his cheek with her fingertips and then she kissed him. 'Why don't you go and turn off that engine and come inside. It's not too late for us to try making a child together.'